THE BARD
AND THE
BONE KING

JAMES
KOVACS

A NOVEL

ACKNOWLEDGEMENTS

First, I would like to thank my dear love, Amy Lamendella for her priceless contributions, feedback, editing and support throughout the process of writing this book. I couldn't have done it without her. Great thanks to Wendy Luckey and Pilar Woodman for their helpful feedback on early versions of the manuscript. Many thanks to my editor, Kevin Miller, for his priceless input. My gratitude also to Marisa Belger and Laura Chandler for reading the final version of the book. Lastly, I'd like to thank Brent Bishop for his inspired design work and artistic contributions.

To hear the author read excerpts from this book, please search for "Bard and the Bone King" on YouTube and the social media environs of the interweb multiverse.

Cover design and map by Brent Bishop: brentbishop.com

*Dedicated to the amazing teachers
who have blessed my life:*

*Master Daniel Johnson
Isa Gucciardi
and
Wendy Luckey*

Thank you for teaching me how to listen

Orkney Islands

DRUID'S KEEP

WILLOW'S GLEN

VALLEY OF THE ALCHEMIST

sawtooth hills

whispering woods

STONEWALL

POOLS OF PEACE

Bog of Despair

obelisk hills

LOCHSHIRE

RING OF BRODGAR

Kirkwall

UNSTAN

May I go where the river takes me.
Destiny's journey will surely shape me.
Into what? I do not know.
Flowering mystery. Live in flow

We are not alone in this world. Since the birth of time alternate realities have existed just beyond the borders of our own, spiral dimensions coiling around Earth like ancient dragons. Beings of immense power and wisdom inhabit these neighboring realities. They are the Guardians of Earth, ever watchful of mankind's unfolding destiny.

When great need arises in the human heart, one of these magnificent dragon dimensions circles closer and, with lightning-bolt talons, touches our world, cleaving open a doorway, through which the Great Ones can enter and do their work. Rarely seen but powerfully felt, these beings have altered human history again and again; compassionate teachers dedicated to helping humanity flower into its boundless potential. The time is ripening for them to return to our world. The winds of change have begun to blow once again on Earth....

ONE

Long ago, deep within the mists of time, there lived a young bard named Aidan Bourne. On the day of Aidan's birth, a vibrant rainbow colored the skies above the village of Willow's Glen. The auspicious omen seemed fitting, because, from that first moment, the young child emanated a soft golden light. Visitors to the newborn felt the touch of divine grace and love in his presence. The villagers were not surprised that such a radiant soul had chosen to be born to Mary and Bran Bourne. They were kind, gentle people with a great love for Mother Earth and all her children.

Aidan's mother and father were wise in the old ways and knew a great deal about healing herbs, medicine making, and many long-forgotten mysteries of earth magic. From a young age, the bard learned how to make medicinal teas and poultices and how to care for herbs in the family garden.

Mary and Bran instilled in their child a sense of curiosity and awe toward Mother Nature and the miracles of life. Perhaps the greatest of all their gifts was teaching Aidan the lost art of listening. "Knowledge speaks, wisdom listens," his father was fond of reminding him.

Bran taught his son how to quiet his mind through meditation. Many of nature's voices are too soft-spoken to be heard by a noisy mind. Becoming more comfortable in the expansive silence, Aidan learned to listen ever more deeply to the whisperings of the world.

Over time, Aidan began to hear the language of birds and animals, insects and trees, rivers and wind. He came to know that everything in this world has spirit. All God's creations had stories to tell and important lessons to teach those who knew how to listen. One had only to open their heart in gratitude, quiet the mind, and listen with humility, patience, and without expectations. Aidan was skilled in this way of listening and, fueled by his great curiosity for life, spent much of his childhood drinking in the wisdom from Mother Earth's many teachers.

The birds and animals near Aidan's home loved the boy dearly for his pure heart and gentle nature. With his curly blond hair, round face, and bright blue eyes, many people from his village said he looked like an angel. His spirit was so pure that, wherever he went, he radiated golden light, like the sun. When he walked in the forest, trees and flowers leaned toward him, and woodland faeries bathed in his luminous light. The bard's songs were so sweet that hummingbirds sipped the nectar of his words, carried along on the breeze.

As a child, Aidan spent most of his days exploring the unusual forest that surrounded his peaceful village of Willow's Glen. Villagers had named it the Whispering Woods due to the gentle breeze that blew through the trees, rustling the leaves and whispering words to passersby. It was an enchanted woodland filled with ancient oak, ash, hazel, and alder trees. The Whispering Woods was the bard's second home, and he had many adventures there while learning from the wise, old trees.

Late one afternoon, a particularly old oak tree with a special gift for storytelling offered to tell

Aidan a tale that all the oaks in the forest knew well. Aidan delighted in hearing stories and couldn't pass up a tale from the ancient oak. So, he sat on a soft patch of leaves and gave the massive tree his ear. As the wind rose in the gnarled branches above, the rustling leaves became a voice like a rippling stream, and out spilled the story of Quercus the Arcane.

"Quercus was a rather quirky wizard who lived long ago in the Irish countryside," the oak tree began. "He had endless hunger for life's mysteries and traveled far and wide to study with the great esoteric teachers of the day. He voraciously studied alchemy, magic, chemistry, herbs, astronomy, and meditation."

As the story unfolded, Aidan realized something strange was happening. He wasn't just hearing the story; he was living it! Aidan had become Quercus through the telling of the tale. He felt the immense joy of learning, the elation of discovery, and the insatiable curiosity of Quercus the Arcane, experiencing the odd wizard's idiosyncrasies as if they were his own.

"Quercus often became so lost in thought that he was oblivious of his surroundings. As a result, he regularly knocked himself unconscious, walking distractedly into walls and tree branches, and broke many bones falling into streambeds and ditches. After decades of this abuse, his arms and legs were knobby and bent in unnatural directions. In pursuit of wisdom, Quercus often forgot to eat or sleep for days on end, until someone forced him to sit down for a meal and get a decent night's rest.

"As the years flew by, and unruly gray hairs sprouted in his beard and eyebrows, Quercus came to the disturbing realization that he would only be able to acquire a fraction of the knowledge he longed for before his human life expired. Even worse, he would not have time to share his wisdom with others to benefit the world.

"Quercus decided that he must, at all costs, prolong his life, so he could continue to learn and share his knowledge. So, he decided to use the power of magic and alchemy to transform himself into one of the world's longest-living creatures...a tree.

"Quercus knew of the Whispering Woods and decided it would be the perfect home for his new life as a tree. The magic was so strong in the forest that he could more easily speak to others and share his teachings. Quercus spent an entire moon taking powerful potions and eating nothing but wood. As the days passed, he became less and less like a man and more and more like a tree. His legs rooted deep into the earth and his twisted, broken arms became the gnarled branches of an oak tree. Over generations, the oak tree continued to gather teachings and became one of the wisest trees in the forest. It still lives today, and loves to share its knowledge with those patient enough to listen."

By the end of the story, Aidan felt like he had literally become an oak tree, rooted to the earth. Since he couldn't move, and night had fallen, he decided to spend the night in the forest. Thankfully, by morning's light, Aidan could walk like a human once again. From that day on, he regularly sat with the wise oak tree, who taught him a great deal about the world.

Growing up, Aidan was delighted to discover that the natural world was full of songs in addition to stories and wisdom. As a boy, he rose at dawn to hear the music of birdsong in the family garden. Listening to the unbridled joy for life expressed in each bird's voice, Aidan longed to share his own song with the world.

Listening more attentively as time passed, Aidan realized that, not only did the birds sing, everything in nature had its own unique song. When he was humble and quiet, songs from plants, rocks, mountains, and even stars filled his mind with their melodies. By singing their songs, Aidan learned to honor the spirits of nature and share their magic with the world. Star songs inspired awe and a sense of belonging in the great cosmos, while tree songs reminded him to stand strong and be rooted in the wisdom of Mother Earth. Every song had its unique medicine for those who heard it.

It was these very spirits of nature that taught Aidan the ways of being a bard. Most bards of his day underwent long apprenticeships with human teachers to cultivate their skills in the bardic ways. Aidan was equally dedicated to his training; however, his teachers were of a decidedly non-human sort.

Once he became a young man, everyone who heard Aidan sing knew he would be a master bard, regardless of his peculiar apprenticeship. A true bard could make someone laugh, cry, and fall asleep through their songs alone. The magic of Aidan's songs could do these things and much more.

Aidan's family lived in a small earthen home with a thatch roof. The circular house had thick cob walls inset with wooden shuttered windows. A wide porch surrounded the front of the house. It overlooked a large garden of fruit trees and garden beds filled with vegetables and medicinal herbs. A meandering stone path wandered past several sitting areas shaded by trees that were perfect for reading, bird watching, or afternoon tea. Bursting with beautiful flowers and plants, the garden was a feast for the senses.

The interior of their cozy home was whitewashed and filled with natural light. Stout tree trunks served as support beams, lending a earthy presence to the interior. The rooms were arranged in a circle around a central garden courtyard with a birdbath, comfortable chairs, and a hazelnut tree for shade. Birds and bees often flew into the courtyard to drink water or visit the many flowers in the garden. With the courtyard doors open, birds, chipmunks, and other creatures wandered into the house from time to time, to the young bard's delight.

Aidan's childhood was filled with the homey smells of his mother, Mary, baking bread, cooking stew, or simmering herbs for medicinal teas. Mary was the village herbalist, and people often came to her to find medicines for what ailed them. She sent them on their way with satchels of herbs and healing salves or sat with them as they drank steaming mugs of medicinal tea.

Watching her one morning moving about the kitchen and singing as she worked, Aidan became lost in the simple beauty of her song. He dreamed of the day when he would be a bard as Mary's clear, melodic voice filled the air

Bees kiss flowers in the light
bathed in perfume and delight
Sipping nectar, oh so sweet,
Golden honey, what a treat

Earth, my mother, plants my kin
Land, my home, I walk again
Over field and under tree
Nature's gifts, I treasure thee

Wander streams and mountains high
Father Sun and clear blue sky
Willow basket, well-worn boots
Harvest flower, leaf, and root

Tending garden, planting seed
Medicine for those in need
Steaming mugs of healing tea
The life of herbs is the life for me!

Mary was truly a woman of the earth. She was gentle and grounded, like the weathered hills surrounding Willow's Glen. Her strong, capable body was healthy and radiant from a life of walking in search of herbs and drinking potent medicinal teas. Looking into her kind brown eyes, Aidan always felt a profound sense of peace and belonging. All who came to her for healing felt unconditionally loved and cared for in her presence.

Mary lost her parents to an incurable fever when she was a young girl. Her powerlessness in the face of her parents' lethal disease ignited a fierce desire to become a healer and to help others. Soon after her parents' death, Mary was taken in and raised by a revered white witch and healer named Sorena, who lived on the edge of the Whispering Woods. Sorena taught her the traditions of herbal medicine and how to learn from the wisdom of nature. Under Sorena's patient instruction, Mary became a master herbalist and a much-respected healer in Willow's Glen.

By far Sorena's greatest gift to Mary was teaching her the ancient path of wisdom known as "the Way." For many generations, druids, witches, and sages had followed the teachings of the Way. Above all, the Way emphasized living in harmony with nature and all beings. Its followers honored Mother Earth's creations as revered teachers and beloved family members. They learned to live with care and awareness so that humankind and all life flourished.

Practitioners of the Way sought to align themselves with the natural cycles of change. They lived in harmony with the seasons of nature and of human life. Embracing the flow of change, they walked their paths with ease, like a river navigating obstacles along its course. By embracing life's challenges as opportunities for learning, they lived with far more joy and peace of mind than those who tried to bend reality to meet their expectations. They moved with life instead of struggling against it. Mary emanated the ease and natural wisdom of the Way in all she did.

She began teaching Aidan about the Way when he was a young boy. One evening before dinner, she sat with him in the garden, enjoying the rich light of the magic hour and sipping chamomile tea as they watched the birds and bees flying about the garden.

"The Way is an energy that moves through all things, like vital, shimmering threads woven through the tapestry of our lives," Mary said, "a power that seeks harmony and allows all life to thrive. It is a creative energy that fills our world with beauty and mystery, and emanates from all living creatures.

"The Way is also a path of wisdom and humble service to the world that all people may walk, if they choose. It is like an ancestor spirit guiding our lives, teaching us to love and honor all of creation. It connects us with the nobility of being human and reminds us of our essential role as caregivers for all life on Earth. We who are open to the Way are never alone in this world. We are family with animals and birds, rivers and trees. If you choose to follow the Way, you will know great peace and a sense of belonging that most people only dream of."

Aidan's eyes sparkled with excitement as he listened. "Please teach me, Mother. Help me learn the wisdom of the Way, so I too can walk this path."

Mary looked at Aidan with her gentle, loving eyes and smiled. "May it be so, my dear son. May it be so."

Aidan's father, Bran, also grew up studying the timeless teachings of the Way. He trained in magic and the ancient mysteries of the druids from an early age. His teacher, Shandor, had a dream revealing that young Bran was meant to learn the secret ways of the druids. After much persuasion, his parents reluctantly agreed to release their son into Shandor's care. Bran left home soon thereafter and began his rigorous training with the wise druid. He spent hours each day in meditation and reflection to train his mind, so he could listen to the silence and begin to commune with the wisdom of the Way.

Shandor constantly challenged Bran by questioning fundamental assumptions about his identity and the nature of reality. Through years of such training, Bran learned to be at peace in the groundless truth of the unknown. From this place of not knowing, he discovered one of the greatest gifts of his apprenticeship: being fully awake to the infinite moment. In the past, he had been constrained by his thoughts, beliefs, and identity to a limited view of reality. By realizing that he knew nothing and listening in wonder with the ears of a child, the mystery of creation revealed itself to him. This was the point when his true learning began.

Like dropping into the depths of a bottomless well, the wisdom of the Way opened to him. Learning from Shandor and dedicating himself to long hours of study and meditation, Bran came to know about many aspects of magic: divination, shapeshifting, alchemy, changing the past and the future, spells for empowerment and healing, and much more.

Shandor taught him the druid's language of power that opened communication with the realm of spirit and magic. Each word of this language was a living being. An intimate relationship with every word had to be maintained to speak the druid's tongue.

In his more advanced studies, Bran specialized in crafting magical objects. He learned the art of working with metal and gems and studied the ways of empowering amulets and jewelry with healing energy for specific purposes. Using the druid's tongue, he infused these objects with power, so that every ring, necklace, and talisman came alive.

Through many years of doing this work, Bran became skilled in the ways of crafting empowered objects. People regularly came to Willow's Glen from surrounding villages to buy his amulets and other jewelry for protection, healing, and good fortune. With his parents as role models and teachers, Aidan slowly grew to know the beauty and wisdom of the Way.

TWO

When Aidan reached the age when most children began attending school, his parents decided on a different course for his education. Wanting to guide his learning toward what they considered most valuable, Mary and Bran decided to join a small group of families who were homeschooling their children. They encouraged Aidan to follow his curiosity and study what he most wanted to learn. Since Aidan was an endlessly curious child, he wanted to learn about almost everything, and that is what he did.

He devoured any books he could find on astronomy, philosophy, history, religion, literature, and herbal medicine. Aidan was also intrigued by the political and social realities of the day and was constantly asking questions of his parents and the other home school teachers.

Being geographically isolated from mainland Europe and the rest of the modern world, the inhabitants of Orkney Island lived in a cultural vacuum. Although Christianity had a strong presence in Orkney, most villagers still lived according to the ancient traditions. The Way still flourished as a guiding force in Willow's Glen. Honoring the Earth and the rhythms of nature was a sacred duty for the people of Aidan's village. Only in Orkney's cities had people begun to abandon the old ways.

Aidan was horrified to hear about the violence and greed that was prevalent in the modern world. In disbelief, he read about power hungry leaders who sought to subjugate their neighbors rather than live in harmony with them.

Kings waged wars against their neighbors in an endless stream of needless violence. People leveled forests, killed animals for sport, and greedily extracted metal and other resources from the ground. When Aidan learned of the witch trials and cruel oppression of people practicing earth-based traditions, it was almost too much for him to bear. He couldn't fathom such hatred and cruelty. How had people forgotten about love and the teachings of the Way?

One afternoon while they were working in the garden, Aidan asked his father about this disturbing trend of violence and separation from the Earth. Bran looked at Aidan with compassion in his clear blue eyes. "Sadly, Aidan, some of our brothers and sisters have lost their way. Many have become arrogant, cold-hearted, and blind to what is real. People take and take from our dear planet and give nothing in return. Even in my work, I must be wary of this. As you know, I require precious metals and gemstones for the jewelry I make. These materials must be mined from the Earth and it is essential that this be done in a caring way, not taking too much and doing work to heal the Earth in places where mining has occurred.

"Many miners have forgotten these practices and ruthlessly exploit Earth's resources with no thought of giving anything in return. I am careful to buy only gems and metal from miners who respect Mother Nature and her needs. I have something to show you. Look here."

Bran reached into his pocket and opened his hand for Aidan to see. In his palm was one of the most beautiful talismans Bran had ever made. It was a circular piece made of gold inscribed with images of mountains and trees. The talisman was inset with emeralds and a deep-blue sapphire that sparkled like water in the sunlight.

"It's stunning!" Aidan exclaimed.

"Do you know who I made it for?"

Aidan shook his head.

"Mother Earth," Bran said with a contented smile on his face. "In thanks for her providing me with the gems and metal to do my craft, I regularly make her talismans infused with prayers of love and healing. Then I listen to where she wants to receive this offering, and I bury it in that place with great care. This is a good way to live, my son."

Bran regularly brought Aidan to his jewelry workshop in town. Aidan loved watching his father work with metal and gemstones, crafting them into objects of beauty. More than anything, he loved watching Bran use the forge to melt gold and other precious metals. Aidan could sit for hours looking into the flames and glowing red coals of the forge. At such times, he imagined he was looking into the fiery magma that burned deep within the Earth.

One afternoon while pouring molten copper into a tiny mold for a ring he was making, Bran began to talk in a tone that spoke of sacred things. Aidan felt the strength of his father's spirit in his words.

"My work is a form of alchemy. I work with the energy of the elements to infuse life and spirit into each amulet and talisman that I create. Working with the elemental spirits is an essential aspect of the teachings of the Way. All life is made up of these elements. Your life and your health depend entirely on their energy. Water allows your blood to flow, and fire warms your flesh. Without air and the bounty of food that grows from the soil, we would all die.

"All life and all creation depend on the ancient spirits we call 'elementals'. By studying how the different elements relate to one another, we can come to a deeper understanding of the workings of the Way. When the elements exist in a state of dynamic harmony, life thrives in all its myriad forms.

"The spirit of the Way maintains this harmony through the generative and controlling relationships between the five elements. In the generative cycle, one element feeds the growth of the next. For example, water nourishes the growth of trees, wood feeds the element of fire, earth gives birth to the element of metal, and so on.

"Through the controlling cycle, the elements exert a limiting influence on each other, so none becomes too strong or out of balance with the others. You can see this controlling influence working when water extinguishes fire, earth channels and guides the flow of water, and, here in the foundry, how I use fire to melt metal, so it can be shaped into tools and jewelry. The generative and controlling cycles are constantly at work in the world and in our own bodies. This is how the Way maintains harmony in the natural world and health and wellbeing in the lives of our people."

Aidan sat in awe of his father's knowledge of the Way. He felt as if Bran had opened the door to an entirely new reality by exposing him to the elements and giving him a view into the inner workings of creation.

"It is by cultivating an intimate relationship with the elemental beings that I can create these protective amulets and healing talismans for people," Bran continued. "Dedication and perseverance are required to learn to dance with the creative powers of the elements. Only then can you safely channel these primal energies to fuel the process of alchemy and craft magic for the purposes of healing."

Aidan's parents emphasized the importance of direct experience in his education. They encouraged him to learn about life through observation and to hone his awareness of the world around him. He learned about medicinal herbs by making medicines and trying them himself. After reading about astronomy in a book, he spent many nights lying in an open meadow on his back and observing the stars. Much of his learning about nature took place in the Whispering Woods with Feather, a girl from his home school group, who lived nearby.

Like Aidan, Feather loved the Whispering Woods and the spirits that lived there. As a matter of fact, she looked like a forest spirit herself. Feather was small and thin of body with delicate, sensitive hands. Wild long brown hair framed her face, and her large green eyes were not of this world. Her penetrating eyes could perceive spirits and other things that were beyond most people's awareness. Mary said that Feather had strong Fey blood in her veins, and, over time, Aidan came to agree. On several occasions, out of the corner of his eye, he saw faeries buzzing around her head as they walked through the forest.

Aidan and Feather were perfect companions. Both had an insatiable appetite for learning and were endlessly curious about the world around them. They spent long afternoons together exploring the mysteries of the Whispering Woods.

The hours flew by as they spied on otters frolicking in the creek, dissected owl pellets, and watched bees busily gathering nectar and pollen. Through their adventures in the forest, they soon became the best of friends.

One day after spending all morning studying herbal medicine, Aidan went for a walk in the Whispering Woods. In the lazy heat of the summer afternoon, he walked along Riffle Creek and harvested mugwort for his mother's dream tea formula. After collecting a good-sized bundle of the herb, Aidan came to one of his favorite hazelnut trees and decided to take a nap. As he drifted along the edge of sleep, he heard the sound of lute music somewhere in the forest. Aidan loved the lute. Several people in his village played, and he wondered who it was.

He couldn't make out which direction the gentle melody was coming from, but as he focused on the sound, the music became more distinct. It was an intriguing wandering melody unlike any he had heard, yet it seemed familiar.

Aidan heard crunching twigs as someone approached through the forest. He sat up with his back against the tree, hoping to meet whoever was playing the lute. Instead, Feather appeared from the trees, walking along the creek. She gave him a knowing smile. "I thought I'd find you here, Aidan."

Feather had a powerful sixth sense. She could feel where things and people were, much like a wolf follows a scent. She seemed to perceive a reality of which most people were not aware. Without realizing it, Aidan's awareness drifted off again to the intriguing lute music, and he became lost in its mysterious melody.

"Uh, hello? Are you there, Aidan, or have the Fey folk taken you?"

"Oh, sorry, Feather." Aidan snapped out of his trance and focused on his friend.

"No problem, silly boy." She smiled impishly. "I was just making fun of you. So, what are you up to?"

"I was just taking a nap, and then I started hearing that lovely lute music. Isn't it a fascinating melody?"

"Lute music? What lute music? Perhaps you have been with the Fey folk after all. I hear more than most, but I certainly don't hear a lute."

Aidan bolted upright. "Really? That's strange."

While he talked with Feather, the music faded into the background of his mind. As he focused on the sound again, it became increasingly distinct. Aidan suddenly realized that the melody was morphing and changing in perfect resonance with the shifting nuances of his mental and emotional state. As he marveled at the masterful improv the lute music was weaving with his feelings, Aidan noticed that the melody had a decidedly fluid and, yes, *watery* signature to it. Realization dawned on him, and he stared at the running water in disbelief.

"It's the creek! Riffle Creek is playing the lute for me!"

"What a crafty little creek," Feather said, her eyes filled with admiration. "Well, I dare say you had better find yourself a lute, my bardic friend, for I can think of no better music teacher than a river spirit!"

A bemused smile spread across Aidan's face. "Yes, Feather, I think you're right."

By winter, Aidan had his lute. After hearing his story about the creek's lute music, Bran sent word to a master luthier on the coast in Lochshire. Bran gave the man an amulet to protect against the many thieves in Lochshire in exchange for a well-crafted lute.

Minutes after it arrived, Aidan had the lute slung over his shoulder and was walking briskly toward the Whispering Woods. As he approached Riffle Creek, the lute music began to fill his mind again. For hours that afternoon, Aidan sat next to the creek listening and translating watery melodies into notes on the fret board. He lost himself in the liquid communion with the music of Riffle Creek. Before he knew it, night was falling. Aidan hurriedly slung the lute onto his back and made for home, where dinner was waiting for him.

Whenever he had time, Aidan went to the Whispering Woods and continued his unusual music lessons. Every time he arrived, Aidan left offerings of rose petals to express his gratitude for the creek's generosity. As the red petals swirled lazily in the watery eddies, he sang songs and listened for the lute music that arose to dance with his voice. Aidan came to love the lute and, with the help of Riffle Creek, created lyrical music to accompany his songs.

Oftentimes, Feather sang with Aidan, as he played his lute along the banks of the creek. Her voice was beautiful and haunting. It spoke of dark mysterious places in the world and within oneself. Her enchanting melodies often caught the attention of the spirits of the Whispering Woods.

One day as they sang together by the creek, Aidan spotted a fox circling near them through the underbrush. A minute later, he saw a movement out of the corner of his eye. When he turned his head, he was surprised to see a large snake on a rock swaying its head in time with the music. As they continued singing, green butterflies began to circle Feather's head. Looking more closely, Aidan gave a start when he realized a tiny Faerie was riding on the back of each butterfly.

The Faeries had long ears and large deep-green eyes that twinkled playfully as they circled through the air on their butterfly steeds. Their pale skin glowed so brightly with magic that they seemed to be made more of light than flesh. Trails of shimmering rainbow dust spread out behind them as they wheeled around Feather's head. Aidan heard a sweet humming sound in the air around him. Then he realized the Faeries were singing with them. Time ceased to exist as they became entranced with the song of the Faeries.

When the song ended, evening was upon them, and they hurried back to the village. Brimming with curiosity Aidan turned to Feather. "Did you understand the Faeries? Do you know what they were singing about?"

Feather looked at him with a playful twinkle in her eye. "Why, yes, as a matter of fact, I do. Here are a few lines I can remember." With her voice full of joy, she began to sing,

Let us sing without a care
There is no then, there is no there
With the wind, we dance and play
Grateful for this blessed day
The Fey are here with twinkling eyes
Flying free in clear blue skies
Nowhere to go, no place to be
With all this lovely company
Forget the 'when's and 'why's and 'how's
Lose yourself in the sacred now

Nectar's song and sweetest lute
Today we feast on spirit fruit
We are one upon this Earth
Flowering in endless birth....

Aidan stared at Feather in wonder, intrigued by the mysterious nature of his dear friend.

THREE

One morning, Aidan was sitting in the garden courtyard of their home happily playing his lute and singing to the birds rummaging through the leaves for food. Holly, a woman from the village, knocked on their front door, and Mary invited her in for tea. Holly had curly red hair and pale skin peppered with freckles from working outside in the sun. Sadness darkened her eyes and she looked as if she had not slept in far too long.

Mary already knew what ailed her. A few weeks earlier, a wild boar had attacked her husband while he was hunting in the forest, and he had died from internal bleeding. Mary had seen her the day before and was trying to support her through the grieving process. This time, Holly had brought her daughter Pearl with her.

"I'm worried about Pearl," Holly said. "Since her father's death, she has not shed a single tear. When I look into her eyes, she doesn't seem to be here. Clearly, she is in shock, but I don't know what to do. Can you help my daughter?"

Mary looked in Pearl's eyes and saw how flat and lifeless they were. "Poor girl," she said, stroking the girl's hair. Mary asked questions and tried to engage with her, but Pearl remained distant and disinterested.

Outside in the courtyard, Aidan was playing a song on his lute. It was a bittersweet, melancholy song about love and loss. Pearl soon took notice, and a sparkle of interest illuminated her eyes.

"Would you like to listen to the song?" Mary asked. The girl nodded, so they walked out into the courtyard to hear Aidan play. As Pearl listened to the sad melody, her eyes came to life, as if the song was watering some parched and withered part of her heart.

Pearl gasped and began to sob uncontrollably. Aidan was about to stop playing, but Mary waved at him to continue. For several minutes, Pearl wept in anguish, mourning the loss of her father. By the end of the song, her sobbing had become less intense, and she was crying quietly in Mary's lap. Mary lovingly placed Pearl back in Holly's arms.

"Pearl is going to be just fine," she said. "Let's go inside and have some tea."

As Mary walked back into the house she turned and gave Aidan an appreciative smile.

After that day, Mary sometimes asked Aidan to sing for people who were grieving or heartbroken. His music was a healing balm for their wounded hearts, filling them with love and a renewed joy for living. As time passed, it became clear that Aidan's songs had the power to heal not only the heart but also the mind and body.

As Aidan grew older, and his abilities ripened, his reputation as a bard spread rapidly throughout Willow's Glen. More and more people arrived at their home asking for Aidan's help with what ailed them. The crowds began to disrupt his family's ability to live a normal life. After reflecting on this problem, Mary came upon a solution that would meet everyone's needs.

Every morning, people were invited to come to the family garden, where Aidan played his music. Among the trees and flowers, a group of villagers gathered to hear him sing. In this way, many people received the benefit of his healing songs, and Aidan's family could still have the personal time they needed.

Mornings in the garden were a magical time for Aidan and the people of Willow's Glen. The flowing, watery lute music weaved together with the healing melodies of his songs. Those with clear vision saw a river of light spreading out into the air from Aidan's lips as he sang. The healing waters of the Way spilled forth from his music and bathed all who were present in its nourishing energy.

If you had wandered into the garden on one of these mornings you might have heard a song like this:

Feel the gentle breeze
Let the wind move you
Listen to the whispers of your soul
Never let the mind take control
Walk the path of your destiny
Remember who you are and simply be
Simply be
Set yourself free
Simply be
Be what you are
A brilliant shining star
Your flowering soul is already whole
Share your beauty
with your human family
And simply be
Be all you can be
Live the life of your dreams
It's as easy as can be
If you can talk, you can sing
If you can walk, you can dance
Fly from the cage
Give yourself a chance

To simply be
Wings open, fly free
Soaring high on the breeze
I see your heart's been burned
in the fires of this world
I know your pain is real,
but everything can heal
It can happen now
Let me show you how
Open up and breathe
Open your heart and feel
Simply be what is real
Real for you now
Now is what you are
Let yourself be
Set yourself free
Life is a dream
Embrace the Mystery....

Many came to Aidan's home to hear these songs of love and healing in the family garden. Sicknesses of body and mind dissolved in the medicine of his music. Whether they shed tears of joy or sadness from hearing the bard's music, people felt cleansed of what ailed them. All who listened to his songs felt peace of mind and joy in their hearts. Aidan was deeply loved by all the people of Willow's Glen—all except one.

On the edge of town, in the shadows of some peculiar, unnerving trees, was a dark, dismal cottage. It could not rightfully be called a home, for a home is a place filled with warmth and the welcoming glow of a fire in the hearth. This lifeless place was as cold as the harshest winter and seemed to consume any rays of sunlight like a gaping vortex of darkness.

Inside the sinister abode lived a cruel, twisted druid named Oscuro, trained in the foul, cunning ways of Black Metal. There is potent magic in the spirit of metal. Good folk like Bran used it to craft golden amulets for healing and objects of sublime beauty. But, if bent to evil purposes, metal can be used to create weaponry of the most diabolical nature and sinister mechanical beings. Oscuro was the proud father of many of these nefarious creations.

While the teachings of the Way are rooted in love and harmony, the path of Black Metal is steeped in fear, greed, and hatred. Oscuro was a jealous man with a lust for power, and, as time passed, he grew increasingly resentful of Aidan's abilities. One winter, his bitterness overcame him and, on the longest night of the year with no moon in the sky, he planted the foul seed of the bard's demise. Oscuro knew he could not take the boy's power for his own. Unlike black magic, white magic could not be used when taken from someone by force.

"Curse him!" Oscuro raged. "I may not be able to use his power, but I'll take it from him all the same."

And so, at midnight, the dark druid began weaving a spell, crafting a curse that would summon a Black Metal parasite into this world. Lighting the coal fire in his hearth, he placed his black cauldron over blue flames, which gave off no light. With his long black hair tied back from his gaunt, pale face, he surveyed the scene around him through eyes of storm cloud grey.

"Let's see now," he sneered, "how about a little homemade soup for a growing lad? It's my mother's secret recipe. First, a cup of snake blood. Then a bucket of badger piss. Next, we'll need thirteen leeches, six vampire bats, nine tapeworms, six hundred and sixty-six mosquitos, and, for taste, three vulture feet. And let us not forget the secret ingredient: nine ounces of pure haedium."

Haedium, more commonly known as Black Steel, was the most malign metal known to humankind, forged in the foundries of hell by the hands of the Dark Lord himself.

As the haedium sank into the bubbling cauldron, a red serpent of smoke coiled up from the soup and hissed malevolently at the dark druid.

"Excellent!" he exclaimed with glee. "The curse is complete. Now let's see what there is to see."

With his pale, bony finger he dipped an especially long tapeworm into the red, viscous soup. His eyes opened wide as he felt an insistent tug from beneath the soup's steaming surface. Carefully, he reeled in the tapeworm and, clamped to its head, was a tiny metallic snake with hungry crimson eyes.

"An ophidian! Excellent! One of the most nefarious creatures ever to slither forth from this cauldron!"

Ophidian, shadow serpents, were beings of utter wickedness. Born of the foul path of Black Metal, they embodied all the hatred and cruelty of its twisted lineage. Their venom was one of the most damaging poisons for the human heart and soul.

The next day, dawn broke to a particularly cold winter morning. "A perfect day to deliver some warm soup to that pathetic golden boy," Oscuro said with a malicious grin.

Oscuro walked outside to his grimy stable, where a filthy horse lived. Ankle deep in mud, the druid brushed dead vampire bats from the back of the toxic animal. Taking care to avoid the green, oozing boils covering its body, Oscuro mounted his sickly steed. Coughing and groaning, the mangy horse reluctantly limped off toward Willow's Glen.

They arrived at midday, just as Aidan was finishing his morning singing for a large group of villagers.

"Perfect!" Oscuro whispered. "He'll be cold and hungry from singing all morning in the chilly air." As the dark druid approached the group, the garden plants wilted slightly as he passed.

Oscuro spotted a senile, old woman sitting on the edge of the crowd and hatched his evil plan. Knowing Aidan didn't trust him, he decided to use the weak-minded elder as his puppet. He handed the old woman the covered bowl of soup and, using his powers of mind control, instructed her to deliver the soup to the bard.

As the old woman approached Aidan, Oscuro took over her mind and spoke through her voice. "Thank you, dear Aidan, for the gift of your music," the old woman said in a feeble voice. "You must be hungry after singing all morning for the people. Please accept this bowl of soup in thanks for your work. It is a seafood bisque made by my hands from an old family recipe."

In the back of his mind, Aidan sensed something wasn't quite right, but he couldn't place what it was. Not wanting to be rude, and realizing he was hungry, he accepted the bowl of steaming soup from the elderly woman.

"Delicious!" the bard exclaimed as he slurped the red broth with relish. Quickly devouring the enchanted soup, he tipped the bowl to drain the last of it down his throat. Then his eyes went wide. "I think I swallowed something hard!"

Oscuro's puppet smiled. "Well, you were eating rather quickly. You'll be fine. It must have been a piece of shrimp."

Knowing his evil plan had been realized, the dark druid smiled wickedly and slinked off like a wraith into the shadows of the forest. With a smug look on his face, Oscuro untied his putrid horse and began the slow journey back to his gloomy abode.

FOUR

Nine days later, Aidan became gravely ill with a mysterious fever. Stabbing pains wracked his chest, as if sharp fangs were piercing his heart. At times, the pain was so unbearable that Aidan fell to his knees, grasping his chest.

As the days passed, Aidan's sickness took a tragic toll on his life. The radiant, golden aura that had always surrounded him faded into shadows, and his eyes became dim. Aidan's vitality continued to decline until he barely had energy to sit up in bed. As time crept on, the ophidian's poisonous venom spawned fears in his mind that he would never be cured, and a crushing hopelessness overtook him. Aidan found himself face to face with a host of negative thoughts and anguished emotions.

Until this point, Aidan's life had been filled with joy and peace. He had, of course, experienced fear, sadness, and other painful emotions, like anyone else does. Yet, even in the midst of the stormy seas of intense emotions, the core of his being was at peace. He had remained rooted in his connection with the Way, experiencing his emotions as different lines of music weaving a tapestry of vitality and teachings into his life.

Oscuro's curse had shattered Aidan's foundation of trust in the Way. Despair and hopelessness shook him to the core, and Aidan began to think something was fundamentally wrong with his soul. The growing darkness from

Oscuro's curse made Aidan question his identity and essential worth as a human being. Ashamed and despondent, he struggled to understand the cruel shadow that had taken root inside him.

Mary and Bran sensed the presence of black magic in Aidan's illness. To confirm their suspicions, they sought the counsel of Mary's teacher, Sorena. After breakfast, Mary made the long trek to Sorena's home at the edge of the Whispering Woods. Her cozy cabin faced out from the forest toward the jagged peaks of the Sawtooth Hills.

Before Mary had a chance to knock, Sorena opened the door and smiled at her student. Her hazel eyes studied Mary's face. Perceiving the sadness in Mary's eyes, the witch's smile faded. "Welcome, my child," she said. "Please come in and tell me what's on your mind."

She sat Mary down on a sheepskin by a low table next to the fireplace and walked off to make some tea. Although in her seventies, Sorena's thin frame still moved with fluid grace. She seemed to float across the floor, her long white hair gently flowing in the air as she walked.

Returning with a pot of Hawthorne tea, Sorena sat on the floor across from Mary and poured two cups. "So, tell me, Mary, what weighs upon your heart?"

With a sigh, Mary began the story of Aidan's illness. Near the end, she told Sorena her suspicions that black magic was at work and asked Sorena's advice on how to cure his affliction. After Mary finished speaking, Sorena nodded. "Let us consult the runes."

Rising to her feet, Sorena retrieved a felted wool satchel from the fireplace mantel. She upended the satchel and poured the rune stones onto the table. After flipping the stones rune side down, she mixed them around and looked at Mary. "In your heart and mind, hold the intention of finding a cure for Aidan. Then pick the five stones that call to you."

Mary closed her eyes and took a deep breath. Clearing her mind of all but her intention, she opened her eyes and picked the runes that called to her. The rune stones were smooth to the touch. They looked like black glass, but when Mary held them up to the light, she saw hints of iridescent purple and blue shining from within them.

Sorena looked closely at the runes etched into the five stones and tilted her head slightly, as if listening to a faint whisper. After a moment, she looked up at Mary. "Your suspicions are correct, my child. Foul magic is at the root of Aidan's illness. Unfortunately, a highly skilled practitioner of Black Metal has placed a curse on Aidan. This much is clear: whoever has done this foul deed has gone to great lengths to conceal their identity. Aidan's illness will be difficult to cure, but do not give up hope. A path to healing always exists. It is simply a question of finding the right medicine."

Leaving Mary to sit with her thoughts, Sorena collected a bag of potent medicinal roots and herbs from her kitchen. After explaining how to prepare the herbs, Sorena handed Mary the bag. "You had best make your way back to Willow's Glen," she said. "It is a long walk through the forest. If you leave now, you can still make it back before dark."

Mary embraced her beloved teacher and thanked her. Stepping out the front door, she turned and smiled at Sorena before starting the long journey home.

That night, Mary prepared medicine from Sorena's healing herbs. For weeks, pots simmered with bubbling medicine over the kitchen fire. With the help of the bitter teas, Aidan's fever subsided, and his energy slowly returned. Tragically, however, Aidan could no longer sing. When he tried to sing, no sound would usher forth from his mouth, and he felt a sharp, stabbing pain in his heart. Even playing the lute wracked his chest with unbearable pain. Without the joy of song and music in his life, Aidan sank into a dark depression. For two months, his parents worked day and night to find a remedy for the sinister curse that had stolen his ability to sing, but to no avail.

One spring morning, while out walking along the River of Knowing on the far side of town, his parents were forced to admit defeat. "This curse is beyond our abilities to heal," Mary said with despairing tears in her eyes. "What more can we do to rid our son of this foul affliction, which has darkened the light of his soul?"

Crushed by the cruel reality of their situation, Bran hung his head and stared powerlessly into the river's emerald waters. A flash of shimmering light from a passing fish sparked a childhood memory of listening to his elders tell stories by the light of the fire on an autumn night long ago.

"Perhaps, my love, we have not yet done all we can do. The elders once spoke of a legend about this fair River of Knowing. It is said that when night and day are of equal length, the spirit of this river will answer any question for those whose hearts are pure. The equinox is only days away! We will purify ourselves and see if the legends are true."

For the next five days, they fasted, purifying their bodies with cleansing herbs and sweating in the village steam hut. On the afternoon of the fifth day, under cloudy skies, Mary and Bran approached the sacred River of Knowing. Weak and thin from fasting, the couple kneeled in prayer at the water's edge, honoring the river's spirit and offering gifts of acorn meal and fresh picked flowers. Then, with love in her heart, Mary looked into the flowing waters and asked her question: "River of Knowing, I come to you with humility and gratitude. Please, tell me, how can my son be healed of the foul curse laid upon him?"

Seconds passed. Minutes. Yet there was still no response from the river. Finally, grief overtook Mary, and she fell to her knees, sobbing.

As her first teardrop splashed into the water, its ripple rapidly grew into a wave that surged across the river's surface. At that moment, a ray of sunlight escaped from the clouds above and fell on the opposite shore, illuminating a magnificent purple flower.

"A dream orchid!" they exclaimed, for this delicate flower was rare beyond measure and seldom seen by human eyes. Drinking the tea brewed from a single flower of the mythical plant could summon dreams of profound healing.

"Thank you, fair river, for hearing our prayers and showing us the path of healing for our son," Mary said with tears of joy in her eyes.

That night before bed, they steeped a mug of dream orchid tea for Aidan. The fragrant aroma rising from the cup filled the air with jasmine and amber, honey and rose. Aidan gratefully finished the precious tea and soon drifted into the land of dreams.

In his dream, the bard found himself floating through a landscape filled with jewels of luminous color. Radiant light emanated from the gems, infusing the air with a sublime, expansive energy. In a state of wonder, Aidan moved through the mysterious realm, drinking in the healing light around him.

The dream shifted, and he suddenly found himself in a royal chamber filled with treasures of unimaginable beauty. His eyes beheld a large pyramid of blue lapis carved with runes, a golden cross with a brilliant ruby at its center, and a tapestry on the wall with a complex, flower-like, geometric pattern. The sacred objects glowed with radiant energy.

Aidan began to sense he was not alone. He raised his head and saw a massive throne at the far end of the chamber. Sitting on the throne was a being, the likes of which he could have never imagined.

A magnificent king sat with fierce nobility in front of Aidan. His regal robes were adorned with the mystical jewels of his realm. The king emanated a power unlike anything Aidan had ever felt. He sat like a stone mountain, so rooted that the winds of time could never loosen his grip on life.

The king's proud, ancient face was devoid of flesh, and made entirely of bone. Beneath his golden crown of luminous jewels, where eyes would have been, were the deepest wells of blackness. The bard felt himself being drawn into their emptiness, as if he were falling down a bottomless well. Countless images flickered through his mind, scenes from Earth's past and its future, strange beings from alien worlds, and realms of sacred geometry. It was as if a doorway had opened into the pregnant womb of creation, from which all life is born. Aidan's mind reeled from the flood of images, so he shook himself out of the trance and returned his attention to the scene before him.

The king's energy was so fierce and stern that the bard became afraid. *Have I stumbled upon a demon king? Some malevolent spirit with wicked intentions?* Aidan found that he could not look away from the bottomless pools of the king's eyes, and something prompted him to stay longer in the presence of the timeless monarch.

The ancient king had not moved from his throne, so Aidan calmed down, cleared his mind, and asked his heart if this great being could be trusted. As he listened with his feelings, he realized that inside this formidable being was a pure heart. Its spirit felt like a kind, loving grandfather with a stern, noble exterior, and it became clear that this being was here to help him.

"Magnificent king of luminous light," Aidan said with respect and humility, "thank you for bringing me here. I am Aidan. I humbly ask for your aid in healing me of this foul curse. Do you have a name, Ancient One?"

"You may call me the Bone King," came an unspoken reply arising from the recesses of the bard's mind, "although I have been known by many other names throughout time."

"Bone King, my greatest wish is that I may return to my life as a bard. I long to once again sing songs of joy, love, and healing for the people of my village."

From within Aidan's awareness, the Bone King's resonant voice spoke. "To heal yourself of this evil curse, you must make a pilgrimage to a sacred site of the ancient ones from the long-dead

Age of Stone. These were the ancestors of the druids. Through their humble devotion to the Way, they acquired immense knowledge and skill in magic. These ancient ones were masters of creating doorways between worlds. Portals to countless dimensions exist within their sacred sites of stone.

"In Orkney, there is a stone cairn by the name of Unstan that the ancients used to help usher souls in and out of your world through the gates of birth and death. It is a powerful place of healing, where people can unwind the knots of heart and soul that keep them imprisoned in fear.

"When dawn breaks on the morning of summer solstice, the chamber of Unstan will be filled with the sunlight. At that moment, a doorway will open between my gemstone realm and your world, through which I will be able to enter. If you are there at that time, we will heal you of this dreaded curse."

Aidan blinked and awoke in his bed with rays of dawn's light warming his skin. It was a family tradition to share dreams with each other before breakfast, and on that morning, Aidan's parents were especially eager for news of his dreaming. As they sat next to the crackling fire, sipping nettle tea with rose petals, Aidan began to speak.

"I know what I must do," he told his parents, then he recounted his dream of the Bone King. He did not mention his other dream, in which he had seen that it was Oscuro who had laid the curse upon him. Although he was seething with anger over the wrong done to him by Oscuro, he was clear that confronting the druid would only bring more darkness upon himself and his family. Aidan remembered a conversation several months earlier, when Mary had spoken of Oscuro.

"Oscuro practices the sorcery of Black Metal," Mary had said as she stirred a pot of medicinal herbs simmering on the stovetop. "Metal is a powerful element and, like a sword, it can sever us from our own humanity. The followers of Black Metal have severed their connection with their own hearts in the name of greed and power.

"There is great wisdom and medicine in the darkness. My teacher, Sorena, is often called a white witch; however, this is only partly true. She and I are, above all, witches of the Way. We are servants of life itself, and life is made of light and darkness. Followers of the Way use the teachings of darkness and light to cultivate wisdom and bring healing to those in need.

"Where we differ from Oscuro is that the Way serves love and harmony, while the teachings of Black Metal are rooted in greed and fear. As the human spirit grows and flowers, it emanates light, like the sun. This radiance is the natural state of a vital, healthy spirit. However, for Oscuro, light and dark are out of balance. He has forsaken the light, and his heart has become poisoned with darkness. All things become poison in excess."

Aidan shuddered at the disturbing memory, but nothing could sully the happiness he felt that morning. With the Bone King's promise lifting their spirits, hope's golden light glowed once again from the family hearth. Joy whet their appetites, and breakfast tasted more delicious that day than it had in a long time. Fresh eggs, scrambled with thyme and dill from the garden, filled the air with a mouth-watering, savory aroma. Aidan added to his plate a steaming slice of seeded wheat bread fresh from the oven, slathered with creamy butter and Mary's homemade thimbleberry jam. All was right in the world on that fair morning, and the family dared to feel optimistic that the Bone King would cure Aidan of his cursed illness.

"I too had a dream about your journey to the sacred cairn," Aidan's father said. "You must be well prepared on your journey, for you may encounter dangers along the way. In my dream, I saw that you must visit the legendary Alchemist who lives in the hills near the druid's cairn of Cuween. He will have something essential for you, an object of power to protect you on your journey. The Alchemist is a reclusive hermit and not keen on human visitors, so you must arrive with a gift that will surely grant you entry to his abode...a dream orchid!"

Aidan's eyes sparkled with curiosity and excitement. Growing up, he had heard stories of the fabled Alchemist and his mysterious powers. As a boy, he had often dreamed of meeting him. Aidan nodded, smiling.

Mary thoughtfully put down her tea and began to share her dream from the night before. "My dreams also foretold of someone you must see before embarking on your journey. You must visit Father David at our local church. Tell him the nature of your quest for healing. He may have something for you that will be helpful on your pilgrimage to Unstan."

FIVE

Several weeks later, all had been made ready for Aidan's journey. The day before he was set to leave, Aidan spent the day in the Whispering Woods with Feather. Sitting on the banks of Riffle Creek, they watched the shimmering shapes of trout swimming among the rocks. They spoke excitedly of their past adventures in the forest and enjoyed their last hours together before Aidan left for Unstan. But their time together was bittersweet, because Aidan could not sing with her, as he once had.

"Don't you worry, my dear bard," Feather said. "When you return from your journey, we will sing together next to the creek, just as we used to do. Perhaps the Fey folk will come make music with us again to celebrate your healing." She winked knowingly at him.

Late in the afternoon as they walked back to the village, Feather wished him well on his journey and they reluctantly parted ways.

The next morning, Aidan was set to begin his travels. His knapsack was filled with everything he needed: loaves of hearty wheat bread filled with hazelnuts and huckleberries, dried salted strips of venison, red potatoes from the garden, a bag of medicinal herbs for various purposes, a map of Orkney, a sharp knife with an elk horn handle that his father had given him, and the dream orchid in a clay pot. The pot had a clay lid with air holes to protect the sacred flower during his travels.

As Aidan prepared to leave, his father approached with an object in his hand. "Son, I have created a talisman to bring you strength and good energy on your journey." Bran placed an intricate gold ring in Aidan's hand. The gold was inlaid with spiraling vines that merged into a heart. Looking more closely, Aidan noticed runes woven into the twining vines and a large red garnet in the heart. Placing the ring on his finger, Aidan felt the darkness and negativity from the ophidian fade into the background of his mind. The bard breathed a sigh of relief.

"This ring will protect you from the curse's damaging effects while you seek a permanent cure. There is great love in this amulet." Bran's sky-blue eyes were tender as he met Aidan's gaze. Aidan embraced his father and thanked him for the precious gift.

Not wanting to delay his departure any longer, Aidan turned to his parents and, with tears in his eyes, said his farewells.

"May the spirit of the Way protect you and bless every step of your journey," Mary said.

With that, Aidan turned away from his beloved family and set off for the parish church to meet with Father David.

The village church was a small, unassuming structure, simple of design and built by the skilled hands of a master stonemason in days long past. Parishioners were greeted at the entrance by two strikingly lifelike carvings of the church's patron saints. On the right of the church doors stood the benevolent figure of Saint Francis di Assisi, a dearly loved saint in Willow's Glen. Saint Francis stood with a bird in his open hand next to the trunk of an ash tree that branched into a canopy of leaves, which covered the top of the doorway. Its branches were interwoven with those of its sister tree, holding watch on the other side of the door. Next to the tree on the left stood a statue of Saint Catherine of Sienna, a saint revered for her healing abilities and love for humanity.

Aidan felt a strong connection with Saint Catherine. The stories of her life, as told by Father David, played a large part in Aidan's wish to become a bard and share his healing gifts with the world. Sometimes when Aidan sang for others, he felt her spirit coming through him. Indeed, one of his favorite songs had come to him from Saint Catherine in a dream. It was a song of forgiveness that had soothed many anguished hearts over the years. He bowed in silent gratitude to the saint before entering the church.

As Aidan stepped across the entryway into the humble house of God, he was struck by the stillness and peace infusing the dimly lit chamber. He let out a sigh as his eyes followed the row of weathered wooden pews back toward the preacher's lectern and the great wooden cross, illuminated from above by a narrow shaft of light. Ribbons of smoke rose from frankincense and myrrh burning on the altar, the wispy white fingers reaching up into the still air with their resinous aroma.

The sacred presence of the church was enhanced by rich hues of liquid light entering through stained-glass windows touched by the morning sun. Kneeling near the altar in a state of reverent prayer was Father David. Aidan walked back toward the altar and sat in prayer for a few minutes as he waited for Father David to finish.

Aidan had always cherished Father David's sermons and Jesus' teachings of communion with

God and unconditional love for all beings. The priest had taught him much about love, generosity, and how to pray. He taught Aidan that humility, gratitude, and wholeheartedness were the keys to true prayer. This advice had helped the bard commune more fully with the divinity in all things.

As Aidan became a young man, he realized that, although he dearly loved Jesus and his teachings, Christianity was not his core faith. The bard's church was the forest, and the divine spoke to him through every bird, river, and breeze. In nature, Aidan felt the sacred dance of Goddess and God animating all of creation. He would always be grateful to Father David for teaching him to commune with the sacred. A wave of bittersweet sadness arose in Aidan as he remembered how spirit used to flow through him when he sang his songs of healing for others.

Aidan looked up to see Father David's smiling, wrinkled face looking down at him, his clear brown eyes filled with radiant joy and gentle kindness that warmed the bard's heart. The elder priest's grey beard and humble wisdom gave him the air of a loving grandfather.

"Hello, my son," the priest said in his soft, soothing voice. "What brings you to the house of God on this beautiful spring morning?"

Aidan told Father David the story of his upcoming pilgrimage to the cairn of Unstan and of his mother's dream that the priest would have something to help him on his journey. Father David knew God had chosen Aidan to bring healing to the world through his songs. Committed to helping the bard in any way he could, the priest nodded knowingly. "Come this way, Aidan. I have something to show you that few people have seen."

They walked through a door near the back of the church and down a long, dark hallway lit by candlelight. At the end of the hallway, they stepped through a doorway and out into the most magnificent garden Aidan had ever seen.

As his eyes surveyed the garden, Aidan's first thought was that he had returned to Eden. Vibrant flowers blossomed everywhere, and ripe fruit hung from the trees. The garden was filled with the happy buzzing of bees and birdsong. Butterflies meandered lazily through the air, enjoying the morning sun. A small stream of crystal-clear water bubbled forth from a spring at the far side of the sacred garden. The entire sanctuary seemed to glow with a soft light. "Welcome to the Garden of the Goddess," the priest declared. "Years ago, before our church was built, this sacred garden was a pilgrimage site for those who loved nature and its healing medicine."

Father David pointed to a large boulder at the head of the garden stream. "The spring waters that emerge from beneath that rock have an immense life-giving force and potent healing energy. The spring is a gift from the Goddess herself. Sprinkling a few drops of this water in one's garden will bless anything grown there with potent vitality. The water can cure many diseases and restore the drinker to a state of radiant health."

Aidan thought briefly about drinking the water himself, but his heart told him the cure for his curse would not be found here.

"For many years, witches, druids, and other followers of the Way came on pilgrimage to this sacred garden. They sprinkled their lands with the spring's life-giving waters, and the surrounding farms and forests thrived for many generations under their care.

"Unfortunately, during the time of Saint Francis di Assisi, power-hungry men of the church and practitioners of Black Metal sought to corrupt these waters and turn their power toward evil. Saint Francis dearly loved these gardens, and when he realized they were being threatened, he came immediately to pray for help.

"Once here, he spent days fasting and making offerings to the Goddess. Early one morning, deep in prayer, Saint Francis begged the Goddess to preserve the purity of the springs and prevent the sacred waters from being used for evil purposes. In a state of divine rapture, Saint Francis felt the Goddess enter his body, animating him with her power. Using his body as her vessel, she spoke through his lips, casting a powerful spell that caused the garden to disappear from human eyes. From that point on, this blessed garden was cloaked in a spell of invisibility, concealing it from humankind's vision.

"Only those invited by Saint Francis himself could penetrate the invisibility spell and enter the garden. The Goddess instructed him to have a small church built around the garden to protect it from the outside world. After building this church, he was to find a priest of pure heart to be its guardian for the years to come.

"Since then, there has always been a father of this church dedicated to protecting the Garden of the Goddess. For as long as I walk this earth, I will faithfully serve as guardian and steward of this holy place. You, Aidan, are now part of a small network of people who have access to this sacred haven."

Aidan was filled with wonder and gratitude for his good fortune. He was honored that Father David entrusted him with access to the garden shrine of the Goddess and humbly thanked him for his kindness.

"A few days ago," Father David continued, "the gurgling waters of the spring whispered to me that you would come and that I should give you this."

He held out a small blue crystal amphora that sparkled in the sunlight like a gemstone treasure. "The amphora contains water from the Goddess's spring. Just a few drops can heal the body. The power of the water is varied and vast. If you find yourself in need, listen to your heart, and you will know how to use it. May this gift serve you well on your journey, and may the Goddess bless your every step."

As they were leaving the garden, a hummingbird with emerald wings and a ruby-red chest flew up to the bard and landed on his shoulder. She leaned toward his ear and began chirping happily in the pleasant, excited way of her kind. To Aidan's surprise, he found he could understand the meaning of every twit and chirp that came to his ear. At high velocity, she told him her name was Ruby and said the Goddess wanted her to join Aidan on his journey.

Aidan was thrilled to have such a cheerful companion on his travels. He noticed a feeling of lightness and joy permeate his being as he became attuned to the high vibration of the hummingbird's energy.

Father David laughed. "It seems you will leave this garden with more than one treasure from the Goddess!"

And so, with Ruby buzzing happily above his head, Aidan said farewell to Father David and parted ways. The priest watched fondly as the young bard and his buzzing companion set off on the winding road up the valley to begin their journey to the home of the Alchemist.

The first day of their journey was filled with clear blue skies, clouds of white cotton, and the crisp air of spring. The grasslands glowed with the vibrant green of fresh, new growth. Ruby buzzed happily from flower to flower, sampling the delicious local nectar of spring's bloom. They traveled many miles that day, winding up the broad valley of Willow's Glen, over the jagged slopes of the Sawtooth Hills, and down the other side into an expansive meadow, where a large flock of sheep was grazing happily.

Walking Orkney's countryside with Ruby as his travel companion put Aidan in good spirits. The sweet smell of grass filled the air. Aidan loved to walk, and his faith in the Bone King's promise put extra spring in his step. The soft, loamy soil yielded pleasantly under his feet. With the energy of Bran's healing ring and Ruby's excited chirping and buzzing about, Aidan felt more hopeful than he had in months.

Near sunset, they stopped to make camp under shelter of a group of large, gnarled oak trees. Resting against the trunk of a stout oak, Aidan enjoyed a dinner of his mother's delicious bread, dried venison, and a salad of fresh greens he had picked earlier that afternoon. As dusk deepened toward nightfall, Aidan felt a weariness come over him from the many miles they had traveled. So, he spread out his bedroll and laid on his back to take in the growing number of stars appearing in the rapidly darkening sky. As he pulled his wool blanket around him and yawned, he looked up at Ruby perched in a tree branch above and wondered if she ever slept. Aidan fell asleep to visions of hummingbirds in hammocks and a night sky filled with twinkling gemstones.

The dew-covered grass sparkled like diamonds in the early morning sun. Aidan rolled up his blanket while Ruby buzzed near his head and chirped her "good morning" to him. Eager to continue their travels, Aidan ate a quick breakfast of bread and venison while consulting his father's map about the next leg of their journey.

Walking through an open expanse of meadow, Aidan began to think about the Bone King and mused about his world. What other powerful beings inhabited the Bone King's realm? With his imagination brimming, Aidan watched the billowing clouds above and crafted stories from the images appearing in the morphing whiteness. Cloud spirits trumpeted massive horns that summoned air dragons, who fought with huge trolls emerging from cloudscape mountains....

Aidan had spent many afternoons watching clouds with Feather, seeing stories emerge from the shifting mountains of mist. He sensed Feather's presence as he spent the day walking in a state of creative imagining.

That evening, Aidan and Ruby made camp near a small stream under a group of alder trees. While there was still light, Aidan gathered wood to make a fire. He loved fire and the ritual of making fire: collecting wood and kindling and creating a tinder bundle from small leaves, duff, and tinder fungus from his fire pouch. After preparing everything, Aidan knelt in prayer. "Grandfather Fire, I come to you with love and gratitude for your radiant spirit. You are the hearth of belonging for our people. Thank you for warming our hearts and illuminating our lives."

With that, he struck flint to steel, and a shower of sparks fell onto his tinder bundle. After he blew gently on the small pile of mugwort and tinder fungus, it burst into flames. He gently placed the tinder bundle in the center of the pile of kindling he had constructed and watched as the fire flared to life.

Ruby was happy to sit next to the fire, for a hummingbird's body tends to get chilled at night without the constant influx of sugary nectar. Perched on Aidan's knapsack, she quietly chirped her contentment to Grandfather Fire. Within minutes, Ruby was completely still, as if in a trance. Aidan became a bit concerned, because soon she was catatonic, as if she had died on her perch. He decided not to disturb her, which was good, for nighttime hibernation is the way of hummingbirds. Ruby's metabolism was so high that she would never survive the night without resting deeply, like a bear in winter, to conserve her energy.

At dawn, Ruby was buzzing about like her normal self again and visiting the flowering purveyors of fine nectar in the area. After consulting his map, Aidan's excitement began to build. If they made good time, they would reach the home of the fabled Alchemist by day's end.

SIX

The Alchemist lived in the hills surrounding a sacred cairn named Cuween. Cairns were stone structures built by the ancient followers of the Way as sacred sites for prayer, rituals, and meditation. Cuween was an important pilgrimage site for the druids of Aidan's time. All that could be seen of the cairn from the outside was a small doorway leading into a hillside. Cuween was built underground and could only be entered on one's hands and knees through a long, narrow tunnel that led deep into the hillside.

A timeless wisdom lived in Cuween's inner chambers. Some people believed life's greatest questions could be answered while meditating in the realms of vast knowledge and mystery within the cairn. Others said the secret magic of the druids drew its strength from the pregnant silence of the cairn's unknowable depths. Indeed, druids spent many days and nights immersed in the darkness of Cuween's subterranean chambers, cultivating their power and drinking from its bottomless well of mysteries. For this reason, they called the cairn the Druid's Womb.

Aidan and Ruby approached Cuween in the light of the late-afternoon sun, happy to have made such good time on their journey. Although Aidan was eager to reach the Alchemist, something made him stop at the entrance to the cairn. As he studied the doorway to Cuween's inner chambers, a breeze rustled the leaves of a yew tree growing next to it. Time seemed to slow, the air around him began to shimmer, and he sensed the wind spirits trying to tell him something. As Aidan listened to the rustling leaves, a strong gust of wind rose up and blew open the door to the cairn. A strange, spiraling vortex of wind formed in front of him and shot dry leaves into the passageway.

"Well, that message couldn't be clearer," the bard mused while stroking his chin. "It seems we must pay a visit to Cuween before continuing on to see the Alchemist."

Ruby had no love for small, dark spaces and, through a string of anxious chirps, she made it clear she was none too keen to join him.

"Very well. I suppose I must go this one alone. I'll take a peek and be back in a few minutes."

Ruby ruffled her feathers nervously as Aidan lowered himself on all fours and shuffled through the small doorway. He crawled through the low, narrow passageway for a long distance until, at last, the space opened into a series of stone chambers where he could walk upright again. With the low-lying sun shining through the distant entrance, the dim light allowed him to explore the inner chambers of Cuween.

The rooms were constructed entirely of stone. Some were spacious, others barely large enough for someone to sit cross-legged. The smell of stone and earth hung in the cairn's still, cool air.

Pausing for a moment, Aidan felt a twinge of fear in his belly, knowing he was so deep beneath the hillside. Shaking it off, he looked into another chamber and recoiled when he saw a human skeleton lying on a stone bench against the wall.

Back at the cairn's entrance, a gust of wind suddenly slammed the cairn's wooden door, plunging the bard into complete darkness. Then

Aidan heard the ominous sound of the cairn door being locked from the outside.

Impenetrable darkness surrounded Aidan on all sides. Nauseating fear gnawed at his belly as he struggled not to panic. Just as he was thinking of crawling back down the tunnel and trying to break the door open, a pale orb of white light appeared down a side passageway leading further into the cairn. The orb's cool, liquid glow was calming and strangely reminiscent of the light of the moon. Aidan's curiosity got the better of him, and he walked slowly toward the glowing orb. As he approached, the pale light moved down the passageway, leading him deeper beneath the hillside.

The pale orb stopped above the entrance to a large chamber. Stepping over the entryway, Aidan was horrified to see that the room was filled with human skeletons lying on stone benches. Then, from the recesses of his mind, came a voice like the wind, older than time itself. "This is the Chamber of Death," it said. Every fiber of his being wanted to turn and flee, but his body was frozen and incapable of moving.

"Who are you?" he asked the eerily familiar voice.

"I am the Ancient One, old as life itself. I am water dissolving stone, fire consuming forests, the darkness beyond all knowing. I am the destroyer, that can never be destroyed. I am the womb of all that will be. I have come for you, Aidan. I am Death."

At that moment, Aidan lost consciousness, crashing into a skeleton before he collapsed onto the cold stone floor.

He slipped into a dreamlike state and found himself in a bedroom with concerned family members sitting around a bed, in which lay a thin, old, wrinkled man. If not for his shallow breathing, Aidan would have thought the man already dead. A sense of déjà vu washed over him as he became aware that the elderly man seemed strangely familiar.

"Meet the man you once were." Death's voice spoke like wind blowing through his mind.

Aidan shuddered as he realized he was looking at one of his past lives, in which his former self was approaching the moment of death. In a flash, Aidan became the dying man and felt immense weakness as the life force drained from his body. He felt the man's fear and sadness at having to leave his family and all that he loved so dearly in this world. The crying faces of his loved ones and the familiar knotted-oak ceiling of his bedroom were painful reminders of a life he felt was no longer his own. A ragged sigh escaped his lips, and a tear rolled down his wrinkled face. Aidan felt the man ache for release from the suffering of life.

The old man inhaled, and time slowed as his eyes were drawn to a movement outside the bedroom window. His family faded into the background as his awareness moved outside the house and into the warm glow of the late-afternoon sun on a clear fall day.

The old man watched as a multi-colored leaf spiraled slowly down from the canopy of a gnarled oak tree in his garden. His entire awareness became immersed in the reality of that one exquisite leaf. Fall colors of red, orange, and green had transformed the leaf into a stunning canvas of nature's sublime beauty. The leaf was engaged in an elegant dance as it fluttered and twirled through the air. His eyes followed its animated descent until it finally came to rest among other fallen leaves on the soft earth.

When the old man's awareness returned to the room, Aidan felt the spirit of Death arrive. The now-familiar ancient voice spoke to the old man. "You have lived a good, long life, Losgann. Your time here is done. Leave this withered shell of your body. Let go of all that you still cling to in this life. Release yourself from your suffering, and be free once again. It is time to return to your eternal home in the great beyond."

Somehow, as Aidan listened through the ears of his previous life, his fear dissolved, and he felt the presence of Death as never before. As his heart opened with the heart of the dying man, he experienced the true nature of Death for the first time in his life. Aidan realized he had been deceived by childhood stories of a merciless Grim Reaper.

As the spirit of Death filled the room, Aidan felt a sense of peace and protection wash over him. It was as if a gentle, knowing mother held him in her warm, loving embrace. At that moment, he realized this beloved world was not the only place one could feel a true sense of belonging. Death and the promise of what lay beyond warmed his heart and filled him with wonder.

Losgann, the old man whom Aidan had once been, relaxed as his mind drifted back to a memory from his childhood. He lay out in a meadow near his home on a night of the new moon looking up at the miraculous expanse of the starry sky. Looking out into the vast cosmos, the boy was overcome with a visceral sense of belonging in this immense boundless universe. Heaven's canopy of starlight and darkness was his home. The twinkling diamonds of the night sky stirred within him a deep longing to set off on a grand, epic adventure.

The old man smiled on his deathbed, closed his eyes for the last time, and released his final breath. Then Aidan saw something so beautiful it brought tears to his eyes. From the man's old, emaciated body, like a flower reaching up from rich fertile soil, Losgann's spirit rose like a radiant angel into the air above. His face shined with joy, love, and a child's curiosity as he soared beyond the walls of the room toward the golden light of the setting sun and onwards into his next great adventure.

Aidan was left with a powerful sense that the old man had been liberated and transformed through the initiation of his passing. In a flash, Aidan realized that part of his life path was to work with dying people so he could ease their passage from this world to the next.

Aidan awoke to the feeling of smooth, cold stone against his cheek. From a nearby bench in the chamber a skull smiled knowingly at him. Turning his head, he saw the pale orb hanging in the doorway. As Aidan got to his feet, the orb moved down the passageway toward the cairn's entrance. The orb led him back down the long crawlspace to the doorway and then faded into darkness. After a few moments of sitting apprehensively in the dark passage, Aidan was relieved to hear the lock on the door click open.

Outside, it was night. The full moon was perched high in the heavens above. It was as if the orb had followed him out of the cairn and continued to guide and protect him from its home in the sky. Aidan reflected that he had always felt the moon guiding him in life, connecting him with his intuition, and drawing him deeper into the mysteries of creation. The moon illuminated his dearest dreams and fed his heart's longing to explore the frontiers of the unknown in the outer world, as well as the vast universe within. He bowed in loving reverence to the moon's wise maternal presence.

Drowsiness began to overtake Aidan as the intense journey into Cuween caught up with him. As if still in a dream, he unpacked his bedroll, got under his wool blanket, and lay down on the soft grass. Aidan drifted off to sleep, grateful for the cheerful company of the twinkling stars above and the liquid light of the moon watching over him.

SEVEN

Aidan awoke to the sound of chirping and the buzzing of wings. He opened his eyes and saw Ruby hovering inches from his face, excitedly expressing her relief that he was alive and unharmed. As the soft pink light of dawn filled the sky, Aidan lit a fire to warm them and cooked some small potatoes for breakfast.

With the smell of roasting potatoes drifting in the air, Aidan told Ruby about his adventures in Cuween and his encounter with Death. Ruby was overjoyed when Aidan spoke of wanting to assist people with their passage through the doorway of death.

Ruby spoke of how she had helped many creatures of all kinds to die bathed in peace and love. Besides the joy and magic of her presence, Ruby used the power of the rainbow to assist people's passage between this world and the next. She used colors to harmonize their energy and support their connection with spirit as they moved into the beyond. Aidan did not entirely understand how the process worked, but he knew he had found a partner for his future path of working with the dying.

After a breakfast of potatoes roasted with fresh rosemary, they packed up camp and made off to find the Alchemist.

In a small valley between two rolling hills, they came upon a shepherd guiding his flock across the grassy terrain. He was a wiry man with hunched shoulders. A long pointed beard covered his thin sun-weathered face. His eyes were more animal than human, and the man looked strikingly like a goat.

"Good day, fair shepherd," Aidan said as he approached the peculiar man. "I am Aidan, and I seek the home of the Alchemist. Can you tell me where I might find him?"

The shepherd stared at Aidan with his beady eyes for an uncomfortable few moments. "Ya' must be daft to seek the Alchemist," he said in a raspy voice, unaccustomed to speech. "He's got his fingers in things that shouldn't be tinkered with. Changing things that shouldn't be changed. I've heard tales of him turning people into toads, and worse. He's a dangerous man, and he's not keen on visitors."

Aidan paused to consider what he was getting himself into before he replied. "I appreciate your concern, but I have no choice. I must see the Alchemist."

"Well, then," the goatish shepherd said, pointing to a peak farther up the mountain. "Over that peak ya' drop into a valley. Follow the river upstream, and ya'll find the Alchemist's home."

"Thank you...kind shepherd," Aidan said, realizing the man hadn't told him his name. "May you enjoy this fine day with your flock."

"Ay, good luck to ya', Aidan," the shepherd said before turning back to his sheep.

"What a curious man," Aidan said to Ruby as they walked toward the peak above the valley of the Alchemist.

Hours later, after dropping into the valley and following the river upstream, Aidan and Ruby came upon the Alchemist's home. It was nestled in a small, forested valley along a peaceful, meandering river. His home was a network of rooms and structures in strange locations. A large treehouse was perched within the thick, gnarled branches of a mighty oak tree. Hanging from one of the tree's largest branches was another room, accessed by a hanging rope ladder. Where a floor would have been, rope webbing spanned the entire space, and the walls were open to the outside. The hanging room was tall, and from the ceiling hung flags, mobiles, and other objects that danced and twirled in the wind. Hammocks hung at different heights, and a number of bells and chimes sounded merrily when the wind spirits moved through the treetops.

Aidan watched, mesmerized, as a breeze rose, and the entire structure came alive in movement and sound. Mounted upside down on a neighboring tree's branches, a handful of small windmills whirled in the breeze.

Down below, a stone path led to another room behind a cascading waterfall in the river. Ruby flew up and sipped from the falling water as it glistened in the sun. Hovering there, she could make out the shifting shapes of blue and green furniture behind the liquid wall of the water room. A small branch of the river had been diverted down the middle of the room and ran under a wide, glass-topped table between two couches. Off to the side of the waterfall room, a wooden waterwheel spun lazily in the sloshing body of the river.

Aidan turned his head and gasped at what he saw. Off to the left in a grassy clearing, glowing brightly in the midday sun, was a huge, boulder-sized quartz crystal emerging from the ground. Amazingly, some kind of temple space had been carved into the giant crystal. Through the transparent walls, he saw that a large altar had been carved out of the quartz itself. On the altar were many precious stones and crystals. The room was decorated with shining candelabras of silver and gold, and a giant mobile of precious gems hung from the ceiling. Cushions lay around the space on top of an intricate silk carpet woven with all the colors of the rainbow.

To the right of the crystal room, under the shade of a large oak tree, was a grassy knoll. Looking closely, Aidan noticed a rounded wooden door that led into the side of the hill. He wondered what surprises he might find in the underground chamber.

"How delightfully unusual!" Aidan said, a puzzled smile on his face. He decided the best course of action was to announce his presence. "I am Aidan," he called out, "a bard from Willow's Glen. I have come to seek the aid of the great Alchemist."

The sound of glass breaking descended from the treehouse above, followed by angry cursing. "Blasted bat barf! Ghastly ghost guano!"

From the floorboards of the treehouse, a round door swung open, and down popped the head of a peculiar old man with an irritated look on his face. His long grey hair stood straight up from his head in a thick solid braid supported by a series of silver rings holding the braid upright. Another set of gold rings created the reverse effect by gathering the hair from his long, hanging beard. It was as if thick chords of grey rope adorned with precious metals sprouted out of his chin and the top of his head. The crotchety old man had a thin pointy nose and the face of a fox. His piercing eyes had an unusual quality that Aidan could not quite place.

"Go away, foolish boy. I have no time to waste on the likes of you." the Alchemist said in a flustered, impatient voice.

At that moment, Ruby flew up within inches of the Alchemist's face and started chirping cheerily. He listened intently and then looked at Aidan. "This delightful creature is your companion? Interesting...well, maybe you're not a *complete* idiot after all."

Aidan was annoyed with this rude treatment but wisely decided to hold his tongue.

"How about this, young man: just to show you that I'm a good sport, we'll have a little fun. I'll tell you a riddle. If you answer it correctly, we can chat for a few minutes. If you get it wrong, you must scurry back from whence you came. Do we have a deal?"

Since he really had no other option, Aidan nodded in agreement.

"Very well," the bothersome Alchemist said, smiling. "Here is your riddle:

"Ancient as the earth, spirit of the stars above, child off fallen trees...What am I?"

Aidan thought deeply for a minute, to no avail. Then a memory came to him of a dream his father, Bran, had once shared with him. In the dream, Bran was shown that the countless stars in the sky were massive, blazing orbs of fire like their own sun. They only appeared to be points of light, because they were so far away. Aidan found the fantastic idea hard to believe, yet the memory caused a thought to ignite in his mind.

"Fire!" the bard said. "Fire is the answer!"

The Alchemist's mouth fell open in disbelief. Then his face scrunched into a frown. "Oh, very well!" snapped the Alchemist. He pulled his head back up into the treehouse. A few moments later, a rope ladder dropped from the doorway, uncoiling like a snake in front of the waiting bard.

"Excellent!" Aidan whispered as he began climbing the ladder into the Alchemist's arboreal realm.

As he climbed up through the door in the treehouse floor, Aidan looked around in amazement. The treehouse was much larger inside than it appeared from below. A number of small stained-glass windows and large crystals inset into the ceiling filled the space with multicolored beams of light. Huge branches of the oak tree intersected the main room, forming support columns and providing staircases to rooms perched near the high ceiling. Smaller branches bursting with vibrant green leaves spread throughout the space, creating an enclosed canopy illuminated by beams of sunlight coming in through skylights. Aidan was surprised to see squirrels scurrying among the branches and birds flying through the expansive canopy.

On the far wall, an impressive library of old leather-bound books filled the shelves from floor to ceiling. The center of the room contained a large open-air kitchen stocked with pots, pans, glass flasks, and beakers filled with mysterious bubbling liquids. Wide shelves in the kitchen contained countless jars filled with dried herbs, roots, flowers, powdered stones and minerals, insects, and some creepy things you probably don't want to know about.

A small cooking fire burned in a wood stove. Steam billowed from a large black cauldron simmering on the stovetop. Next to it on the floor was broken glass from the flask Aidan had heard break earlier. Looking up from the floor, Aidan's eyes locked with those of the clearly impatient Alchemist.

"Well, are you going to stand there gawking all day, or are you going to introduce yourself properly?" the Alchemist asked.

"B-beg your pardon," the bard stammered. "My name is Aidan. I am making a pilgrimage to the sacred cairn of Unstan to discover a cure for a foul curse."

"Hmm…I see." The Alchemist raised a bushy eyebrow with curiosity. "I am Cambius, the Alchemist. You are certainly not a typical country boy. I am interested to hear more about this curse. Please, tell me the story from the beginning."

Cambius poured them both steaming mugs of delicious floral tea. After sipping his tea, Aidan sat down and began telling the story of his dark curse and the reason for his journey.

Shortly after starting his tale, the bard felt the powerful tea take effect as a warm wave of euphoria filled his body. "Nice tea," Aidan said dreamily. With a relaxed smile on his face, he told his entire tale to his curious companion. Aidan found himself unusually chatty and spoke as if he were talking to an old friend. He finished his tale by sharing his father's dream, that the Alchemist would have an object of power to help Aidan on his journey.

"An interesting tale indeed…," the Alchemist said, pensively stroking one of the gold rings binding his ropy beard. Whether from the tea or Aidan's story, Cambius had softened significantly from his earlier crabby state and appeared much more amiable. Looking into the Alchemist's eyes, Aidan realized what had seemed strange about them earlier: they changed color! His eyes had been light blue when the bard first saw them. While telling his story, Aidan thought they had changed to brown but wrote it off as the potent tea altering his vision. But now there could be no denying it. Cambius's eyes had morphed into a vibrant shade of purple!

"Oh, I almost forgot!" the bard exclaimed as he reached into his knapsack. "I have a gift for you."

He pulled out the tiny pot containing the dream orchid. Lifting the pot's perforated clay lid, Aidan revealed the journey-jostled plant.

"A dream orchid!" Cambius's jaw dropped open in disbelief. Then he began pacing excitedly and ranting to himself, "A dream orchid! Impossible! I thought it only a plant from legend. Unheard of! A priceless treasure! Unbelievable!"

After a minute or so of carrying on in this way, he calmed down and gratefully took the rare plant from Aidan's hands. Cambius looked down lovingly at the somewhat wilted orchid. "We must do something for you at once, my little travel-weary friend."

He gently repotted the slightly limp plant into a large bowl, placed it on a well-lit table in the living room, and then pulled a bundle of dry herbs from an apothecary jar in the kitchen. He used a beeswax candle to light the bundle on fire and then walked back to the dream orchid. Blowing out the burning herbs, he fanned the smoke gently over the wilted plant with his hand as he whispered under his breath. Aidan watched the plant perk up significantly, and by the time Cambius had finished, the dream orchid looked perfectly healthy and vital once again.

"Much better, dear one." Cambius smiled with fatherly pride and then returned to his seat across from Aidan with an intrigued look in his chameleon eyes. "Young man, the spirits of this world look favorably upon you. Your heart must be pure indeed. I will help you however I can on your quest for healing. We must consult the spirits about this powerful gift I am meant to give you."

At that moment, a brown wren flew down from the canopy and landed noiselessly on the Alchemist's shoulder. She chirped in his ear in the gentle way of wrens. Cambius listened intently, looked at the bird with a perplexed expression in his now-green eyes, and said, "Are you sure, my dear? Wouldn't that be far too risky?" The wren seemed quite confident that its advice was sound, so Cambius conceded. "Oh well, maybe the boy will have better luck than I did. I suppose it's decided then."

He turned to Aidan. "You have come for a gift of power, and it appears you shall indeed have one. I only hope it does not prove too powerful to contain."

With Ruby and the wren having a cheerful conversation on his shoulder, the Alchemist took Aidan over to a large, squat lockbox with thick metal walls sitting on the floor of the living room. When Cambius opened the box, Aidan saw it was lined with an even thicker layer of stone, and inside was a small, square object. Cambius picked it up, revealing it to be a masterfully crafted box made of lapis and bluish, silver metal engraved with runes. Built into the front of the box was a small thick glass window. Standing inside, looking out at him with warm friendly eyes, was a tiny red imp-like creature!

"It's a fire sprite," the Alchemist said, cringing slightly as spoke. "It's one of the most dangerous creatures known to this world."

Aidan looked closely at the fire sprite's smiling amiable face and stroked his chin. "He doesn't look very dangerous."

"Do not be deceived by his appearance," Cambius warned. "That would be the gravest of mistakes."

For a moment, Aidan thought he saw a fiery spark flicker in the sprite's eye.

"The fire sprite's power makes dragon fire look like a candle flame in comparison. Once released from this rune box's protective spell, his energy can be difficult to contain. I would recommend only releasing him from the spell in a time of gravest need.

"Let me tell you a story. As you may have noticed from the construction of my home, I am rather obsessed with elemental energies. I built the different rooms of my abode to embody the energies of the elements: water, air, wood, metal, and earth. Elemental energies are essential to the practice of alchemy, and I have invited their primordial spirits into my home, so I may commune with them and learn from their timeless wisdom."

Aidan thought for a moment. "Is the metal room the giant crystal?"

"Yes. Metal embodies energy in its most distilled, concentrated form. In addition to silver and other metals, crystals also contain the spirit of metal. Crystals contain concentrated, pure energy. In many ways, they are a union between metal and light. But let me not digress from my story.

"A few years back, I designed a fire room that was meant to be a home for this fire sprite. The structure's outer walls would be pure fire kept burning by the sprite. Through potent spells of insulation, the temperature inside could be set to use as a sauna or increased to the heat of an oven...or beyond. The fire sprite would stay in a protected enclosure that distributed his energy out into the walls, keeping the entire room ablaze.

"Unfortunately, in creating the fire-distribution system, I significantly underestimated the fire sprite's power. The inferno within him overloaded the system, and the room exploded. Without the help of the river, I would have undoubtedly burned this entire valley to the ground. I hope you have better luck with the fire sprite than I did. Powerful spirits seem to look over you, Aidan. Perhaps you can learn how to manage the fire sprite's power safely, where I could not."

After placing the rune box back in the stone safe and locking the lid, the Alchemist taught Aidan the spells to release the fire sprite from his containment and to lock the rune box once again.

"Please stay here tonight as my guest," Cambius said. "You can have a good night's rest and leave refreshed in the morning."

Aidan was happy to oblige, since he found the Alchemist to be fascinating company and was eager to explore his interesting home. Besides, Ruby was clearly enjoying the companionship of the many birds living in the canopy of the treehouse.

Cambius told Aidan he had work to do before dinner and, not so subtly, shooed him away. After watching the Alchemist drop a bat wing into a simmering beaker of bright blue liquid, Aidan decided to leave him alone and explore the elemental abode.

Descending the rope ladder from the treehouse, Aidan stepped onto the grass and surveyed the scene around him. A path of multicolored stones and crystals connected the various rooms of the Alchemist's home. In the afternoon light, the path shined with all the colors of the rainbow. Aidan's eyes were drawn immediately to the crystal room glowing brightly in the sunlight.

Approaching the massive quartz structure, the bard ascended the crystalline stairs and stopped at one of the most unique doorways he had ever seen. The door was crafted entirely of silver metal with a bluish hue. Adorning the door's surface were geometric symbols inlaid in gold and highlighted with precious gems. The doorknob was an enormous, clear gemstone, which sparkled with rainbow light as he turned it and pushed the door open. Closing the door behind him, Aidan saw a padded mallet hanging from the inside doorknob. Although there was no gong in sight, the inside of the door was inset with a circular shape, like a cymbal. Aidan struck the door with the mallet, producing a resonant tone like a temple gong. As he listened, the sound waves infused his mind with peace.

The space was saturated with brilliant multi-colored light. Sunlight brought the crystal walls alive with a luminous glow accented with streaks of rainbow from imperfections in the quartz. Aidan felt drawn to sit at the altar on the far side of the room. The altar's surface was carved into the crystalline wall of the quartz room. Covering the altar was a tapestry with an intricate geometric design. Crystals and golden bells on the altar pulsated with energy, beckoning Aidan toward them.

Removing his shoes, Aidan walked across a lustrous silk carpet of brilliant gold and silver and sat cross-legged on a cushion in front of the altar. Closing his eyes, he began to meditate by turning his awareness inwards, as his father, Bran, had taught him.

Bathed in the radiant, pure energy of the crystals and precious metals on the altar, Aidan's mind easily became focused and concentrated. A brilliant field of refined white light filled his awareness. The words "Diamond Mind" came to Aidan, and he sensed that priceless teachings would come to those who sat with open awareness in the temple's refined energy.

His father's words, "Knowledge speaks, wisdom listens" came to Aidan, and he realized how Bran would love to explore the mysteries of that sacred space. Aidan wanted to stay and meditate longer, but his curiosity about the other elemental rooms called to him.

Leaving the crystal room, Aidan followed the stone path past the treehouse and out to the river. The surface of the waterfall shimmered with color in the light of the evening sun. The water room beckoned from behind the rippling wall of green and blue. Aidan followed a raised stone path behind the cascading water and found himself in a space straight out of a fairy tale. It looked as if he had walked into the home of a water nymph.

The chamber was bathed in undulating blue light from the sun's rays filtering through the waterfall. The walls and ceiling were sculpted out of stone into flowing lines reminiscent of water in a river. Ripples, waves, and eddies created a feeling that the walls were in constant motion. The couch, chairs, table, and bed were all constructed with similarly fluid lines and shapes.

Aidan sat on the edge of the bed and was startled when the mattress gave way like liquid.

The bed was filled with water! Lying back on the bed's wavy surface, Aidan basked in the space's watery atmosphere. Just being there, his body began to feel less solid. His mind became more fluid and creative, wandering as if in a dream.

As his eyes followed the wavy lines in the ceiling, Aidan noticed several lanterns hanging from chains. The lanterns were made of blue and green glass, so the candles created a watery glow at night. Aidan longed to spend the night in the water room and see what dreams would come.

Pushing himself with some effort off the bed, Aidan meandered across the space to the waviest couch he'd ever seen. It was cushioned with a thick carpet of soft green moss. A small stream wandered through the living room and passed beneath the glass coffee table in front of him. The bottom layer of glass touched the stream's surface, giving a clear view into the watery world below. Aidan was delighted to see large trout swimming among the rocks under the coffee table.

"I wish I could live here," Aidan said longingly. He had always had an intimate connection with rivers, so the water room was a dream come true. Aidan was pulled out of his reverie by the sound of the Alchemist's voice calling him to dinner.

As he walked back toward the treehouse, Aidan noticed an area farther up the hill where there had been a horrible fire. The charred remains of a building littered a large area of blackened earth. Aidan swallowed hard as he realized he was looking at the remains of the fire room. As he climbed the rope ladder to the treehouse, he reminded himself that the fire sprite had created that fire. Clearly, his new travel companion was not to be taken lightly.

As Cambius prepared their dinner, he and Aidan spoke of alchemy and music. Upon hearing of the healing songs that Aidan used to sing for people, Cambius mused that alchemy and music had much in common. Both involved transformation of energy in fundamental ways. Aidan's songs were like alchemy for troubled minds and anguished hearts. The soothing sounds of his songs transformed people's suffering and heartache into states of peace, acceptance and love for life. Cambius saw that the function of the bard's music was not merely entertainment but human alchemy and healing of the spirit.

While Aidan and Cambius lost themselves in conversation, Ruby buzzed about in the branches above, chirping excitedly with robins and sparrows.

As the aroma of simmering soup and sautéed mushrooms drifted in the air, Aidan's eyes surveyed the many unusual items in the Alchemist's home. On a pedestal in the far corner, he noticed something that made his mind reel in confusion: a clear glass orb. From a metal post within, small bolts of lightning shot out toward the surface of the glass. Aidan could not believe his eyes. It was magic, the likes of which he had never seen or heard spoken of before. Baffled, he pointed an inquisitive finger at it. "What is that thing?"

"That, dear boy, is one of my greatest alchemical discoveries. Using the power of my windmill and waterwheel, I have learned how to summon the spirit of lightning. Once harnessed, the lightning can be used as a power source for many purposes. You must never speak of the Lightning Orb to anyone. If humanity knew how

70

to harness the energy of lightning, it would utterly transform reality as we know it. Most humans are far too foolish and shortsighted to use such power in a responsible way. Greed and lust for power would reap immense destruction in its efforts to control this immense source of energy. The world will just have to wait to discover the ways of lightning."

Aidan walked over to the Lightning Orb and stared at it in fascination. He was delighted to find that when he touched the orb, tiny fingers of lightning followed his finger. He was finally coaxed away from the orb by Cambius's announcement that dinner was ready.

While they ate wild mushrooms sautéed in butter and a savory soup of roots and herbs, Aidan spoke of his encounter with Death in the chambers of Cuween.

"You are fortunate indeed," the Alchemist said. "Death is one of the greatest allies a person can have in life. Death teaches us to see clearly what we cherish most, so we can fully devote our lives to those things. Delusion and confusion dissolve when Death is near, allowing us to let go of things of little importance. In this way, we can listen to our hearts, focus our energy on the things we hold most dear, and be fully alive."

Although Aidan wanted to continue his fascinating conversation with the Alchemist, soon after dinner sleep began to beckon. Watching Aidan nod off multiple times, Cambius chuckled, then led the half-asleep bard to his bed on a platform high up in the branches of the oak canopy. Aidan wasted no time laying his head on the pillow. In the company of squirrels and birds also readying themselves for dreamtime, he fell into a deep sleep.

EIGHT

The next morning, the smell of freshly baked bread coaxed Aidan to leave his comfortable bed. Dawn's early light sent beams of yellow and red from stained-glass windows into the leaves above his head. *What a blessed abode,* Aidan thought as he rose and dressed himself. Climbing down the ladder from the lofty perch, he joined Cambius for a breakfast of hearty acorn bread with butter and honey and roasted hazelnuts with dried berries.

Aidan was reluctant to leave the Alchemist's fascinating company, but he knew they needed to resume their journey to Unstan. After breakfast, he and Ruby said their farewells and thanked Cambius for his help and hospitality. With obvious hesitance, Cambius handed Aidan the lapis rune box containing the fire sprite.

"The fire sprite feeds on sunlight and fire. Make sure you leave his box out in the sun for some time every day. May your need never be great enough that you are compelled to release him."

Aidan promised to return with the fire sprite after his journey was complete. Ruby clearly was also eager to return. After the hummingbird said her sad farewells to her new feathered friends, she and Aidan descended from the treehouse and set off to continue their journey.

The morning was clear and crisp as they hiked the valley of the Alchemist back to Cuween and descended the rolling hills to the main road. As they walked, Aidan gathered yarrow, angelica, and other plants for his medicinal herb satchel. Throughout the long day of travel, he chewed yarrow leaves to sustain his energy. Ruby had plenty of energy, thanks to sugary nectar from flowers they passed along the road. She buzzed about with curiosity and startled slower birds by rocketing past them at high velocity. She also surprised several squirrels and sheep by appearing out of thin air and hovering within inches of their faces.

Aidan tied the fire sprite's rune box to the outside of his knapsack during the afternoon, so it could feed on the energy of the sun. The sprite sprawled out on his back like a supremely contented sunbather.

Just after nightfall, the travelers came to the town of Stonewall, where Aidan hoped to find a warm meal and a comfortable bed for the night. Stonewall took its name from the tall stout wall of stone that enclosed the settlement. The wall's large grey rocks fit together perfectly, built by a master stonemason long ago. The wall was created not only to protect the town from attack but also to deflect the raging winds that blew in from the ocean during the cold, dark winter.

Entering through Stonewall's formidable wooden gate, they found themselves on a dusty street lit with the flickering glow of lanterns hanging from lampposts carved with vines, dragons and trees. The intricate carvings came to life in the oil lanterns' shifting light. Most of the storefronts were closed for the night, and only a few people were out walking in the chilly night air.

Aidan smelled roast mutton on the breeze and knew an inn or tavern was not far away. His mouth watered from the savory aroma, and he longed to sit down for a meal. Shivering from the cold, he decided to put on his wool cloak before they continued. Aidan didn't know what kind of people lived in Stonewall, so he decided to be cautious and not open his knapsack in view of people on the main street.

Stepping off into a empty side street, he knelt and untied his knapsack. He had just removed his cloak and was retying his knapsack when he heard footsteps behind him.

Turning quickly, he stood up to see three unsavory drunken men in coarse, stained tunics sneering at him with a cruel look in their eyes. A large, stocky man with a dark beard and even darker eyes stepped forward.

"You must be growing tired of carrying that heavy knapsack, young master," he said with a mischievous, drunken slur. "Perhaps my friends and I can help relieve you of your burden." His friends laughed heartily, thinking his words were quite clever.

"I don't think that will be necessary," the bard said haltingly as fear tied his stomach into knots.

Anger flashed in the thieves' eyes, and the leader pulled out a dagger with a notched weathered blade. "Perhaps you don't understand your situation, young master. Either you give me your knapsack, or I will take it and leave you bleeding here in the dirt."

Before Aidan could reply, Ruby appeared and hovered aggressively within inches of the man. Red-faced, the thief slashed wildly at the hummingbird with his dagger. With the skill of a boxer, Ruby swooped left and right, up and down, dodging his attacks. Then she retreated toward Aidan, and a strange thing happened.

Intense ruby-red light shot out from the hummingbird's body, bathing the three men in its luminous glow. For a moment, the men looked confused, but then they seemed to become even angrier. The red light fed their anger, and they appeared to be enjoying their rage. They began attacking each other with blows and wrestling in the dirt.

Ruby's light shifted to a rich orange, and the men's anger slowly subsided. They released each other, laid down on their backs, and looked happy and radiant, as if they were basking in the sun. A minute later, the light emanating from her morphed into a rich golden yellow, and Aidan was surprised to see the thieves transmuted into noble, almost regal, versions of themselves. Rising to their feet, they looked strong and proud, their faces softened into benevolent smiles. Finally, the light shifted to the vibrant green of new spring growth. By then, the men looked utterly transformed, as if they had been reborn. They beamed with fresh vitality and undeniable joy.

Aidan could not believe his eyes. Clearly a significant healing of the heart had occurred. Their ill intentions had dissolved, and now they embodied higher versions of themselves.

At that point, the green light shining from Ruby disappeared, and the men looked around, bewildered. They stepped toward Aidan, fell to their knees, crying, and begged his forgiveness for threatening him and trying to steal his knapsack. Still confused, the bard looked over at Ruby, who nodded to him as she buzzed around contentedly.

Aidan happily forgave the men for their attempted theft, and they rose to thank him and Ruby for their kindness. "I am Janus," the leader said. "Is there anything we can do to repay you for this great blessing of the light, young master?"

"Well, actually," Aidan said, "It would be quite helpful if you could tell us where to find a warm meal and a comfortable bed for the night."

The three men cheerfully led the bard back onto the main street and towards their destination. Aidan found it strange how kind and happy the men had become and vowed to ask Ruby more about her powers when they had a moment alone.

They stopped in front of an inn with a giant boar's head over the door. It was bustling with activity, and the sound of merrymaking spilled out from its open windows like a giant wave of ale.

"Welcome to the Boar's Head!" Janus announced with pride. "The finest food in Stonewall. The proprietor is a lovely woman named Fionna. You'll feel right at home here."

With that, they bid their farewells. As they were leaving, Janus slipped a couple of coins into Aidan's hand. "The first round of mead is on me!" he called back over his shoulder.

Amused, the bard looked at Ruby, who was perched on his shoulder. "What interesting spells you weave, little magician. I've never heard of thieves giving money instead of taking it."

The smell of roast venison brought Aidan's awareness back to his empty stomach. He pushed open the thick wooden door, and they stepped into the Boar's Head Tavern.

As he walked through the door, Aidan's senses were flooded with the smell of boar stew, roast venison, pipe tobacco, and the aroma of a roaring fire mingled with the musk of human bodies. Sounds of clinking mugs of mead, loud conversation, fiddle music, and singing greeted his ears. The large room was dimly lit with the soft light of oil lanterns hanging from the ceiling, and the air was thick with tobacco smoke.

Folk of all sorts filled communal tables in the center of the room, while smaller groups sat in wooden booths against the walls. To the left, a long bar stood in front of wooden barrels filled with wine, ale, and mead. Behind the bar, steam billowed from the inn's bustling kitchen. On the far wall of the main room, a large stone hearth glowed with the warm light of a welcoming fire. A group of revelers stood around the fire singing raucously as a fiddler played his tune.

A radiant woman with pale freckled skin and long braided red hair stood at one of the tables carrying more mugs of mead than Aidan would have thought possible. After delivering the mugs to the table and joking with her customers, she wiped her hands on her apron, looked up, and caught Aidan's eye.

Walking up to Aidan, she looked at him with blue eyes full of warmth and kindness. "Welcome to the Boar's Head, young sir. I am Fionna, the owner of this establishment. You must be tired and hungry from you travels. May I offer you a plate of hot food and a mug of our local mead? Our home-cooked venison is particularly good tonight."

"You have read my mind, fair lady," Aidan replied gratefully. He introduced himself and Ruby, who was still perched on his shoulder looking around excitedly at all the activity. Bewildered, Fionna looked at the bard's tiny companion. "Miss Ruby, can I offer you anything to make you feel at home?"

Ruby looked at her and then chirped in Aidan's ear. With a look of surprise, he said, "She will have a small glass of your sweetest honey wine, if she may."

They took their seat at one of the booths near the fire and were soon delivered a steaming hot plate of food and a small glass of blackberry honey wine. "I also brought you a taste of my famous boar stew, on the house," Fionna said, sliding a steaming earthen mug toward Aidan. He was ravenous by then and laid into the food with relish.

Fionna's venison, roasted with onions and rosemary, was the finest he'd ever tasted. The delicious stew and hearty peasant bread reminded him of home. Aidan longed for the company of Feather and his family and wished they could be with him enjoying Fionna's excellent cooking. After finishing his supper, Aidan sat back, content, and looked up to see Ruby perched on her glass, sipping merrily from her honey wine. With his belly full, the bard became intrigued about the magic Ruby had used to deal with the thieves and asked her to explain what had happened.

Perched on the edge of her wine glass, Ruby chirped rapidly in response. "I practice rainbow medicine, which uses the energy of light and colors to transform and harmonize a person's energy. In the case of our three angry thieves, I first bathed them in pure red light. Red best matched their angry, hot, violent energy. Pure red energy was so familiar to them that it was like a homecoming to sit in their native color.

"Then I shifted the energy to orange and then yellow, slowly cooling them down until they were ready to move into the green light. Green is one of the most healing and harmonizing colors. It is fully aligned with life and nature. Green is also the color of spring growth and new beginnings, which those men desperately needed."

Aidan had never imagined that color could be so powerful. He had newfound respect for his curious traveling companion. As she perched on the edge of her glass, contentedly sipping blackberry honey wine, Aidan began to wonder how alcohol affected hummingbirds.

Out of the inn's smoke-filled air, Aidan heard a woman's rich, resonant voice rise in song, weaving itself together with the slow, sad melody of a flute. He looked over to the fire and saw that the beautiful voice came from the owner of the Boar's Head. Fionna sang of a man and woman who were deeply in love until the man was struck by lightning and killed. So filled was the song with passion and emotion that the entire tavern remained quiet and listened intently to the tragic tale. When the song ended, the patrons let out a collective sigh.

Not wanting to leave her customers in such a somber state, Fionna launched into an upbeat, boisterous song accompanied by the cheerful melody of a fiddle and the driving pulse of a frame drum. As she sang of the joys of spring and the festival of Beltane, people rose from their seats and sang along, dancing arm in arm. The music was so infectious that Aidan soon found himself dancing by the fire with a smiling red-cheeked milkmaid twice his age. To his surprise, he saw that even Ruby was dancing in twirling flight around the room. The song continued, chorus after chorus, keeping the revelers dancing without break. Finally, when Aidan thought he might collapse from exertion, the music stopped, and everyone fell back into their seats.

Returning to their booth, Aidan drank thirstily from his clay mug of mead as Ruby dipped her beak into her blackberry honey wine. The bard looked up from his mead to find Fionna looking down at him. "I'm glad to see you have been enjoying the music...and your little friend also." She nodded toward Ruby who was back doing her aerial dance as the fiddler played another buoyant tune.

"I enjoyed your song a great deal," Aidan said. "That first song was so heartfelt and full of sorrow."

Aidan knew the woman could have been a bard herself from the power of her song. Bards were known to be able to bring people to laughter or tears through the spirit of their voice. Fionna certainly had that ability. Thinking about such things brought pangs of sorrow to Aidan's heart as he remembered how dearly he loved to sing for the people of his village. Aidan returned from his thoughts and looked at Fionna. "Did you write the first song yourself?"

"That I did, young master," she said somberly as a look of sadness came to her eyes. "The song was about the love of my life, who passed on several years ago. John was a shepherd, a sweet man of the earth who loved nature. We had a wonderful life together tending sheep near our home in the hills outside Stonewall.

"John had already been struck once by lightning and lived. He had an intense passion for weather—among other things," she said with a knowing smile. "He would go outdoors in the most extreme winds and lightning storms. They seemed to feed his spirit. Sadly, the second lightning strike took his life and stole him from this world.

Considering his love for the weather spirits, I suppose it was a good way for him to die.

"I was crushed with despair for a long while after his death and wondered if I would ever recover. But for those with a love of life and God, there is no giving up in the face of tragedy. So, I decided to start a new life and bring something good into this world. I sold our home and our flock of sheep and used the money to open the Boar's Head. Providing good food, drink, and music to townsfolk and travelers was healing to my soul and, over time, joy slowly returned to my heart."

"You are a courageous woman," Aidan said. He had a growing affection for the strong, generous owner of the Boar's Head. "Thank you so much for sharing your gifts with us all."

"It is my pleasure, young master," Fionna said as she walked off into the boisterous revelry of the tavern.

Tired from his long, eventful day, and feeling the strong mead, Aidan fell into a dreamlike state watching the dancing and merrymaking around him. Ruby's swerving aerial dancing became wilder and more raucous as time went on. At one point, she accidently careened into the brown curly hair of a young woman dancing next to her. It took a bit of squirming and buzzing for Ruby to extricate herself from the woman's locks.

"I think your friend may have had a bit too much honey wine!" Fionna said with a laugh as she passed by carrying a large number of mugs brimming with ale.

A few minutes later, a thick blanket of drowsiness descended on the bard, and he decided it was time for Fionna to show him to his room. Still in the midst of her drunken revelry,

Ruby clearly had no desire to sleep. Aidan took a last look at the cheerful, rowdy scene in the tavern before ascending the stairs to his room and the cozy sheepskin bed that awaited his grateful arrival.

Later that night, Aidan slipped into a dream. He was outside in the dark of night in the middle of a violent storm. He could barely stand as the biting winds and rain battered his body. In the midst of the howling gale stood a lone oak tree. Its branches creaked and lurched ominously under the wind's brutal onslaught. Aidan feared the tree would be toppled.

The next moment, the Bone King appeared between Aidan and the oak tree. Seemingly impervious to the savage winds, the ancient monarch stood rooted like a mountain. His robe was decorated with small gemstones and an intricate network of fine lines of pulsing light. The fabric appeared to be alive, as waves of light rippled across its surface.

Framed by the image of the violently lurching tree, the Bone King's fleshless face stared at Aidan. The ancient teacher raised his arm, pointed at Aidan with a long, bony finger and said, "Like this tree, your resolve will be tested in the stormy winds of adversity. Stand strong when ill winds threaten to topple you. Walk the path of your destiny no matter how difficult it becomes. Root yourself in the power of your resolve.

"The challenges you will face are essential for your healing. When a tree bends in the face of howling winds, its roots become stronger, and so shall yours, if you persist. When the roots of your spirit run deep, no challenge can divert you from your path."

The image of the Bone King faded as the dream dissolved into darkness.

NINE

Aidan awoke to the pink light of dawn spilling its soft beauty into the room. Inches from his face, he saw the strange sight of a hummingbird nestled into the thick wool of the sheepskin bedcover. When Ruby opened her eyes, she looked thoroughly unwell.

"Looks like you overdid it last night," the bard said as he gingerly carried her over to the window. Opening the shutters, he placed Ruby next to some flowers in the planter box outside the window. "You just need a little breakfast to set yourself straight." After a minute of sipping nectar from the flowers, she was buzzing around happily again and seemed to have fully recovered.

Over a delicious breakfast of scrambled eggs and thick bacon, Aidan laid out his map and spoke with Fionna about the next leg of their journey.

"There is only one path over land that will lead you to your destination," Fionna said with hesitation, "and it is filled with peril."

Pointing to the map, she said, "A day's journey from Stonewall, you will be forced to cross the dreaded Bog of Despair. There is great evil at work in the bog. Many travelers have been lost to the swamp's foul waters. When crossing the bog, you must never stray from the path. If you slip into its dark waters, you will surely die—or worse."

After breakfast, Ruby and Aidan thanked Fionna for her advice and her warm hospitality, said their farewells, and left the Boar's Head. The main road through town was bustling with townsfolk and merchants selling their wares. After buying some salted cod from a fishmonger, Aidan and Ruby made their way toward Stonewall's front gate and the next leg of their journey.

Those who lived to tell of their journey through the Bog of Despair spoke of the place in hushed whispers. It was said that cruel spirits inhabited the bog's dark waters and they fed on the souls of travelers who lost their way. As they traveled across the pastoral countryside, Aidan's mind grew uneasy thinking about what they would encounter in the cursed swamp.

As the afternoon wore on, a cold, biting wind arose, stealing the heat from any exposed skin. Aidan wrapped himself tightly in his wool cloak and pressed onwards through the rising wind. Ruby didn't seem to mind the cold. Sipping on flower nectar, she kept her body warm and her spirits high.

Not having the benefit of nectar to nourish him, Aidan's spirits had grown sour by the time evening arrived. The chill, gusty winds had further unsettled his troubled mind. They set up camp for the night within sight of the bog. A hazy layer of darkness blanketed the distant bog and prevented the light of the setting sun from illuminating its interior. Even from so far away, a foul, rotten smell permeated the air.

"I don't look forward to tomorrow's travels through that dark, putrid land," Aidan said, his nose wrinkling in disgust. Ruby also seemed hesitant. She had noticed that the flowers did not taste quite so sweet as they drew closer to the bog. She chirped her wish that Aidan had wings and that they could simply fly over the fetid waters.

"If only that were so, Ruby." The bard sighed as he lit a fire. The friendly, crackling flames brought some cheer to their hearts, as did the rose tea Aidan brewed for them.

As Ruby sipped rose tea while perched on his knee, Aidan voiced his fears that perhaps the Bone King was only a dream and that he might never recover his ability to sing. With sympathetic chirps, Ruby assured him that their quest would be successful, and he would be healed of his affliction. But doubt speaks convincingly when fear clouds the mind. Later that evening under overcast skies, Aidan still felt uneasy as he lay beneath his wool blanket and readied himself for sleep.

That night, disturbing images haunted his dreams. Aidan dreamed that the bog's toxic water rose up like a serpent, plunged into his open mouth, and filled his body with its poison. Black tendrils spread like hungry roots into his heart and filled his mind with anguished thoughts. As the shadow spread within him, Aidan felt his will to live dissolving. Unable to take another step, he collapsed into the swamp, and the foul waters swallowed him like helpless prey.

Moments later, to Aidan's horror, he saw his form rise from the putrid waters. He had been transformed into one of the walking dead, with pale skin and cruel, red eyes. Aidan knew he was cursed to spend the rest of eternity in the Bog of Despair.

Suddenly, a ray of sunlight penetrated the grey mists and surrounded him in its radiant glow. Like a plant reaching for the sun, his heart sprouted white wings, took flight from his undead body, and soared off beyond the horizon.

Aidan awoke in a cold sweat with the waning moon looking down at him from the hazy night sky. He had no stomach for more sleep or dreams, so he decided to calm his mind using the druid's meditation his father had taught him as a boy. He spent the remaining hours before dawn focusing on his breath. As Aidan dropped deeper into the meditation, his sense of self dissolved into a vast expanse of awareness. With no sense of individual identity remaining, fear and doubt evaporated like mist.

As the sun rose on the eastern horizon, Aidan felt renewed and ready to face the bog. He realized his quest was not about him at all. Singing was about being a vessel for the spirit of the Way, and playing the role he was meant to play in life. He resolved to do everything in his power to end the curse, so he could bring his healing music to others once again. Aidan ate a quick breakfast of his mother's hearty bread and a cup of rose-petal tea. The tea warmed his heart, and its aroma helped to counter the bog's foul reek. He decided to fill his water skin with rose tea for their journey.

Bard and bird set off from their camp in high spirits. But as they approached the bog, the foul smell became worse. It emanated from the thick mist rising from the dark waters. The rank odor reminded Aidan of dead, rotting animal flesh mixed with something even more odious. And it wasn't just the smell. The air created an acidic feeling in his lungs and throat, as if it were eating away at him.

The Bog of Despair spread out before them. Its dim expanse was shrouded in mist that prevented the sun's light from entering. Day and night, the bog existed in a realm of shadow. Within its hazy interior, Aidan saw a faint trail winding along a convoluted maze of passable land through the swamp. A tangle of bogweed, swampvine, and dart thistle bordered the trail, their roots wading in the silty water.

The water was unusually black and thick with an iridescent sheen, as if oil covered its surface. Although liquid, it had none of the transparent qualities of water and Aidan wondered what lay hidden beneath the surface.

"Well, my feathered friend," Aidan said, "you are lucky not to walk through this godforsaken land. May your feet rarely touch ground as we travel." Reluctantly, they set off into the swamp.

With every step along the trail, Aidan felt the marshy ground sink beneath his feet. All was eerily quiet in the swamp. Nothing moved. There was no breeze, no birdsong, no life whatsoever except bogweed, swampvine, and dart thistle. Aidan moved gingerly around any dart thistle he encountered. When touched, the dart thistle plant shoots poisoned darts into the offending body part. The sting is similar to that of a scorpion, and Aidan resolved to avoid the experience.

Before long, the bog's caustic stench gave the bard a splitting headache. As they traveled deeper into the swamp, the foul vapor began to cloud Aidan's thinking, and dark thoughts proliferated in his mind. At first they were only minor irritations, like resenting Ruby for being able to fly while he had to walk. Over time, they became stronger and more grim. Aidan began to doubt his strength of heart and his worthiness to be a bard.

Try as he might to resist such thoughts, they continued to grow like cancer in his mind.

Aidan felt pain growing in his heart as Oscuro's ophidian fed on the bog's evil energy. The cruel energy of the curse darkened his heart like the waning light of the moon during an eclipse. Feet growing heavier with each step, Aidan continued to plod forward along the soggy trail.

Doubt assailed his mind, and a voice began to whisper in his thoughts. *How arrogant you are to think you are a vessel for the power of the Way! You sing to others only to feed your selfish pride. You are a hoax and a liar. Give up your grandiose visions of self-importance. You are nothing. Give up your foolish quest!*

Aidan realized to his dismay that there was truth in the dark voice's words. He felt self-importance when he thought of being a bard in Willow's Glen. *Is it true?* Aidan asked himself. *Have I been motivated by pride all along? I don't think so. My desire to serve others is my true motivation. Isn't it?*

Confusion and doubt clouded his thinking. He was ashamed by his own arrogance. The ophidian fed off his self-critical thoughts, causing a surge of searing pain in his chest.

"So, this is the true nature of the ophidian curse," Aidan whispered with a heavy heart. "Oscuro hopes I will make an enemy of myself and be destroyed by my own shadow."

Aidan tried to ignore his shadow's voice, but its words weighed heavily on his soul. Try as he might to resist his own negativity, the oppressive weight of shame and despair eroded his will to keep walking. Fears and doubts assailed his mind like locusts, while the bog sapped more of his energy with each step. As Aidan's strength declined, the evil ophidian parasite within him sensed his weakness. Excruciating pain wracked his chest as the ophidian sank its serpentine fangs into his heart. Stopped in his tracks from the unbearable pain, he remembered his father's protective ring. Aidan held his hand with Bran's ring over his heart, and the agony subsided enough that he could continue.

The marsh's mist had descended, and the air was thick with an eerie pale glow. The only sound penetrating the blanket of fog was the slow squishy rhythm of Aidan's boots as he walked. For what seemed like eternity, he willed himself onwards. It was a constant battle to bolster his resolve against the crushing despair haunting his mind and the terrible pain in his chest. Only the energy of Bran's ring over his heart gave him the strength and courage to continue shuffling along. Yet, as time ticked on, Aidan felt the bog's foul energy like a tide of rising darkness threatening to drown and consume him.

Even with his father's magic ring, the pain in his heart finally became so unbearable that he fell to one knee, dangerously close to a dart thistle. His mind was spinning, and he could barely see through the darkness that had overtaken him. Through his clouded vision and muddled mind, two strange images came to him. One was seeing Ruby snatched in mid-flight by the lunging jaws of a giant red bog lily flower. The other was that he was being surrounded on all sides by slithering snakes (or were they swampvines?) with pale, yellow eyes....

Coiling themselves around Aidan's ankle's as they hissed spells of despair in his ears, the swampvine serpents yanked him to the ground and dragged him toward the waterline. Aidan reached for the knife at his side, but it had slipped from its sheath as he fell. Struggle as he may, he was unable to dislodge the serpentine coils from his legs.

As his feet reached the tarry water, he felt his flesh burning from a bone-chilling cold. Nausea overtook him, and he vomited black bile onto the bogweed-covered trail. The voice of his shadow and the weight of despair was so unbearable that he longed to submit to the bog's lethal waters.

Aidan knew he had little time left, so, with the last ounce of his will, he reached deep within himself, beneath his shadow's cruel words, beneath the ocean of evil threatening to drown him, he descended into his curse-scarred heart. There he found it—the flickering flame of strength that could never be extinguished. From that place in his heart, he sent out a fierce prayer for help to the forces of light in the world. His cry rippled out beyond the murky hell of the bog.

Hours or moments later (he could not tell which), Aidan opened his eyes to the curious sight of a small acorn woodpecker standing on the ground in front of his face. Before he could think, the woodpecker hopped forward and knocked nine times between Aidan's eyebrows. The sharp pecking was painful as the hollow knocking resonated loudly through his skull.

Then something awakened in Aidan's mind, and a clear vision of a rose came to him. Aidan remembered the rose tea in his water skin. With a surge of energy, he reached for his knapsack, seized the water skin, and squirted some rose tea into his mouth. Rose is good medicine for an anguished heart and can bring light to a darkened spirit. Its effect was immediate. The bog's cruel voices and Aidan's shadow faded, and the weight of despair began to lift. Quickly, he squirted the tea on the swampvines gripping his legs. They relaxed their grip enough for him to wiggle free.

Rising to his feet, Aidan caught sight of the tightly closed flower of a red bog lily with his squirming friend, Ruby, inside it. He dripped a few drops of rose tea on the bog flower. Slowly, the flower relaxed, opened, and Ruby tumbled into Aidan's outstretched hand. Poisoned by the bog's evil secretions, Ruby was unable to fly. Aidan tilted the water skin to let Ruby drink. After a few drops, the hummingbird was flying again and eager to get going.

"I agree, my friend," Aidan said. "Let's not delay a moment longer in this foul place."

Ruby shot into the air, and Aidan began walking with determination along the marshy path. When voices of doubt and shame assailed him, he took another sip of the rose tea. It caused the dark thoughts to recede and allowed him to feel compassion for himself. He was humbled by the arrogance he felt about being a bard but did his best not to judge himself harshly.

As he walked, Aidan reflected on his true motivations for being a bard. Connecting with his heart, he was grateful to see that his primary motivations were not selfish or arrogant. At the core, it was his love of music and his desire to help others that inspired him.

Aidan sighed with relief. *Thank the Way that my intentions are not totally impure. If I ever sing again I must be vigilant and make sure that I do not fall into feelings of arrogance and self-importance.*

By continuing to sip the rose tea, Aidan was able to endure the long hours of travel without succumbing to the swamp's dark enticements.

Soon after sunset, they finally reached the end of the bog. Not wishing to camp near its cruel waters, they continued walking for a good while by moonlight. At last, when there was no trace of foul vapor in the air, and the Bog of Despair was nothing but a memory, they made camp next to the pleasant gurgling of a meandering creek sheltered by alder and willow trees. Aidan had barely covered himself with his blanket and laid down his head when he dropped into sleep.

Aidan found himself floating free in the vast cosmos surrounded on all sides by twinkling starlight. His vision was drawn to a strange sphere of darkness off to the left, where no stars were visible. It was a black hole devouring all light that came near it. Before he knew it, Aidan was hurtling into the black hole at a terrifying speed, pulled in by its immense gravity. Like a titanic cyclone in space, the black hole spiraled him violently around its center, dragging him deeper into its core. He felt his body expand and contract in impossible ways as the forces around him became even stronger. Approaching the central core of the black hole, time and space imploded, and Aidan was flooded with visions of the past and future and alien worlds beyond imagination.

Then everything stopped. Aidan found himself looking out eyes that were not his own. He gazed at a nightmarish scene. Everything was grey and lifeless. A rock quarry shrouded in cold mist was filled with people moving slowly and stacking stones. Although their bodies seemed human, they were clearly something different; somehow diminished, lifeless. They moved with the stiff, rigid gait of people whose spirits had been broken. The vital spark of life in their eyes had been extinguished. All that remained was a dark cloud of fear and malice. The wretched slaves were the walking dead.

Aidan realized he was looking through the eyes of their master. The slaves looked at him in utter horror when he caught their eyes. He felt their master's cold cruelty and his loathing for humankind. He wanted nothing more than to enslave humanity and steal their souls. The slave master's hatred burned like an inferno, and Aidan knew he would not stop until he had destroyed all life on Earth.

Aidan awoke, terrified, but he calmed down as he heard the soothing sounds of the stream nearby and realized where he was. Patches of starlight shined through the tree branches above.

"What a foul dream!" he whispered to himself. "The residue of the bog must have brought evil visions to my mind." Deep down, he sensed there was more to the nightmare than simply the lingering darkness of the bog. Not eager to return to the land of dreams, Aidan stayed awake for a while as he tried to calm his thoughts.

He was not the only one with a troubled mind that night...

Far away to the north, the dark druid Oscuro tossed and turned in his bed. His mind was ill at ease, for he had just learned of Aidan's journey to heal himself of his curse. Earlier that day, Oscuro went to the market in Willow's Glen to replenish his stock of Brugmansia flowers. While walking the rows of merchants and craftsmen, he came upon a traveling witch, named Raven, who came through town from time to time.

Raven was a short, squat woman with brown, inquisitive eyes. She wore a purple shawl woven with small bells that jingled gently when she moved. Her brown curly hair was tied back and adorned with raven feathers that shined with iridescent blackness in the sunlight. In the midst of the bustling market, she sat at a table filled with magical charms, herb satchels, and medicinal candles. Raven was known for her skills as an oracle and fortune teller. Oscuro decided to stop at her stall and see if she had anything he might need.

"Hello there, Oscuro," Raven said. "Please, sit down, sit down. How may I help you?"

The two sat across from each other without speaking. Raven looked into the druid's eyes for several moments before she spoke. "Today I will read your fortune from the bone oracle."

Oscuro nodded his assent, for he trusted her oracular abilities. Rarely did he ask the witch for something specific, preferring to wait for her to tell him what he most needed to know.

Raven produced a black felt satchel and emptied its contents onto the purple tablecloth. Out poured a pile of small bones, fox teeth, and a raven's beak.

"Take the objects in your hands, and cast them onto the tablecloth," she instructed. Intrigued, he gathered the items and tossed them back onto the table. The witch looked at the pattern of objects intently for a minute. Looking up at Oscuro, she fell into a trance and began to speak.

"Your destiny is intertwined with that of the bard."

Oscuro shuddered at the mention of Aidan.

"Aidan has set off on a journey to heal his curse. He travels to the sacred site of Unstan. A great deal rests on the outcome of his quest. The course of history hinges on Aidan's fate."

The witch snapped out of her trance and looked around, disoriented, as if she didn't know where she was. Seeing Oscuro's face seemed to bring her back to the present.

"I hope the reading was helpful."

"Quite," Oscuro replied, although he looked shaken and even paler than he typically did.

Sitting in bed later that night, still pondering the witch's words, a growing fear begin to sicken the dark druid's stomach. Abruptly, he rose from his bed.

"I will destroy the bard before he reaches Unstan and meddles in the turning of history," he hissed. "But first, I must summon the power of Black Metal and create an ophidian army to crush that pathetic cherub and any who stand with him!"

Hatred and jealousy curdled his blood like poison, but Oscuro's twisted mind became more at ease knowing that Aidan's quest would fail. "Ahhh, that's better. Perhaps now I can sleep."

He sighed with relief, but there can be no true peace for the wicked. Hatred breeds evil, and dark were his dreams.

TEN

Aidan opened his eyes to the pink light of dawn filtering through the alder leaves, illuminating the streambed. He yawned, stretched, and shivered with the lingering memory of the Bog of Despair. He decided to take advantage of the stream and wash away any remaining residue of the foul place.

Bathing in the chilly, refreshing stream Aidan gave thanks for water's ability to cleanse the body and mind. Ruby found a partially submerged rock in the shallows and frolicked in the water near him. He watched in amusement as she flapped her wings excitedly and sprayed water everywhere.

Sitting on a rock with his legs dangling in the river, Aidan daydreamed of water as liquid diamonds falling from the sky, raining purity and beauty upon the lands. In his imagination, the stream became the body of a liquid diamond dragon weaving through the world breathing not fire but rainbow light to bless the world with its magic.

Rivers and streams are lovers of dreaming, and this particular stream was intrigued by Aidan's vision. As the young bard sat in his dream-drenched reverie, the stream's babbling became louder and began to whisper his name. It whispered not "Aidan" but his name nonetheless, for it whispered the pure essence of his soul in water language. Although it is impossible to express the rich feeling and nuance of water language with the written word, Aidan's name could crudely be translated as "Hearth of the Golden Light." Most human names have lost their vital spirit and, at best, capture only a fraction of their owner's true nature. With water names, it is quite different. The person and the word are one. Both are equally vibrant and alive.

Hearing his name spoken in water language, Aidan encountered his soul essence in its pure form. He felt seen and honored to the core of his being. Water language is the most intimate of languages, and it brought tears of joy to Aidan's eyes. Without thinking, he opened his mouth and found himself speak the name of the stream...in water language!

Watery words spilled from his mouth like a stream of glistening liquid winding through the air. The words were so pure that Ruby couldn't resist sipping some of their refreshing essence as they passed by in the gentle breeze. The stream's name, roughly translated, was "Flowing Rainbow Nectar."

Streams love to babble, so Aidan found himself in a long conversation that wandered far and wide, as river folk are prone to do. Feeling an immediate kinship with the bard, the stream shared teachings with him about the ways of rivers and the wisdom of water. Flowing Rainbow counseled him to be at ease as he walked his path through the world, to let the intuitive knowing of his heart guide him, and to move with the currents of his life rather than resist and struggle against them. To Aidan's delight, Flowing Rainbow gurgled forth some poetry that her dear mother ocean had shared with her from lands far to the east:

Rocks in rivers teach
Beauty's born of obstacles
Flow with all life brings

And this one from an old man of simple wisdom:

When a man is in turmoil how shall he find peace
Save by staying patient till the stream clears
How can a man's life keep its course if he will not
let it flow
Those who flow as life flows know
They need no other force
They feel no wear, they feel no tear
They need no mending, no repair[1]

Hours flowed by amidst the watery meanderings of their intertwined minds. Aidan developed a strong affection for Flowing Rainbow's bright, youthful spirit and the generosity with which she shared her timeless wisdom. Like many streams, she was a sensitive soul and was grateful to commune with a caring human being.

Startled out of his watery trance by Ruby's impatient chirping, Aidan realized that most of the day had gone by, and the late-afternoon sun reminded him that they needed to move on while there was still some daylight.

Aidan gave thanks to Flowing Rainbow for her companionship and for the ocean of teachings she had bestowed upon him. Before leaving, he offered her a gift of dried rose petals, which eddied lazily for a few moments before being received by the current and carried downstream.

As they continued their travels, Aidan felt strangely altered from his time with the stream.

---

[1] With credit to Witter Bynner, The Way of Life, According to Lao Tzu.

He felt the energy of pure invigorating water flowing down through his body and out the bottoms of his feet. The sensation was highly pleasurable, verging on ecstasy. His steps had also become decidedly more fluid and relaxed, and he felt he could walk for days without tiring.

Shocked, he stopped in his tracks as a realization dawned on him: he could see—no, feel—the exact location of every stream, river, lake and spring on Orkney Island. Letting his awareness expand further, he could feel oceans and clouds connecting to far-off lands with their own intricate networks of streams and rivers.

Aidan's head swam, and he became dizzy with this flood of new awareness. Sitting down for a moment, he marveled at the remarkable gifts Flowing Rainbow had bestowed upon him.

"The Flow!" Aidan said to himself in stunned disbelief. "It may take a while to get used to this new awareness. Wait until Feather hears about this!"

The Flow, or water magic, may come to people who have a strong connection with water. Followers of the Way have also been known to hold the elemental magic of Flame, Wind, and Terra according to their elemental makeup. Aidan's parents had told him stories of people who became vessels for elemental magic, but he had never met anyone with this gift.

With liquid legs and windswept wings, they traveled through the peaceful meadows north of the Obelisk Hills. Wildflowers bloomed in a colorful mosaic as far as the eye could see: purple lupine, orange poppies, and white bursts of angelica. Ruby had boundless energy for travel, with plentiful nectar to be found. Although he had eaten nothing that day, Aidan was energized by the refreshing liquid light of the Flow coursing through his body.

With light hearts, they traveled through the blooming grasslands until the sun lay its golden head on the horizon and prepared for sleep. However, there was no sleep to be had for our travelers. With far too much energy to make camp and settle in for the night, they decided to continue walking by the cool light of the waning moon.

Musing about his day, Aidan found he could still communicate with Flowing Rainbow's spirit. She had woven her being into the waters of his body so her guiding spirit was always near at hand.

As they walked through the still night, the moon walked its own path across the starry sky. When the eastern sky began to blush with the coming dawn, they reached the edge of the Obelisk Hills. The ancient, weathered hills were populated by mounds of huge granite boulders and obelisks, like kings of stone on earthen thrones; majestic and proud, protecting their realm through the endless march of time.

Climbing the first of the hills, Ruby and Aidan discovered a cave amidst the massive cluster of boulders. Having finally grown weary from their long night of travel, they decided to nap in the shelter of the cave. The cave was long and narrow with no unpleasant smells or animal droppings. It was cool and dry inside, so they made themselves comfortable and dozed off.

After sleeping for a spell, Aidan slipped into a rather odd dream in which two massive snowcapped mountains were debating with him about whether it was better to be a human or a mountain.

"The life of a human is but a blink of an eye!" the taller mountain bellowed through his crusty granite lips. "We mountains live to see entire civilizations rise and fall. Fickle human life fades like a wilting flower, while we remain."

"That is certainly true, wise mountain" Aidan replied. "But you can never swim in a river or feel the cool water on your skin."

"I know rivers like no man ever will!" the other mountain boomed. "Look here at this sweet river flowing down the valley behind my ear. She has been my beloved for thousands of years, always whispering watery poetry in my ear." His forest-bearded face smiled smugly at Aidan.

"Hmm...well, that does sound quite lovely," Aidan mused, stroking his chin, "but we humans can sing and make beautiful music for each other."

"Foolish boy." The taller, granite-skinned mountain laughed. "When the wind blows, my voice bellows its haunting melody to the sweet music of the forest's rustling leaves. Add to this the singing of birds and chirping of insects in my realm, and you can see that mountains are a virtual symphony of music."

"I suppose I hadn't considered that," Aidan said, a bit taken aback. He stood pensively for a good while, and then his eyes lit up. "Aha! But humankind can travel the world freely, exploring lands your eyes will never see—and we can dance!"

The tree-bearded mountain looked down at Aidan with his twinkling sky-blue eyes and laughed so heartily that the wind rose up, pushing the bard back with its breath. "You have never seen a mountain dance?" He smiled mischievously.

At that moment, both mountains began to hop up and down, causing the ground to quake violently. Aidan struggled to maintain his footing, but he was quickly thrown to the ground, colliding with the dancing earth.

ELEVEN

Aidan awoke to violent shaking all around him. The cave's walls looked like they would collapse on him at any moment. With Ruby already racing ahead of him, he jumped up and sprinted out of the cave and away from the huge mound of boulders. Through eyes squinting from the bright light of day, Aidan looked out on a truly terrifying sight.

The boulders and obelisks on the hill had come alive and were fighting a battle against a different boulder clan attacking from below. The giant warriors fought with stone clubs and hammers, the height of Aidan's own body. Every crushing blow created a deafening clap that shook the earth. As quickly as he could, with the ground moving beneath him, Aidan ran down the hill and away from the warring titans. From a safer vantage point below, he saw the stone giants' stern, grim, faces as their fierce blows rained down upon each other. Some of the more lethal attacks fractured their stone bodies and sent showers of rock shards into the dusty air.

Aidan realized that two of the stone people defending their hillside home wore crowns of stone inset with purple gemstones and gold ingots shining brilliantly in the light. They were the king and queen of the Larimar clan with sky-blue larimar eyes, fighting side by side to defend their beloved home. Their faces were etched with determined, proud nobility.

The attacking clan was led by a king and queen that made Aidan's skin crawl. Their faces were sunken and twisted with cruel malice, and their coal-black eyes seethed with hatred as they pressed on with their attack. They wore stone crowns inset with red gemstones and ingots of cold bluish silver. The king of the Black Coal clan sensed Aidan's gaze and stopped in his tracks. Looking around, he spotted the bard and locked eyes with him. Aidan felt beams of malice boring into him before the king returned his attention to the battle. Aidan resolved to flee if it looked like the Black Coal clan would be victorious.

The battle wore on for some time, with both sides taking crushing blows. As the fighting built to an earth-shattering climax, the Larimar Queen picked up a boulder and hurled it down the hill toward the Black Coal king. It sailed through the air like a comet and struck the king's face with shocking force. The blow shattered the king's cheek and right eye and he stumbled backwards, falling to his knees. Attempting to rise to his feet, dizziness overtook him, and he collapsed.

With the crushing defeat of their king, the Black Coal clan lost their taste for battle. They tended to his tar-oozing wounds the best they could and uprooted two trees to form a giant stretcher. Carrying their wounded king, the defeated stone giants turned their backs on the hill and began the slow march back to their home.

On the battleground, the dust settled, and the earth was still once again. Aidan's eyes were drawn to the top of the hill, where the Larimar Queen stood bathed in sunlight. Two large, diamond tears fell from her eyes, whether due to the attack on her home or her lethal blow to the king, he knew not. Her eyes turned toward Aidan, and she motioned for him to join them on the hill. Feeling it was not wise to refuse, he and Ruby made for the hill to speak with giants.

"Welcome to our humble home on the hill," the ancient queen said with a booming voice. "I am the Larimar Queen. Better that violence had not tainted our first meeting, but this battle was not of our choosing. Warfare among our kind is rare. You have witnessed a sight few mortals ever see."

After introducing himself, Aidan asked, "Why did the evil band of...*stone people* attack you?"

"They are not evil, simply foolish and greedy. The Black Coal clan is a young family, only fifty thousand years old or so. They were born from a vein of hot magma and coal that erupted from the earth. Lava still runs hot in their adolescent veins. The foolish fire of youth has not yet cooled, so they still lust for power and conquest.

"We of the Larimar clan are a much older family. Our stone ancestry extends far back in time. A deep vein of larimar runs beneath our hill. It is the living root of our lineage and our strength. Our home is known throughout the Obelisk Hills as a place of great power. The Black Coal clan craves this power for their dark purposes. They have paid a grave price for their greed and aggression. Thankfully, we did not pay so dearly."

Aidan looked around at the aftermath of battle. The Larimar King moved about assessing the damage and tending to family members in need, but the stone bones of the Larimar clan were strong indeed, and none were badly injured.

At first it was an unsettling experience to be among the towering stone giants, feeling the ground shake every time they moved. But before long, Aidan and Ruby settled in and began to appreciate the stoic strength and nobility of their people. Stone people are holders of ancient wisdom tested over eons of life and death through the endless seasons of our world. They are keepers of the stories of our ancestors and epochs long forgotten or shrouded in myth. For those with the patience to slow the mind to the pace of the earth, much can be learned from these elders.

"Our people have a great love of stories," the Larimer King's rumbling voice boomed. The family of giants had gathered in a clearing at the top of the hill around a huge fire pit. "But for the occasional passing druid or witch, we rarely hear stories from the human realm these days. We would love to hear any stories you have to share, young man." The circle of giant stone faces nodded in smiling, crunchy unison.

So, as afternoon lumbered toward evening, Aidan shared many stories of his home, his life, and his quest for healing. When he came to his story of the Alchemist, the Larimar King's eyes opened wide in disbelief. "The Alchemist is still alive! That crafty, old fox. He has managed to live a bit longer than most of your kind."

"How old is the Alchemist?" Aidan asked.

"Oh, about five thousand years—give or take a few centuries."

Now it was Aidan's eyes that widened in astonishment. After recovering his composure, he continued the story of his adventures. When he spoke of meeting Flowing Rainbow Nectar, a crusty smile cracked on the face of the Larimar Queen.

"Flowing Rainbow is a dear friend," she said. "We have spent many hours on her banks sharing stories of water and stone."

By the time Aidan finished his tale, the sun had grown tired of standing and was resting leisurely on the western horizon.

"The sacred cairn of Unstan is a powerful place of healing," the Larimar Queen was saying. "It contains doorways between this world and many others. We also know of the Bone King and his gemstone realm. He is the Ancient One, existing since time beyond time. The stone people are but children compared with the span of his life. Fortune follows you, young bard, if the Bone King has summoned you."

As darkness deepened toward night, one of the Larimar clan gathered wood from a giant pile and stacked it in the fire pit. Then he casually struck his metal fingernail on his stone palm, sending a sparking, molten mass into the woodpile. With no kindling needed, the fire burned brightly in no time.

Aidan prepared a meal of salted cod, bread, and wilted nettles he had picked earlier that day. "If you would be so generous, I would love to hear what stories you have to tell," Aidan said to the circle of stone giants as he chewed on a piece of bread that hadn't grown any fresher during his travels.

After thinking for a long moment, the Larimar Queen said, "You would be long dead before we could tell a fraction of our tales. However, a story comes to me now that wishes to be told....

"Thousands of years ago, in the Stone Age of humankind, your people lived in harmony with the natural world. They were aligned with the wisdom of the Way. Your ancestors were a gentle people and knew their rightful place in the great tapestry of life. Love and reverence for the Earth and its creatures guided their ways. Knowing themselves to be one with all beings, they lived in harmony with the Earth by learning from trees and birds, rivers and animals, wind and stone."

"Did the Larimar Clan have contact with these people?" Aidan asked.

"Yes, your ancestors were dear friends of the stone clans. They honored our wisdom and stories, and we taught them how to build with stone in the ancient ways. Everything they built is a living being. Their homes and temples, sacred cairns, and rings of stone are a marriage between the spirit of the Earth and the heart of humanity. Every standing stone they erected is alive with its own unique spirit. These stone monoliths strengthened their communion with Mother Earth and fostered peace and bounty in this fair land.

"Through their deep listening to the music of the spheres, they also learned from the vast cosmos itself. Through countless seasons, they observed the movements of the stars and learned to live in unison with their heavenly dance. They sensed that the stones they used for building and the stars above came from the same origins. A resonance exists between the metals and minerals contained in stone and the blazing bodies of the stars above. A living network of energy connects the constellations of the heavens with the earthen rings of stone."

Several craggy heads around the circle nodded reverently in agreement. The stone people's kinship and communion with the stars gave them a strong sense of belonging in the universe.

"The Ring of Brodgar, here in Orkney," the Larimar Queen continued, "was built by your ancestors as a bridge to connect Earth's energy with the movements of the cosmos and, in doing so, bring humanity into harmony with all creation. This is the essence of living in accord with the Way.

"Brodgar and other stone circles track the movement of the sun, moon, planets, and constellations, allowing your people to align themselves with the progression of the seasons and the mysterious cycles of change in the cosmos. They knew their place in the world and lived as one with the celestial mobile of heavenly bodies spinning like dervishes through the ages."

Aidan's eyes lit up as the Queen spoke of the Ring of Brodgar. He had read about the sacred site during his studies of history and astronomy. Inspired by ancient people's ability to track the movements of the cosmos using nothing but stone, Aidan planned to visit Brodgar on his way to Unstan.

"This lived connection with the Way," said the Queen, "opened the door to vast realms of knowledge and power for your ancestors. They learned to use the elements of air, earth, fire, and water to guide the forces of change and, in doing so, gave birth to the revered practice of alchemy. Their culture flourished, and life prospered in Orkney. Farming and gardening became high arts, and food grew abundantly for humans and animals alike.

"This era gave rise to the druids, holders of essential wisdom and teachings for humankind. They spent long hours listening to the silence and delving into the mysteries of the Way. The druids trained their minds to be clear like diamonds and steeped their hearts in humility and gratitude. In return, life's greatest secrets were revealed to them.

"Alas, all things must come to an end, so too this golden age of human evolution, for humankind's shadow rose to power and began to eclipse your ancestors' radiant light. Pride, greed, and lust for power began to haunt their minds. Love for the world decayed into a desire to dominate all life. They lived in abundance yet thirsted for more...and more. Wanting to be like gods, these deluded people searched for a source of power that would allow them to rule like omnipotent kings.

"Delving deep underground, they found what they were searching for. Mining the earth, they discovered brilliant veins of metal. Metal is an element of concentrated power, and your ancestors used it to fuel their twisted dreams of superiority and subjugation. When the first sword was forged, it severed their connection with the Earth, and their own hearts. Forging weapons of iron, they waged war on their neighbors. Aggression, violence, and fear ruled their lives.

"It was during these dark times that the evil teachings of Black Metal came to your world. Sorcerers with a lust for power were drawn to this path of greed and hatred. But the price of following this foul path was terribly high. Black Metal became a poison that diminished the spirit of any who practiced it. The Iron Age had dawned, and the blessed age of stone was lost to the tides of time. Sadly, your people have not yet recovered from this tragic fall from grace."

Aidan was deeply pained by the stone queen's words. A somber mood settled into the circle of stone giants around the fire. Aidan was ashamed of humanity's blind arrogance and looked at the Queen with sadness in his eyes.

"Have hope, fair bard," the Larimar Queen said. "Change is certain in life, and this time of human ignorance cannot last forever. You have great love for the Earth, Aidan, and there are many others like you. It may be that the tide is already turning. Perhaps a new story of your people is being written as we speak."

"May it be so," Aidan said, drying a tear from his face. The Queen's encouraging words inspired hope in his heart. Aidan sighed and looked into the blazing fire, his eyes following the sparks rising into the night as they merged with the stars above. He prayed that humankind would reclaim its humble nobility and remember the teachings of the Way.

The night was growing late, and Aidan's lack of sleep from the previous days was catching up with him. Yawning, he stretched his arms. "Fair people of stone, sleep is calling me. I must bid you goodnight."

"Oh, that won't do at all!" the Larimar King bellowed. "We have many stories still to share before the night is through. Perhaps a bit of tea will bring you back to life."

Aidan doubted anything could keep him from sleep, but he did not know the strength of larimar tea.

"Here you are, a hot mug of larimar tea. That should do the trick."

Aidan took the steaming mug and quickly realized it was no regular cup of tea. A glowing sky-blue liquid swirled in the cup with eddies of rusty red and light green. The brew emanated an intriguing energy that he could feel seeping through the mug and up his arm.

Before the Larimar King returned to his seat, he spotted the fire sprite in the rune box perched on Aidan's knapsack. The sprite was basking in the light of the bonfire with a contented look on his face. The Larimar King shuddered and stopped in his tracks. "If the fire elemental has appeared again," he said, in a low, rumbling voice, "then great change is truly upon us. I only hope your kind will survive the transformation."

Aidan looked at the fire sprite with apprehension for a moment before returning to his glowing mug of tea. As he drank, he felt a cool wave of energy wash through him. Once the tea took full effect, he had no further worries about falling asleep. Larimar tea is remarkably energizing for soft-skinned beings. Halfway through his cup, Aidan could barely contain himself. He began dancing around the fire and doing cartwheels. But, all the while, his mind was crystal clear and could focus perfectly on the stories of the Larimar clan as he jumped around like a monkey to the amusement of the stone beings. In the hours before dawn, Aidan heard many stories of the Larimar clan and Earth's long-forgotten past.

When the light of dawn bathed the circle of stone giants in its gentle light, Aidan found he still had boundless energy and was eager to continue their journey. He thanked the Larimar clan for their kindness and wonderful stories. Before they took their leave, Aidan drank the rest of his larimar tea to fuel the day's travels. He considered offering some to Ruby but then thought better of it. Imagining what the tea would do to a hummingbird was a bit frightening.

So, with a brisk pace driven by larimar legs and nectar-fueled wings, Aidan and Ruby covered many miles through the Obelisk Hills. Not wanting to encounter the Black Coal clan, they gave wide berth to hills covered with boulders.

Around midday, a small shadow passed in front of Aidan. Looking up, he saw a majestic, golden eagle flying low in the sky. The raptor looked down at them with its piercing gaze and veered towards an oak tree ahead of them. Perching in one of the branches, it seemed to be waiting for them to approach. Hummingbirds are fearless, so Ruby flew over to investigate. In a flash, she was back on Aidan's shoulder and, with a puzzled look on her fuschia-feathered face, chirped excitedly in his ear.

"Eagle has been searching for you for many days. She wishes to speak with you."

"How unusual," Aidan said as he approached the tree. The intensity of Eagle's gaze was a bit unnerving, but Aidan greeted her with due respect nonetheless. "Noble lady of the clear blue sky, I honor your soaring flight and unparalleled vision. What news do you bring?"

As Aidan's eyes locked with her gripping gaze, Eagle began to communicate without sound, speaking directly to his mind. *Hello, fair Aidan. My vision is keen, but I come on behalf of one whose eyes are far sharper than my own. I bear a message from the Seer. He is one of the wisest druids and urgently wishes to meet with you. The Seer has information that is essential for your quest.*

Aidan hesitated. He had grown wary of druids since his fateful encounter with Oscuro. "How does the Seer know of me, and why should I trust him?"

Eagle's eyes spoke without speaking, *As I said, the Seer's eyes perceive a great many things, and you among them. As for trusting him, you must search your heart and decide for yourself.*

Aidan asked his intuition to guide him and got a strong sense that he could trust the Seer. As he accessed the knowing in his heart, Aidan suddenly felt the watery presence of Flowing Rainbow rising within him. Rivers love feeling, and the opening of his heart had awakened her spirit. With her crystal-clear intuition, the water spirit confirmed the Seer's good intentions.

"Very well," Aidan said, grateful for the presence of his watery sister, "we shall pay a visit to the Seer. Where does he live? How many days' travel for those without wings?"

One would never reach him on foot, unless you can breathe underwater. The Seer lives on an island to the north of Orkney. But for those without wings, there are other ways to travel. Follow me.

With that, the golden eagle spread her huge wings and took to the sky once again. Ruby shot off after her like an arrow while Aidan was left to follow at the ponderous pace of an earthbound human.

TWELVE

At midday, Aidan heard Eagle screech in the sky above him. Looking up, he caught her steely gaze, and she silently spoke to his mind. *We go to the Pools of Peace further to the east. It is an enchanted place, revered by druids and witches. The magic that lives there will aid us in our journey to the Seer.*

As soon as he spoke the name of the place, Aidan saw the spring-fed pools as if he were there in the flesh. The Flow allowed him to feel the location of distant bodies of water as simply as touching his own hand. Aidan felt a timeless peace permeating the pools and sensed a presence...someone he once knew? Eager to be at the pools, Aidan quickened his pace through the windswept grasslands of the hill country.

They arrived at the Pools of Peace as the late-afternoon sun bathed the forested refuge in golden light. Fed by natural hot springs, the grouping of pools surrounded a large swimming hole formed at the base of a charming waterfall. Cold water from the stream had been diverted into the pools, so the temperature could be adjusted to one's liking. Multiple distinct thermal springs converged in the healing sanctuary. Sulfur, calcium, magnesium, and other minerals all fed different pools, allowing bathers to experience the unique healing properties of each type of water separately.

A peaceful, nurturing energy permeated the pools, and the travelers felt at ease as soon as they arrived. Aidan sensed the presence of strong magic everywhere. Rocks and trees glowed with energy and seemed to be breathing, expanding and contracting in unison with his breath. Threads of rainbow light danced in the shimmering cascade of the waterfall. *This is an enchanted place, indeed,* Aidan thought, washing his dusty face in the cool water of the swimming hole.

He looked up to the amusing sight of the stoic golden eagle standing on a branch next to the restless, chirping hummingbird. They were an interesting pair, the proud, stern intensity of the raptor and Ruby's joyful, chatty, buzzing energy. Nevertheless, they seemed to enjoy each other's company.

We will stay here for the night, Eagle said. *We cannot do what we came to do until morning. Tonight let us enjoy the healing waters of the pools.* The feathered duo flew off to a tiny pool that seemed to have been made for birds and other small creatures to enjoy.

Aidan looked around and found himself drawn to a solitary pool set away from the others under the shade of a hazelnut tree. Removing his travel-soiled clothing, he lowered himself into the welcoming waters. The pool had been glazed completely white over time by the mineral content in the springs. The water sparkled like diamonds in the dappled sunlight filtering through the forested canopy.

Aidan felt his skin tingle slightly, and his body relaxed as the warm medicinal waters took effect. As he soaked, a sense of wellbeing and peace permeated his body and mind. He felt the Flow rising within him to commune with the spirit of the pools. The connection allowed him to feel the energy of the healing waters irrigating him with their purity. Pockets of heavy, stagnant energy in his body began to dissolve, leaving him filled with clean, white light. Aidan began to understand what drew travelers to this sacred place.

Slipping into a blissful state of relaxation, his mind drifted into a dreamlike trance. Time dissolved as Aidan dropped into a profound sense of stillness. The rustling of the breeze-brushed leaves in the forest whispered poetry in his ears. Lyrics for new songs whirled through his mind. Near sunset, a gust of wind arose, and the smell of sweet flowers filled the air. Opening his eyes, Aidan thought he must be dreaming.

Approaching through the trees was a woman, spinning like the wind. The soft, white fabric of her dress spiraled hypnotically in the breeze. Her graceful form came to rest in front of the pool, and she stood in front of him with a playful look in her eyes. Or were they eyes? When Aidan looked directly at her face, all he saw was a bursting vision of magnificent flowers. Although she had the body of a lithe, attractive woman, she clearly was not human. Her spirit felt strangely familiar. She reminded Aidan of the magical days of his childhood, spent exploring the Whispering Woods.

"Hello, young bard, I am Daphne, the steward and guardian of the Pools of Peace. I welcome you to my home in this enchanted realm of healing waters. For countless generations, I have served the spirit of this land and its vital role in our world. The energy of the Way permeates the springs that feed these sacred pools. All who soak in these waters become steeped in the nourishing energy that allows life to thrive."

Listening to Daphne speak, Aidan became entranced by her mesmerizing voice and the alluring movements of her body. She moved with seductive, fluid grace. Every gesture of her hands was infused with magic and meaning.

"Throughout history, those who serve love and freedom have come to the pools for cleansing and healing. They fill the vessels of their beings with the waters of the Way, so they can share its medicine with the world. Servants of the Goddess and Mother Earth leave this sacred land renewed and inspired to continue their work for the benefit of all beings. I am glad you have finally come to soak in these waters. Welcome home."

As she spoke the word "home", Aidan suddenly remembered how he knew Daphne. She had been there when he was a child learning the ways of a bard from the nature sprits in the Whispering Woods. When the breeze rustled through the leaves, he had heard her watery voice encouraging him to sing. With love and gratitude welling up within him, Aidan realized she had also come to him in his dreams and taught him healing songs while he slept. The magical being was his muse and had guided his path in becoming a bard.

"Good. You remember our history, Aidan," Daphne said, reading his thoughts. "Yes, we have known each other for a long time. Our meeting now in the flesh is timely. You are being called to serve the Way. The time has ripened for you to play your role in the healing of humankind's connection with the heart of Mother Earth. More will be revealed to you soon, but for now, simply know that you have friends to aid you on your journey.

"Aidan, I am an ancient spirit born of this land. I am a child of wind and water, forest ˉ flowers, moon and mystery. Many spirits o call me kin and support my work for our dear Mother Earth. Consider me a trusted ally if ever you find yourself in need."

He was confused by her words yet grateful for her support and friendship.

"Please, take this rune stone necklace as a gift. This is Eolh, a powerful rune of protection and friendship. If ever you need my help or wish to return to the pools, hold the rune stone in your hand, speak my name, and we will be together again."

The rune stone was smooth as glass. Aidan thought it was black until he held it up in the sunlight and saw that it was actually dark iridescent blue. Looking at the rune stone was like gazing into a deep pool.

Aidan placed the leather-corded stone around his neck. When he looked back up to thank Daphne, she was gone, leaving only a flower-scented breeze receding back into the woods. For a time, Aidan remained transfixed by the enchanting image of Daphne in his mind. Eventually, the pools' soothing energy allowed him to relax once again. He slipped deeper into the steaming water and invited its healing energy into his being.

That night, Aidan dreamed of Daphne. In the dream, he followed her far into the forest along the course of a small brook. The scene was dripping with magic, and the air rippled in Aidan's vision as if he was moving underwater. They followed the stream until they reached a lush grotto covered in ferns surrounding a deep pool.

Aidan had never seen a place of such pristine beauty. Stillness permeated the grotto, as if the pool existed outside the movement of time.

Dappled sunlight touched the water in places, sending beams of emerald light shining into the pool's mysterious depths. There was no bottom in sight.

A hazelnut tree stood at the far end of the pool, surrounded by golden light. The tree was magnetic, and Aidan felt it drawing him, calling him. The grotto was steeped with presence, as if it were a living being. Aidan was filled with a sense of belonging that he had never felt before. He longed to remain in the grotto and leave the rest of the world behind.

"This is the Spring of Mystery," Daphne said. "Its pristine waters bubble up from deep within the earth and irrigate the Pools of Peace with the energy of the Way. This spring is the source of this beloved sanctuary's healing energy. It is also the place of my birth and the origin of my power. We are inseparable, one and the same.

"Wisdom and magic from the heart of Mother Earth animate this spring. Any who drink from these waters will find themselves forever changed. But one can never know what seeds within your soul will sprout when you partake of the Mystery. You may drink from the waters if you choose."

Aidan knelt reverently at the edge of the pool, filled his cupped hands with the cool water, and lifted them to his lips. As soon as the water wet his tongue, the Flow surged into his body with a power far beyond what he had experienced in the past. Aidan felt his entire body dissolve into liquid, and he spiraled down, down, down into the emerald depths of the pool.

Merged with the eddying currents, Aidan descended into the watery expanse. The cool water enveloped him in its peaceful embrace. Tiny bubbles sparkled like stardust in shafts of sunlight from above. Aidan floated, transfixed by the beauty surrounding him. The rich emerald-green waters glowed from beams of sunlight penetrating the water.

The dream shifted, and Aidan found himself in a subterranean cavern on the shores of a vast underground lake. The placid water and the cavern's stone ceiling extended far off into the distance, disappearing into darkness.

Standing on the shore of the lake, Aidan felt serenity suffuse his being. The water of the lake was completely still, and the cavern was immersed in silence. The lake brimmed with potential, like a pregnant womb.

"What is this place?" Aidan asked.

Daphne's graceful form appeared beside him. "This is the Mother Spring of all fresh water in our world. It feeds all the springs on the Earth's surface. Rivers, streams, lakes, and ponds are all fed and nourished by these tranquil waters. This place is their home, their foundation, and the origin of their elemental power.

"In a way, this Mother Spring is the earthly counterpart to the moon. The moon encourages water into motion. Lunar energy causes the tides to rise, women's menstrual blood to flow, and activates the energy of water. And on the full moon, the watery energy of human emotions get riled up and awaken the wild side of people."

Daphne smiled mischievously and then gestured gracefully toward the tranquil waters. "While the moon activates the energy of water, the Mother Spring is the source of peace and renewal for the water element. The Mother Spring's calming spirit permeates the Pools of Peace and is the source of their healing, restorative energy."

In the dream, Aidan found himself becoming sleepy. In a quiet, soothing voice, Daphne said, "Perhaps you would like to rest here for a bit and soak up the Mother Spring's good energy."

Aidan lay down at the shores of the underground lake. As his eyes flickered and then closed, Daphne receded into the darkness of the cavern and disappeared.

The next morning found Aidan more rested and refreshed than he ever remembered feeling. Ruby and Eagle had soaked in the pools long into the night, eventually wandering off to find a sleeping perch in the enchanted woods surrounding the pools. Aidan's dream remained strong in his mind, and he knew the experience had changed him in some fundamental way. He felt intimately connected with Daphne and her mystical realm. The whispering of the wind and gurgling of the stream seemed to speak directly to him. The Flow was so strong within him that he felt more like a stream than human. Reality had taken on the quality of a dream yet somehow felt more real than ever before. Gathering wood from fallen branches, he made a small fire to cook their morning meal. In his walk through the forest, Aidan was overjoyed to find a large lion's mane mushroom, chickweed, and miner's lettuce for breakfast. Using the last of his butter, he cooked the slices of mushrooms, filling the air with an earthy, mouthwatering aroma. As the mushrooms cooked, he gathered hazelnuts from a nearby tree and roasted them slowly at the edge of the fire while he enjoyed his savory breakfast.

By the time he was finished, Eagle had returned. *It is time to move on,* she said. Aidan doused the fire, packed up the hazelnuts for later, and they reluctantly left the complex of steaming pools.

Eagle led Aidan and Ruby up beyond the waterfall and into a small clearing with a large white stone in its center. The wide, flat stone had been carved into a shallow basin and dug into the ground. A small channel brought water from the creek to fill the basin. Eagle dislodged the rock with her beak, and the water began gurgling excitedly along the channel and spilled into the white stone basin. When it was full, Eagle rolled the rock back to stop the flow and then flew to the edge of the basin.

As the water stilled, its surface became like a mirror, and Aidan saw the white clouds and blue sky reflected from above.

The Crystal Doorway brings clear vision to those who peer into its water, Eagle said. *Among other things, it can show you the most direct path to the Seer's dwelling.*

Tentative yet curious, Aidan kneeled at the mirror's edge. Looking into the water, he saw his own face staring back at him, but within moments, the image began to morph. He found himself transported to the secret Garden of the Goddess in Willow's Glen. The garden was empty except for him and the birds singing sweetly in the trees. It warmed his heart to be back in Father David's beloved garden. He could smell the flowers and feel a gentle breeze on his cheek. Walking to the spring of the Goddess, he knelt down to touch its sacred waters.

Suddenly, he found himself conveyed back to the Pools of Peace near the swimming hole. Aidan sensed a connection between the two places. Earth magic and the energy of the Way rooted both sacred sites in good, healing medicine.

As the bard pondered this connection, he was transported to a third location unfamiliar to him. Looking around, Aidan found himself in a garden filled with medicinal herbs and exotic plants. Peace also pervaded that place, and he felt the power of the Way permeating the air. But there was also a potent sense of the unknown and the unknowable. Many parts of the garden were shaded, and Aidan felt himself drawn to explore the dark reaches of its interior and the whispered secrets he sensed within.

Feeling eyes on him, Aidan turned around and was startled to find himself face to face with a tall, pale-skinned man wearing the black cloak of a druid. The man had a narrow face with high cheekbones and a long, pointed nose. His jade-green eyes seemed to see right through Aidan, piercing his soul with their gaze.

"Come to me, Aidan," the Seer said, his voice hypnotic and as strong as stone.

With those words, Aidan's body dissolved into rainbow light and flowed like water into the basin. Ruby's rainbow silhouette shot after him and vaporized into the pulsing mirror.

THIRTEEN

The next moment, Aidan found himself standing in front of the Seer. Somehow, he had been transported over land and sea to the Seer's island home.

"Uhhhh...what just happened?" the delirious bard said as his body slowly pieced itself back together and tried to catch up with his swiftly moving spirit.

"Welcome to Druid's Keep. You have traveled through the Crystal Doorway," the Seer said with an amused sparkle in his eye. "The mirror's magic dissolved your body into rainbow light. Your spirit could then travel at speeds beyond imagination through the doorway's portal to bring you here, to my home on the Isle of Odin Preferable to swimming, don't you think?"

"Whoa, I feel very strange..." Aidan said, slurring like a drunken cherub.

"Don't be concerned," the Seer said, smiling. "It may take some time for your spirit to catch up with your body. Here, drink some of this angelica tea. It will help with the transition. Please, have a seat."

Sipping his tea, Aidan looked around in a daze at his surroundings. Being more accustomed to high-velocity travel, Ruby was already buzzing around happily and visiting the colorful flowers in the Seer's garden. Looking more closely, Aidan realized most of the plants and trees in the garden were unknown to him. "I am familiar with most varieties of plants in the northern isles," he said.

"Where are the native lands of these herbs and trees?"

"These green spirits have come to me from the far reaches of this good Earth. This garden is a living treasure of rare and exotic plants and medicinal herbs. One could spend a lifetime here exploring the hidden mysteries of their medicine."

"That would be a life well spent, indeed!" Aidan exclaimed. He told the Seer about Mary and his family's love of herbal medicine. The stoic druid nodded with approval.

Aidan was beginning to feel more like himself and his eyes eagerly surveyed the amazing variety of plants growing in the garden. Looking back at the Seer, Aidan saw the druid's piercing green eyes probing him.

"Time is short, so let us speak of why I summoned you here," the Seer said. "An immense wave of change is rising in our world. An opportunity exists for humankind, the likes of which has not been seen for an age. The ineffable workings of the cosmos are auspiciously aligned to support the flowering of human potential. Celestial energy is focused on our world like a concentrated beam of light, illuminating the unseen realms of darkness and ignorance within us all. This divine light can also reveal the seeds of our remarkable unborn potential."

Aidan felt a bit jarred by the rapid turn in their conversation, but he was intrigued by the Seer's words.

"Humanity's greatest obstacle to evolution," the Seer said, "is the delusion that we are independent beings, separate from Mother Earth and all her creatures—and separate from each other. The idea that we are self-reliant is pure arrogance. Without plants and the bounty of

Mother Earth, we would starve. We cannot live without the clean air and water our world provides. And without the love and protection of our parents, we would have never survived through infancy. No one survives, much less thrives, in isolation.

"Our world is an interdependent web of harmony that supports all life. Mother Earth's generous spirit has created a vast array of sentient beings throughout the ages. Her blood runs in our veins. The ancient followers of the Way lived in harmony with the web of life on Earth and, in doing so, they, and our world, thrived."

Looking into the Seer's eyes as he spoke, Aidan's awareness grew more focused. It was as if reality had contracted around them and nothing existed except he and the Seer.

"Modern people have abandoned the wisdom of the Way," the druid continued. "Seeking to rule like arrogant gods and bend the world to meet their desires, they tried to sever our connection with Mother Earth and claim dominion over all life."

"Yet, as we harm nature, we are slowly destroying ourselves. Polluting the rivers, we poison our bodies. Carelessly cutting down ancient forests, we starve our lungs of air and our souls of beauty. Hunting animals to extinction, we kill essential parts of ourselves. The only separation that exists between humans and the rest of life on Earth resides in our minds. The heart of our people withers in this state of delusion."

With passion in his eyes, the Seer said, "The time has come to end this isolation, step out of the cage of our own making, and reunite with our forgotten family...not only our human relations but our extended family of all life on Earth. We need to heal these connections and remember that every human being is one of our brothers and sisters. And we must renew our kinship with the neglected voices of nature, the noble spirits of birds and beasts, trees and rivers, earth and air. It is time for us to realign with the spirit of the Way that animates all life. This is our lineage. This is the path we are meant to walk."

All of a sudden, Ruby materialized a foot from the Seer's head, hovering in the air, and listening curiously to his words. A moment later she stood perched on the druid's shoulder, preening herself contentedly.

The Seer acknowledged Ruby's presence with an amused smile, then turned back to Aidan and said, "Shall we take a stroll in the garden and continue our conversation there?"

With the Seer's words still swimming in his head, Aidan replied, "I would love to."

The two walked in silence for a time along the garden path. Ruby immediately shot off to a flowering plant along the bank of a small pond. Taking in the serene beauty of the pond, Aidan saw a silvery flash as a fish surfaced to snatch a bug.

As they walked, the Seer pointed out different medicinal herbs growing along the path. Aidan stopped regularly to crouch down and get a closer look at the unfamiliar plants.

Soon the Seer fell silent, lost in his thoughts. After considering his words, he returned to their previous conversation.

"Honesty and humility is essential if humanity is to heal its rift with the natural world. We have forgotten our sacred role as caregivers for life in this world. Like children, our people selfishly take from Mother Earth with little thought of giving in return. We need to open our eyes and see the damaging impact of our ways. Actions based in greed and violence feed the dark side of human nature. The shadow has come to rule the lives of our people.

"If humanity is to grow and evolve into its full potential we must heal the relationship with our shadow. Our brothers and sisters need to work honestly with their negativity and transform it through dedicated inner work. The arrogant minds of our people ignore and repress the inner shadow and, in doing so, fracture our essential nature. This leads people to feel ashamed and afraid of these denied aspects of themselves. Shame and denial have transformed our shadows into anguished monsters who are destroying our communities and life on Earth."

With a heavy heart, Aidan listened to the druid. Hearing the truth of the Seer's words, he thought about the cruelty that Oscuro and the path of Black Metal had brought to his life, and to all of Orkney. Anger rose within him, flushing his face. It took some effort to return his focus to the Seer.

"In this world," the druid was saying, "all things have a shadow side. Part of our path as human beings is to integrate the shadow into our lives in a healthy and harmonious way. We must love and accept our shadows, so we can transform the negativity created by denying and demonizing our own darkness. With honesty and humility, we can do this essential work of healing our hearts and souls."

Aidan reflected on Oscuro's curse and his harrowing experience in the Bog of Despair, which revealed the anguish of his own shadow. Clearly, he still had a long way to go to heal his relationship with the shadow.

The Seer stopped in the shade of a crimson leafed maple tree and looked at Aidan with compassion in his eyes. "When the light and shadow aspects of ourselves dance together as one, we will return to wholeness, and humanity will be reborn. This will allow us to see our lives more clearly, and honestly assess the results of our actions, so we may better serve our families, communities, and our world. Then we can return to the noble path of living in harmony with the Way and fulfilling our role as guardians of this great Earth. It is time for humanity's next adventure into the unknown. May we create a beautiful future in the unwritten pages of history. May coming generations tell the story of our lives with pride and gratitude in their eyes."

The Seer paused for a moment, watching the dappled light play off the water of a nearby stream. Looking back at Aidan with an amused smile, he said, "Perhaps you are wondering, young bard, why I have brought you to my island home to tell you this story?"

"I have been asking myself that question ever since I arrived," Aidan replied.

"Very well then," said the Seer. "How to begin?" After thinking for a moment, he continued. "Every human being has their own precious gifts for this world. Mine is clear vision of that which normally goes unseen. I have seen that you have an essential part to play in the unfolding of humanity's destiny. My vision cannot perceive your specific role, for our future's direction is not yet determined. But I can see that the gifts you carry are of profound benefit in these uncertain times. You live with humility and listen sincerely to the wisdom of other people and the forgotten voices of nature. Your love for all beings and your open mind will serve us well as humankind charts its course into an unknowable future.

"Your work as a bard is of great value in these times. Spirit sings through you and your songs help people's hearts to heal. Aidan, you are a vessel for the Way, overflowing with good medicine for our people. If we are to step into a more loving, peaceful future for this world, our brothers and sisters will need to heal their hearts and minds. You are one of a growing number meant to aid in that healing.

"But I must warn you, Aidan, fear and ignorance still poison the hearts of many. Change terrifies them, and some will resist the rising tide of humanity's transformation. The forces of greed and violence already sense that change is on the horizon. People who are still ruled by fear and negativity threaten the success of our cause. Before long, we will be forced to confront the powers that oppose humankind's awakening.

"And this you must know: the forces of evil have heard whispers of your name. They sense that you are a threat to their destructive ways of living. You are in grave danger, for these dark forces are rising against you. They will do everything in their power to hinder your quest for healing and the role you are meant to play in the history of our times."

Aidan felt like he had been punched in the stomach. With shaky legs, he sat down on the grass with his back against the maple tree. He was confused and distraught by the Seer's words. Thoughts of cruel beings trying to harm him caused him to shrink in fear. But as the Seer spoke, Aidan had felt a growing certainty that the druid's words were true. Since childhood, he had sensed that an era of crisis and transformation would come during his lifetime. He knew he had some role to play in this time of extraordinary change.

Hearing the Seer's words, feelings from his childhood reawakened, and chills of realization rippled down his spine. Feeling a flood of déjà vu, Aidan sensed the pull of destiny calling him. Bringing love and healing music to others was his greatest joy. If he could support humanity's healing in some way, he would make any sacrifice to play his part. Filled with excitement, Aidan closed his eyes and silently promised to serve the cause in any way he could.

Pushing himself back to his feet, he met the druid's eyes.

"Thank you for the clarity of your vision," he said. "I will do whatever I can to serve the forces of love and healing. However, I don't know how best to proceed. Should I continue with my journey to Unstan? Or is there some other path I should follow?"

"Certainly continue with your quest for healing, Aidan," the Seer said. "If you wish to serve others, you must tend to the healing of your own heart first. But perhaps I can give you some counsel about how best to proceed at this time. I will look to the Book of Mysteries and see what it reveals about the next stage of your journey. But first, let us rest for a bit, have a meal, and speak of simpler things. You will need some time to digest all I have shared with you."

"Thank you for your counsel, and I gratefully accept your offer for lighter conversation," Aidan said with a weak smile. Still feeling overwhelmed, he was relieved to take a break from thinking about the perils that awaited him on his journey.

"Excellent," the Seer said, a look of tenderness on his normally stern face. "Let us have some tea and soup, and I will tell you about some of the more interesting plants that live in my garden."

The druid poured Aidan a small cup of tea from a clay teapot. "This is puerh tea from lands far away to the east. It comes from one of my old friends, Great Harmony. He is a Taoist recluse who lives in the hidden peaks of Kunlun Mountain. The tea is aged like a fine wine for many years before it is ready to drink. Over time, its taste and energy become rich, earthy, and balanced."

The hearty brew tasted of the earth, with interesting notes of aromatic wood. Sipping the dark tea, Aidan began to feel centered and grounded. His mind became calm and clear. He thought how much his father, Bran, would appreciate drinking puerh tea before one of his long periods of meditation.

The Seer smiled. "Great Harmony and I have spent long hours drinking puerh together and having lively discussions. The last time I saw him, we got into an entertaining debate about the true birthplace of the Tao. Being a Chinese Taoist, Great Harmony naturally believes that Taoism was born in China, as do most people. He was quite amused when I told him I believe the roots of Taoism originated in England and Scotland and then eventually spread to China. Great Harmony laughed so hard he almost fell out of his chair. Yet I fully believe this to be true.

"I have never felt the primordial spirit of the Tao more strongly than when I meditate in Orkney's ceremonial cairns built during the Age of

Stone. These cairns were built over five thousand years ago, thousands of years before Lao Tzu and the rise of Taoism in China."

Aidan knew of the Tao from his father. He considered the Seer's words for a moment as he looked down at his bowl of soup and brought a spoonful to his lips. It was an aromatic vegetable soup with potatoes, carrots, turnips, and several other roots that Aidan couldn't identify. The savory broth was flavored with exotic spices unknown to his palate.

"The far east is renowned for its rich traditions of herbal medicine," the Seer said. "Over the years, Great Harmony has sent me many seeds from the powerful medicinal plants of his realm."

The Seer took Aidan to where he grew ginseng, the mushroom of immortality, and camelia tea, similar to the puerh they were drinking. Aidan whispered prayers of gratitude to each plant, as his mother had taught him, and sat with each one for a few minutes. Clearing his mind, he sat in silence and asked each plant to commune with him. As he slowed his mind to the pace of the natural world, the plants opened up and shared a glimpse of their true nature with him.

After communing with all three plants, Aidan was amazed by their potent medicine and wisdom.

The Seer was pleased that Aidan showed them such respect and spent the time to connect with each plant. "Your soup contains ginseng and the mushroom of immortality. They are both famous for fortifying the body and extending one's lifespan."

Aidan noticed a potent, bone-nourishing energy filling his body after he finished the earthy soup. "I have a question for you, wise druid," Aidan said, a puzzled look on his face. "When I looked into the Crystal Doorway, before I was transported here, the images of two other sacred places appeared to me: the Garden of the Goddess in my local parish church and the Pools of Peace, from where I just came. There seems to be some kind of connection between your home and those two places that I do not fully understand."

"Yes, you are correct," the Seer said, a twinkle in his jade-green eyes. "To fully explain, I must expand on the history lesson you received from the Larimar clan."

The fact the Seer spoke as if he'd been with Aidan during his visit with the stone people was a bit unnerving. He wondered if anything was beyond the Seer's vision.

"The Larimar clan spoke to you of a time thousands of years ago, when humanity lived in harmony with nature and honored the sanctity of all life. It was the golden age of those who lived according to the Way. During this time of reverence for the Earth, sacred sites of great power were discovered in places where the energy of the Way was particularly strong. These sacred sites became centers for healing and prayer. The power of the Way rippled out from them, spreading harmony to surrounding villages and bringing bounty to people's farms and gardens. Druid's Keep, the Pools of Peace, and the Garden of the Goddess were three of the most important of these venerated sites. Together, they were known as the Sacred Havens of Orkney.

"People traveled long distances to benefit from the good medicine of the Sacred Havens. Travelers would often remain for periods of personal retreat to commune with nature's energy and the spirit of the Way. During these retreats, people renewed the deep stores of energy and inspiration that allowed them to walk their paths in life and to fully give their gifts to the world. Others would come seeking clarity on important issues and decisions. Mother Earth's wisdom speaks strongly in the Sacred Havens. Sound decisions arise in the minds of those who pray for clarity in these beloved sanctuaries of the Way."

Aidan reflected on his time at the Pools of Peace. Spending a longer retreat in that magical place would be heaven. He resolved to return to Daphne's sacred land after his journey to Unstan.

"Although their functions overlap," the Seer continued, "each of the Sacred Havens has its own unique spirit and medicine. The Garden of the Goddess near your home is a haven for the healing of the physical body. Water from the garden's spring is renowned for its ability to heal many varieties of disease and injury. The spring water from the garden also brings healing to Mother Earth. Land that has been damaged by human disturbance or natural forces can be healed with this sacred water.

"The garden is also a sanctuary for communing with the Goddess, Mother Earth, and the spirits of nature. Birds and animals are known to materialize in the garden to share their wisdom with those who wish to learn. It is no surprise that Saint Francis deeply loved this sacred garden.

"The Pools of Peace are a place of nourishment for the human heart and soul. Grief, loss, and emotional suffering of all sorts can be transformed or dissolved in the pools' healing waters. Many pilgrims have found their hearts replenished with joy and peace during their stay.

"The Pools of Peace are also a place for communion with the mysteries of nature and the primordial energies of the elements. The spirits of fire and water carry out their spiraling dance in the sanctuary's steaming pools. The wind spirits are often heard whispering songs and poetry to visitors who soak in the sacred waters, their gentle words weaving themselves into the dreams of those who slumber.

"Enchantment is woven into this place and its mysterious guardian, Daphne. Daphne is more wind than flesh, more river than bone. She is an ancient elemental being, a caretaker of the Way since days long before the birth of humankind.

"A large part of the healing energy of the Pools of Peace is its ability to renew a person's sense of awe in the mysteries of creation. Returning to this place of joyous reverence for life reconnects people with the curious heart of the child within them and can bring significant healing. Daphne is a powerful being; more powerful, I think, than any of us know. She does not make herself visible to many people. You are fortunate to have her as an ally."

Aidan gently stroked the smooth stone of the rune necklace Daphne had given him. Remembering his dream of Daphne's secret grotto, he longed to return to the pools and further explore the mysteries of the Sacred Haven.

Realizing the Seer had stopped speaking, Aidan returned his mind to the present. The Seer nodded and said, "My home here at Druid's Keep is the third of the Sacred Havens. Whereas the other two havens focus on healing of the body, heart, and soul, Druid's Keep is primarily a sanctuary for cultivation of the mind. This haven has always been a place for contemplation and reflection. In the past, many druids and others engaged in mind training came here for extended periods of meditation to cultivate inner peace and awareness. Myself and other teachers guided dedicated students along the path of liberating the mind.

"Also, the library here at Druid's Keep was known far and wide for its vast collection of books related to herbs, magic and many other fields of study. In years past, the keep was filled with druids and other seekers of knowledge engaged in dedicated study of these ancient tomes. I have fond memories of the times when druids sat in the garden reading and monks walked the grounds chanting prayers. The air was charged day and night with the potent silence of so many people engaged in learning and meditation. Those were good days indeed.

"In terms of its connection with Mother Earth, Druid's Keep is a sanctuary for plants from all over of the world. Herbalists, witches, and druids gathered here to commune with the wise spirits of the plant realm. This was a thriving center for the study of medicinal herbs. Many powerful medicines were crafted in the kitchens of this keep."

Aidan decided to return to the keep one day with Mary and Bran. Smiling to himself, he thought the Seer might find it difficult to get his family to leave.

"Those who were devoted to healing and self-cultivation took extended pilgrimages to all three of the Sacred Havens. In this way, they could foster the growth and wellbeing of body, heart, soul, and mind and come to a place of wholeness and harmony in their lives. These pilgrims achieved profound inner clarity, enabling them to live in alignment with their authentic nature and the harmony of the Way. This allowed people to realize their true gifts and to be of greater service to others in their villages and communities.

"Sadly, as people's minds regressed into fear, greed, and violence during the Age of Iron, the Sacred Havens became threatened. Those who wished to dominate others sought to harness and control the power of these places and use it for evil purposes.

"A council was held by followers of the Way to decide how to protect these beloved sites. Guardians were chosen for each of the Sacred Havens to keep them safe and conceal them from the selfish, violent forces gaining strength in the human realm. You have now met all three of the current guardians in Orkney: Daphne, Father David, and myself.

"Spells of concealment and forgetting were cast upon these places, so they would disappear from humankind's awareness until the era of ignorance passed. These three havens of the Way have been strongholds of hope during the long years of humanity's ignorance and folly. The time is ripe for humanity to reclaim its role as servant and guardian of Mother Earth and to reconnect with the wisdom and energy of the Sacred Havens. Across this great Earth, there are many other hidden centers of power preserving the spirit of the Way for our people.

"For many years, I have served faithfully as guardian and protector of Druid's Keep. Ancient magic exists here. It is the source of my power and that of many others who follow the Way. Aidan, you have been brought to all three Havens to root yourself in their good medicine. The spirit of the Sacred Havens and their guardians are now your allies. You are not alone on this difficult path of your destiny. I will do whatever I can to aid you on your journey."

Aidan felt immense relief, knowing he had such powerful beings supporting him. He knew he could never do it alone. Then a thought struck him. "Tell me, great Seer, can I not heal my curse using the potent medicine of the Sacred Havens?"

"I pondered the same question myself," the Seer replied, "but my vision has shown me that the Sacred Havens hold no remedy for your curse. There exists a unique key to every individual's path of healing. For some reason, your healing is intimately connected to Unstan and the Bone King. Perhaps it is time to consult the ancient Book of Mysteries and see what council I can give you about the next stage of your journey."

The tall druid rose to his feet and walked determinedly toward the stone wall of the keep. Aidan followed him through a stout wooden door into the keep's interior. The keep's walls were surprisingly thick, but the passageway was well lit by windows built into the intricate stonework.

They passed through a long hallway and entered an arched stone doorway carved with ancient runes. The doorway opened into a vast library larger than any Aidan had ever seen. Rough-hewn wooden shelves rose almost to the ceiling and were filled with countless leather-bound books and ancient tomes. Walking through the library, Aidan noticed that some of the books had a peculiar glow around them and thought he saw a few of them moving restlessly as he passed. He considered asking the Seer about his peculiar library, but the druid was walking briskly, intent on his destination.

At the far wall of the library, they walked through a doorway into a small circular room with no windows. Candles set into the stone walls filled the chamber with soft, flickering light. In the center of the sparsely decorated room stood a wooden lectern with a large, leather-bound book on it. The tome had three metal clasps and was decorated with golden script in a language unfamiliar to the bard.

"This is the Book of Mysteries," the Seer said. "A wise spirit inhabits this tome. He calls himself the Scribe. His knowledge is rooted in the deepest mysteries of the druids. Upon these pages, he writes the whispers of the Way that are beyond mortals' ability to hear. Nothing that can be known is unknown to him. The Scribe is a dear friend of mine. He has a mind of unparalleled genius. However, he is a tad drunk on knowledge, and his unbounded mind can have an unsettling effect on people." Aidan's eyebrows rose with curiosity.

The Seer lit frankincense resin from one of the candles on the lectern and set the bubbling dish next to the Book of Mysteries. As the fragrant smoke curled and rose like a dancing snake, he stood in front of the book and began to whisper into its open pages.

After the words had been spoken, Aidan felt a rushing sensation in his mind, like a strong wind. Insights and wisdom proliferated in his awareness like fields of rapidly blooming flowers. His mental processes seemed to accelerate, and he felt an unquenchable thirst for knowledge overtake him. Aidan's consciousness felt infinitely vast and he sensed the mysteries of life were within his grasp. Not only were they within his reach, he yearned to know them all--now! The sensation became increasingly intense and uncomfortable as time passed.

And then, in a flash, the feelings disappeared from his mind, and he returned to his native mode of consciousness.

Looking knowingly at the disoriented bard, the Seer smiled. "I see you have met the Scribe. Most people find his mind to be a bit...overwhelming. Even I have had to cultivate my relationship with him slowly over time to avoid going mad. It's probably best that you not read from the book as I confer with the Scribe."

The Seer sat in front of the Book of Mysteries and began to commune with the Scribe in silence. Aidan was surprised to see ornate writing appear on the page without hand or pen to ink them. His brief glance at the flowing script catapulted Aidan into the mind of the Scribe.

Aidan's consciousness exploded into the far reaches of the cosmos. In a flash of light, boundless understanding illuminated his mind. Complex geometric models of multi-dimensional reality saturated his vision, and he was overcome with emotion as the blazing epiphany left him spellbound with the beauty and perfection of the universe.

A moment later, Aidan had the alarming feeling that the foundation of his mind was going to crack, that he had seen more than he should have. He quickly shook himself out of his trance and looked away from the Book of Mysteries. The room began to spin, and a powerful dizziness threatened his ability to stand. With a splitting headache rapidly taking hold, Aidan stumbled toward a nearby bench and sat down with his head in his hands. Using his meditation training, he tried to steady his reeling mind. Focusing on the sensation of his breath, he became more centered within himself. Aidan was relieved to feel his mind become contained once again and was content to return to his more limited view of reality.

When the Seer was done with his questioning, he closed the Book of Mysteries and rose to his feet. Aidan felt a wind rise and leave the room as the spirit of the Scribe returned once again to his home in the endless labyrinth of druidic knowledge.

As the druid approached him, Aidan realized that, in many ways, the Seer's energy was the opposite of the Scribe. Instead of being highly energized, ungrounded, and hurried, the Seer emanated a sense of deep peace and stillness. He felt grounded like a mountain, yet they both had minds of immense insight and wisdom. *What an interesting pair,* Aidan thought.

"I have important news to share with you, Aidan. Let us move into the library, and I will share what the Scribe has written."

The druid led him into the library to a wooden table whose surface was carved with runes. Aidan sat down in a comfortable leather chair while the Seer paced back and forth, stroking his chin pensively.

"It is fortunate that we have consulted the Scribe, my friend. Things are moving quickly, and we must prepare you for what is to come. The forces of darkness are moving against us faster than I had imagined. News of your catalytic role in this era of transformation has reached the ears of sinister forces. The dark druid, Oscuro, now knows of your journey to Unstan. He plans to create more ophidian to use against you and any who support your cause. The dark druid is on the move and bent upon your destruction."

"What exactly is an ophidian?" Aidan asked with hesitation.

"Ophidian are shadow serpents created by practitioners of Black Metal. They are parasitic snakes that consume their victims' life energy. Your curse is caused by one of Oscuro's ophidian." Pondering the reality that an ophidian had taken root within him, Aidan felt sick to his stomach.

Suddenly, a sharp pain pierced his chest, as the ophidian sank its tiny fangs into his heart. After steadying himself, Aidan looked at the empowered ring his father had given him. He shuddered to think what the parasite would do to him without Bran's protective amulet.

"And I'm afraid it is far worse than that," the Seer continued. "A being of much greater power than Oscuro is rising against you. He is Makhol, the demon warlock. Makhol is an ancient being aligned with evil whose immense cruelty is paired with a brilliant, penetrating mind. Makhol lives farther north on Graystone Island, where he rules over a population of the walking dead. Over the years, he has raided coastal villages with his war galleons and taken slaves from the local population. Makhol fractures the souls of his captives with fear and black magic. Then he casts curse, transforming them into zombies who will do his dark bidding. Makhol drives them to destroy life and feed on human flesh. These poor slaves live in a true hell realm. Although you did not realize it at the time, you have already seen visions of Makhol and his undead slaves. You dreamt of him several nights ago."

Aidan remembered the disturbing dream, where he became the cruel master of a group of soulless slaves and shuddered in recognition. The

Seer was right. He had become Makhol in the dream.

"Makhol has divined that you are a threat to his sinister way of life. Soon, he may set sail with his war galleons and try to intercept you. The stakes are rising quickly, Aidan, and we must prepare to face the shadow that seeks your undoing."

Aidan was dumbstruck with the crushing news. Fear was like a mountain on his shoulders. He was grateful for the support of the chair underneath him.

"You will need friends to accompany you on your journey," the Seer continued. "Unfortunately, I cannot join you myself. It is essential that I stay here and serve my role as guardian of Druid's Keep, for all the Sacred Havens may be threatened in these dark times. However, I will watch over you from afar and do what I can to support you on your quest for healing.

"Thankfully, the world is full of powerful allies for those of us who follow the Way. The Scribe has written that you must align yourself with our allies if your mission is to be successful. It is here that I can help you, for I am an old friend of many of these defenders of the Way. The time has come to tell you of a secret forgotten to all but a few in our world.

"A community of powerful witches and wizards exists on Earth. For thousands of years, they have concealed their true nature from our people. When humanity severed its connection with nature during the Iron Age, these beings knew that humankind would be threatened by their power and seek to destroy them. So, these magical beings went underground, so to speak, hiding their potent sorcery from the world. They have assumed a humble physical form that goes unnoticed by those who lust for power. The witches and wizards I speak of are none other than the herbs and plant spirits we love so dearly. Some of the most powerful sorcerers in the plant kingdom are the medicinal herbs. These powerful plant spirits are known as the Green Mystics.

"In the past, the plants had the same physical forms we know so well. But while their physical bodies remained rooted to the earth, their spirits traveled far and wide and were visible to the eyes of our people. The Green Mystics are magnificent sorcerers with powers that were much respected by the people of Earth. They used their potent magic to help humankind grow and evolve. Plants are a bridge between Heaven and Earth, bringing spirit into the world and teaching our people how to live in accord with the Way. Working with the ancient stone peoples, like the Larimar clan, the Green Mystics used their wisdom and witchcraft to help our ancestors build the stone circles, cairns, and other sacred sites, so humanity could live in harmony with the cosmos."

Aidan was mystified by the Seer's revelation about the Green Mystics. Looking out the window at the plants in the garden, his reality began to feel much less solid. The plants and trees seemed to undulate like water, and the air was thick with sparkling energy.

"Working with the spirit of Mother Earth," the Seer continued, his eyes full of passion, "they wove powerful spells into the land and helped create the three Sacred Havens. The Green Mystics revealed many other places of power and Earth magic, where people could commune with nature and nourish their hearts and minds. They taught people how to honor and care for these places, so their healing energy would continue to grow and thrive. Under the guidance of the plants, the wisdom and harmony of the Way flourished, and all of Mother Earth's children prospered.

"Due to humanity's greed and aggression in the Age of Iron, the Green Mystics withdrew themselves from their visible role in human affairs. But it appears this era of concealment may be coming to a close. The plants sense that the potential now exists for our people to honor the Way once again and remember our noble role as caregivers for all life on Earth. The Scribe has shown me that these powerful plant sorcerers will play a key role during these transformational times. They have heard of your influence in the turning of history and seek to align themselves with your cause.

"Thankfully, your connection with the plants is already quite strong. You have learned the ways of herbs from your parents and spent many years listening to the teachings of the plants. Perhaps you have even had glimpses of the hidden power of the Green Mystics?"

Aidan nodded in agreement.

"The time has come to for you to deepen your relationship with the Green Mystics and to behold their true nature. Come with me, Aidan. I have something to show you."

The Seer led Aidan back out to his garden of exotic plants, where Ruby was excitedly exploring all the foreign flowers. He walked up to a patch of ginseng plants, got on his knees, and motioned for Aidan to sit beside him. Whispering words long forgotten, the druid summoned the spirit of ginseng,

Roots of gold and ancient earth
We celebrate your blessed birth
Noble warrior, ancient sage
Teach us of the way of power
Come to us on this great day
Help our souls to ever flower

The air around the plant began to shimmer, and an earthy, resinous smell permeated the garden. Then, before their eyes, a tall, imposing being materialized. The Green Mystic had a body of gnarled light-brown wood and stood ten feet tall. His body was strong and sturdy, like a tree. He stood before them with the nobility of an ancient warrior king. In his hand was a giant sword. The sword pulsed with a fiery golden glow. His strong, wrinkled face was covered with a beard of root hairs, and long regal hair crowned his head like a lion. Blazing eyes like the sun looked down upon the awestruck bard. The ginseng spirit brimmed with golden light, and a fierce power radiated from his being.

"I am Renshen," the Green Mystic said. "We are well met, young bard. It is a pleasure to finally lay eyes on you in the flesh."

"The pleasure is all mine," Aidan replied reverently. "Thank you for revealing yourself to me, great teacher. How can I serve you, Renshen?"

"We will serve each other before our journey ends," Renshen replied in a voice of rooted power. "Our causes are one and the same. I am one of your inner circle of Green Mystic allies. In your time at Druid's Keep, you must find the other members of your inner circle. These teachers will be your most important plant allies in this life. It is important that you cultivate relationships with these plant spirits during your time here."

Renshen's booming voice vibrated in Aidan's chest as he listened. Aidan was grateful that Renshen was his ally and not his foe.

"And this is for you," Renshen said, extending his arm toward Aidan. "You may need it before your journey is through."

In his palm appeared a masterfully crafted sword. The leather scabbard was adorned with intricate metalwork in the shapes of interwoven vines and leaves. Aidan hesitantly took the sword and pulled it from its sheath. The blade was forged from a type of metal Aidan had never seen his father work with in the foundry. It was pale yellow, and it glowed with golden light.

"I thank you for your generous offer, Renshen, but are you certain this sword is meant for me? I am no warrior. I know nothing of swords or battle. The thought of hurting someone makes me ill."

Renshen smiled. "It is good that you feel this way, for violence is to be avoided at all costs. However, on your journey, you may encounter those who wish to do you harm. If you are attacked, you must be able to defend yourself. And this is no normal blade. It is a Sword of Light.

"The magic in this blade is attracted to hatred and delusion. When you wield the blade, it is drawn like a magnet to these dark energies in your opponent. The Sword of Light will not harm the person's body; however, it will sever the hatred from their being and awaken them from the darkness of deluded thinking. This is a healing sword, Aidan. After being pierced by this blade, your opponents may fall, but they will not die. The heavy energies of hatred and delusion will return to the Earth, and the attacker will fall asleep while they integrate the blade's potent healing."

Aidan looked at the sword in wonder, but then doubt darkened his face. "But Renshen, I know nothing of swordsmanship. Even a magic sword is useless in the hands of a novice."

"You are right," Renshen said. "Your training must begin at once. The Sword of Light is connected with my spirit. When you practice with the sword, it will teach you how to attack, defend, and how to move with it. Every morning you must practice with the sword. Begin tomorrow.

"Now, I must go, Aidan. Remember the words of invocation for my spirit. Though my physical form remains here in the garden, my spirit can travel instantly to the far reaches of Earth. Distance is illusion in the realm of spirit. If need arises, invoke my spirit, and I will come to your aid."

"Thank you, Renshen," Aidan said as the ancient warrior disappeared into the shimmering air around him. Aidan left an offering of rose petals in front of the ginseng plant to express his gratitude to his new ally.

"As Renshen said, you must remain for a bit longer at Druid's Keep to connect with the Green Mystics...and to practice with your new sword," the Seer said with a smile. "Those who work with the Green Mystics may have many plant spirits with whom they cultivate relationships. But as Renshen said, there will be a core group of plant allies that are like family. You will develop a stronger connection with these Green Mystics, for they have essential teachings to help you grow and thrive. These plant allies will teach your body, mind, and spirit to flourish and live in harmony with the Way. They will help to support and protect you as you continue on your journey.

"But before you meet the other members of this inner circle, you must study in the library to expand your knowledge of the Green Mystics. And we must make haste. Your lifetime of love and reverence for plant spirits is about to pay off, young bard."

FOURTEEN

For the next two weeks, as the moon waxed into fullness, Aidan studied diligently in the Seer's library. He spent long days and nights reading about the Green Mystics' magical powers. During his time at the keep, Aidan slept very little. His great love for plants and the energy of the swelling moon inspired him to read the ancient texts long into the night. He was also bolstered by the powerful energy of Druid's Keep, which supported all learning and pursuits of the mind.

At night, Aidan studied by candlelight at one of the desks in the library. The Seer's library was no stale, dusty place but was pulsing with life and magic. There was never a question of what book to read next, because when Aidan entered the room, one book would jump around expectantly, trying to escape from the shelves. Inevitably, when he located the rowdy, dancing book, it would be about plants, medicinal herbs, or ancient invocations for the Green Mystics. Once he sat down with the restless book, it opened to the page he was meant to study. When Aidan began to read, the book settled down and become quiet or purred like a contented cat. Thanks to steaming mugs of memory-enhancing teas and a spell of remembering cast by the Seer, by the end of his first week in the library, Aidan had absorbed an unbelievable amount of knowledge.

During the day, Aidan studied in the garden, sitting on one of the many benches along a winding path through the trees. The dynamic, beauty of the landscape kept Aidan inspired during his long hours of study.

The garden had been tended masterfully so that when walking along the path, a new stunning view revealed itself around each bend. Trees, rocks, and plants were placed to inspire the mind and bring peace to the heart. A small, gentle stream meandered through the garden, creating cascades and small ponds that added to the natural beauty. Everything about the garden conspired to keep the mind engaged and clear in order to support meditation and academic study. The scent of rosemary and mint filled the air, keeping Aidan's mind alert while he read ancient texts about the Green Mystics. An invigorating breeze seemed to arise at the exact moment his mind became muddled, or, when his motivation began to lag, the beauty of the dappled sun through the leaves would inspire him to continue. At other times, he refreshed himself by splashing his face with cool water from the gurgling stream.

One afternoon after a large lunch of mutton stew, Aidan felt drowsy as he tried to study in the garden. His dreamy mind wandered lazily as he watched the birds and butterflies flitting about in the afternoon sun. Aidan found his attention drawn to a small tree nearby, whose vibrant green leaves glowed with white light. As Aidan watched, transfixed, a glowing figure rose out of the soil in front of the tree. Standing before him in the bright-colored clothing of a traditional African shaman was a short, thin man with dark-brown skin. The man looked as old as time, yet he emanated undeniable power. White light streamed from his knowing eyes. Aidan knew without a doubt that he was an elder of profound wisdom.

"Hello, Aidan. I am Akon Aba. I am here to teach you the ways of the Diamond Mind, how to be fully present to all that life is, so you can perceive reality with clarity and depth. It is fortunate that your father taught you the ways of meditation from such a young age. We will build on this foundation and refine your mind until it is as clear and pure as a diamond." Akon Aba regarded him with unwavering eyes that looked deep into Aidan's soul.

Aidan swallowed. "I would be honored, wise one. Thank you for sharing your teachings with me." Kneeling at the feet of the Green Mystic, Aidan made an offering of rose petals in gratitude.

Akon Aba nodded in approval. "Very well," he said in a voice strong as bone. "There is only one time, and that time is now, so let us begin.

"To be a vessel for the purity of the Diamond Mind, we must first remove mental and emotional obstructions from your being. These obstructions are like debris clouding the waters of clear awareness. This may be unpleasant. Shall we begin?" The ancient teacher wore the unyielding expression of a stern grandfather.

"Uh...I suppose so," Aidan said with more than a little hesitation in his voice.

"Good," Akon Aba replied. "Begin by closing your eyes and bringing your awareness to your breath."

The last thing Aidan saw before closing his eyes was Akon Aba's eyes sparkling like gemstones with brilliant intensity. Once his mind had become settled and centered on his breath, Aidan felt the Green Mystic's awareness entering his mind. A moment later, it was as if a rushing flood of liquid diamond had been unleashed in his mind. Every fiber in his brain coursed with concentrated, brilliant liquid light. His arms and legs twitched and jerked with the intense energy running through his nervous system.

"Relax, Aidan. It is the Diamond Light that now surges through your body and mind. This is the source of the Diamond Mind. Breathe and allow it to move through you. Soon we will begin the cleaning. You must fully accept whatever arises in your mind."

Aidan wasn't sure he liked the sound of the "cleaning," but he trusted that it would be best to relax in the face of the rushing river of energy. Then it began.

Painful memories and images from his past rose into his awareness: being beaten up by a cruel group of boys in Willow's Glen and the powerlessness he'd felt; feeling superior to one of his classmates and judging him as inferior; seeing a drunk man strike a woman outside a tavern and being horrified by humanity's violent ways. One memory after another arose in his mind. All the images were distressing to see and challenging to sit with.

As soon as Aidan had fully accepted an image without trying to change it, the memory disappeared. Soon thereafter, another painful memory arose, and the process repeated itself. If he resisted the scene in his mind or the feelings associated with it, the image became stronger and more distressing until he fully accepted it as it was.

In this way, Aidan relived many painful events from his life. Then a stream of images came to him from other people's lives. Images of violence, warfare, and horrific cruelty assaulted his awareness. It was all he could do to keep his mind centered and stay present. His fears made him want to run and hide from the miserable truths being revealed to him.

After what seemed like hours or days, the flood of images subsided, and the intense white Diamond Light filled his mind with blazing illumination. He felt the Diamond Light flowing unimpeded through the pathways of his mind like a vast network of liquid truth.

Aidan's mind had never felt cleaner, clearer, or more focused. His presence was fierce and rooted. He was filled with energy and felt like his mind had been born anew. When he emerged from the meditation, Aidan realized his vision and hearing were vastly heightened. He could hear an ant walking on the tree next to him, and he had eyes like a hawk.

"Welcome to the Diamond Mind," Akon Aba said.

"What did you do to me?" Aidan asked in disbelief.

"Diamond Light is the elixir of pure truth. When it enters the mind, you are forced to sit with the painful truths you've avoided seeing. By bringing these memories into the light, you become free of them and can root yourself in the immense power of truth. When you are able to be fully present with all that life is, no matter how painful, the Diamond Mind flowers in its full brilliance."

"I cannot thank you enough for all that you have given me," Aidan said. "Please, tell me, how can I nourish the Diamond Mind and keep its energy strong within me?"

Akon Aba looked at him with ancient, penetrating eyes. "Continue this practice of sitting with the undiluted reality of your life, no matter how painful. Apply this in your meditation and throughout your day. Fully accepting the truth of your life experience and your inner being is the best way to cultivate the Diamond Mind. Also, ask the Seer for tea from the root of my tree. This will help your practice."

With that, Akon Aba nodded to the bard and then sank into the soil of the garden. Aidan had the distinct sense that Akon Aba was an essential part of the ancient Earth, like its mind or nervous system. He also knew without a doubt that he had found another member of his inner circle of plant allies.

Every morning, Aidan awoke early and prepared a steaming mug of Akon Aba's root tea. Then he walked into the garden to practice the Diamond Mind meditation. After Akon Aba's cleansing, Aidan found that he was much clearer and more focused than in the past. Negative thoughts and feelings still arose, but they had less allure than usual. After bringing awareness and acceptance to them, the thoughts naturally dissolved back into the brilliant light of the Diamond Mind. Pure awareness filled his mind like a vast horizon. Aidan felt more awake and present than he had ever thought possible.

After the Diamond Mind meditation, Aidan moved into training with the Sword of Light. As soon as he unsheathed the sword, it moved his body through a series of attacks and parries. In a graceful dance of thrusts, slices, sidesteps, and counterattacks, Aidan flowed through the garden like a graceful dancer.

It felt amazing to have the sword's magic coursing through his body and teaching him how to move with grace and speed. As he trained, Aidan felt Renshen's warrior spirit fill him with power. His body quickly grew stronger with the daily sword practice. By the end of his stay at Druid's Keep, Aidan's sword skills had already progressed immensely.

Early one morning, in the soft light of dawn, Aidan sat in the garden preparing to practice the Diamond Mind meditation. He sat under a hazel tree enjoying the scent of the moist earth and the aromatic plants around him. Aidan thought about his mother and how much she would love the gardens. It would be heaven for her to stay with the Seer and learn about the endless varieties of plants living in Druid's Keep. Memories of his family, Feather, and his life in Willow's Glen bubbled up into his awareness, and Aidan felt a painful longing for his home.

Perhaps thinking about his old life opened time's doorway in the garden, for the air around Aidan began to shimmer, and he felt himself transported into years gone past, when Druid's Keep was bustling with people dedicated to cultivating the mind. He saw dreamlike images of strange-looking druids studying ancient texts and brown-skinned monks in robes chanting in an unknown language. The air was charged with a passion for knowledge harmoniously blended with the serenity of meditation. The people in the garden were shining examples of bright, healthy, peaceful minds. Although saddened that the keep was no longer bustling with activity, Aidan was grateful to be part of this lineage of mind training.

Just as the image began to fade, Aidan spotted the shimmering form of Cambius, the Alchemist, walking down the trail deep in thought. He turned toward Aidan, smiled, and winked at him, then disappeared like smoke, leaving the bard alone in the garden once again.

At the end of the first week, the Seer came to Aidan in the library. "You have studied diligently, young bard. Now it is time for us to put down the books and make the natural world your classroom."

Aidan spent the following week walking far and wide with the Seer in the lands surrounding Druid's Keep. They stopped to learn from any plants that called to them. Some plants glowed brightly, some appeared to stand up, and others simply created a strong knowing in the bard's mind that they wished to commune with him. After making a tobacco offering to the plant with love and gratitude, the Seer taught Aidan the words of invocation for the Green Mystic that had called to them.

In this way, Aidan spent his days learning from the Green Mystics. His newfound allies of the plant realm helped calm his fears of the rising darkness the Seer had warned him about, and his heart was strengthened by his growing kinship with the green guardians of the Way. As Aidan came to understand the powerful magic of the plant spirits, he became increasingly grateful that the benevolent beings had agreed to support his cause.

In the days that followed, Aidan communed with the spirits of many plants: powerful yarrow, mysterious elder, dreamy mugwort, and many other local herbs. He was filled with awe at the unique energy and wisdom held by each of the Green Mystics. For the young bard, the days were filled with the joy of discovery. Ruby shared in Aidan's delight as she sampled the nectar of a range of exotic flowers beyond a hummingbird's wildest dreams.

Working with the Green Mystics, Aidan saw how each plant was essential to maintaining the vital harmony of the Way. They all supported different populations of bees, butterflies, birds, and beneficial insects with their flowers. Plants benefitted the health of the soil and provided food and medicine for the world. Aidan realized more clearly than ever before how selfless and giving the plant kingdom was. The humble Green Mystics were completely dedicated to nourishing the health of all life on Earth.

As the days passed, Aidan began to feel the dynamic pulse of the web of life around him. He sensed how each plant, animal, and human was a vital thread in the fabric of the Way. His time with the plants, little by little, opened him to a direct experience of unity with all life on Earth. He walked the lands around the keep in a state of wonder at the beauty and perfection of the interwoven tapestry of creation. Within the harmonious workings of the Way, all creatures served their roles, and life flourished. Aidan knew his humble ancestors from the age of stone had also lived in this state of mystical union with the Way.

From this place of heartfelt connection with all life, Aidan experienced a profound sense of belonging in the world. He knew that just as each plant and animal played its role in the world, he too must serve his purpose in life. This clarity gave Aidan the courage to continue his quest for healing, so he could once again serve his role as a bard for his people.

As Aidan's second week at the keep drew to a close, the Seer came to him. "One more member of your inner circle of plant allies wishes to meet you before you leave the keep. Perhaps you should take a walk in the garden and ask to meet this new ally."

Buzzing with anticipation, Aidan walked through the garden and asked to meet his ally. Soon thereafter, he noticed that his feet had a mind of their own, and before he knew what was happening, he found himself standing in front of a beautiful flowering rosebush. He knew instantly that this was one of his core Green Mystic allies. As a child, Aidan had always felt a special connection with roses. Kneeling in front of the bush, he made an offering of tobacco and thanked Rose for being his ally. Then, with love and reverence in his heart, he spoke the invocation for Rose that he had learned in his studies at the keep.

> Sacred Rose with wisdom old,
> your smell so sweet worth more than gold.
> Pure love blossoms in your flower.
> Life's painful thorns I shall endure
> My wounded heart is ever pure
> I call to you in this fated hour
> to teach me of love's humble power.

As the final words left Aidan's lips, the largest rose on the bush began to grow and blossom. From within its petals stepped a female figure of stunning beauty. Her skin was smooth, like dark, polished wood, and she wore a dress and robe of dark-green silk with crimson trim. Her elegant face emanated nobility, yet her full, red lips were earthy and sensuous. Kind, green eyes looked at him with a love so pure that it dissolved all suffering. Blossoming from her chest was a great, red rose, which beat like a heart. Aidan was speechless.

"Hello, my child," Rose said. "We meet again. For your entire life, I have watched over you, Aidan, and as your heart knows, I am one of your core allies of the plant folk. You and I have a special bond, because your path in this life is the path of the heart. Others walk the path of the warrior or the druid's way of the mind, but your destiny is to live from the heart and to bring love into this world. You have walked this path well, fair Aidan. Your love for other people and all of life is an inspiration. You have always sought to help others and aid their healing through your music and song."

Sadness clouded Aidan's eyes. "The world of song has been stolen from me by this foul curse," he replied. "Truly, I wonder if I shall ever be a bard again. I can barely remember what it is like to sing. If I am meant to be a bard, why has this foul curse taken my song and poisoned my heart?"

"All things can be healed, my love. Healing of the heart is powerful work. Never lose hope that you will find healing from your ill-fated affliction. Perhaps the muse wishes to know the depth of your devotion to being a bard. Who can say why destiny has laid this curse upon you?

"One thing, however, is certain. Scars on the hearts of those devoted to love allow the soul to evolve into greater compassion, depth, and wisdom. These are the gifts that life's suffering bestows. Those who can fully love amidst the pain of this world are like wine of the spirit, aged through suffering into exquisite complexity. Maintain your courage, Aidan, for this Earth is not a place for the faint of heart.

163

"And know you are not alone in this journey. If ever you are in need, summon me, and I will be there. Commune with me as you have in the past by drinking rose-petal tea. It is good medicine for you and will keep your heart rooted in love.

"The time has come for me to go, my son." Rose looked upon him with a mother's love in her eyes. "Farewell on your journey. You are always in my heart."

With that, the Green Mystic folded back into herself until she merged once again with the vibrant red rose on the bush in front of him.

His encounter with Rose left Aidan with a feeling of warmth and strength in his heart. Fear of Makhol and Oscuro dissolved from his mind, leaving him with a knowing that all was as it was meant to be. He felt that he was in the midst of the greatest adventure of his life.

During his short yet seemingly endless time at Druid's Keep, new frontiers of reality blossomed in Aidan's mind as the magic of the plant kingdom revealed itself to him. He could scarcely believe the parallel realm of the Green Mystics existed beyond the awareness of most people. It made him ponder what other realities existed beyond people's ability to perceive.

Contemplating the potential answers to this question late one night in the garden under a vast canopy of stars, Aidan lay on the ground with his hands behind his head and marveled at how little he knew about life's mysteries. For some reason, the impossibility of comprehending reality seemed hilarious, and he felt as if he were the butt of the cosmic joke. Laughing like a fool, he felt paradoxically that, at that moment, he understood life's greatest mysteries more fully than ever before.

One night, as the time neared for them to depart, Aidan sat with the Seer next to a crackling fire at the druid's hearth. Sipping from misty mugs of tea while watching the dancing flames, they spoke of the next leg of Aidan's journey.

"The Scribe and I agree that you will need other traveling companions on your journey. As you know, the road has become more perilous, and you will need all the help you can get. The Green Mystics, Ruby, and your fiery friend in that little box are powerful allies, but I have seen that others are meant to join your cause."

Smiling, Aidan looked down at the fire sprite, which he had placed on the table to bask in the glow of the firelight. The strange creature was lying back contently with his legs crossed and looking dreamily at the fire through the window of his little rune box home.

"In my visions, I have seen a accomplished warrior and one other who may be supportive of your cause. The Scribe agrees they may play an important role in the events to come. I visited them in the dream realm and explained our situation. When you find them, mention this dream, and perhaps they will consider joining forces with you. These two live south of the Pools of Peace in the town of Lochshire. They frequent an alehouse called the Northwinds. I doubt they will be hard to find, for one of them is a wolf."

Aidan's eyebrows lifted at this last comment. "I certainly can use all the help I can get, but what strange travel companions I attract!"

The Seer laughed. "Strange company for strange times I suppose. The day after next, you must depart from Druid's Keep. You will travel back through the Crystal Doorway to the Pools of Peace. I warn you not to linger at the pools but to immediately take your leave. Unfortunately, the eyes of the demon warlock, Makhol have penetrated the concealment spell of the Pools. That place is no longer safe, nor are any of the Sacred Havens. Soon Makhol's vision may fall on my home here at Druid's Keep. Evil is desperate to maintain its hold on our world. These have become dangerous times for us all."

Aidan spent the next day packing for his journey and saying farewell to the Green Mystics he had befriended in the druid's garden. The Seer provided him with fresh loaves of bread, dried fruit, nuts, and salted mutton for his travels. He also gave the bard a small pouch of felted wool embroidered with flowers and butterflies. Inside the pouch were dried ginseng, rose, akon aba, and other medicinal herbs from the Seer's garden.

"Continue your communion with the Green Mystics by partaking of these teas on your journey," the Seer said. "May their medicine keep you strong in body, mind, and spirit. Your plant allies are powerful and wise. They will help to guide you on your journey. If need arises, use the invocations you have learned to call the Green Mystics to your aid. Also, there is one more of your core allies from the plant realm that you have not yet met. Listen to your heart, and you will be guided to this plant spirit during your travels."

Aidan was not eager to leave Druid's Keep, for he had grown fond of the Seer and the many plants in his garden. He also feared what dangers might assail him on the open road. However, he knew it was time to continue and was heartened with the knowledge that the Green Mystics now supported his cause.

On the morning of his departure, Aidan and the Seer said their farewells before the Crystal Doorway in the druid's garden. The wise druid looked compassionately into Aidan's eyes. "May every step of your journey be blessed by the Goddess and the power of the Way. Know that you are never alone on this great Earth. May you find the healing you seek, young Aidan, and may the clear light of your heart guide you when darkness obstructs the way."

With that, the Seer told Aidan to look into the still water in the white stone basin of the Crystal Doorway. Ruby buzzed around his head and readied herself for the journey. Taking a last grateful look into the Seer's deep, green eyes, Aidan turned his gaze to the water.

FIFTEEN

Back at the Crystal Doorway near the Pools of Peace, Aidan braced himself against a tree and waited for the wave of dizziness to pass. Traveling through the Crystal Doorway was not a particularly enjoyable experience. The journey left him disoriented and unsteady on his feet. After a few minutes, Aidan found he could walk again, and the Seer's words of warning not to linger near the pools came to mind.

Aidan did not need further convincing. As his senses came back into focus, an unsettling feeling descended upon him. He felt the eyes of a malevolent being watching him. Aidan had the strange feeling that the shadows beneath the trees were plotting against him.

"Let us make our leave, Ruby. It appears the Seer was right, and Makhol or some other evil force now watches the pools."

As the two set off toward the town of Lochshire, a group of shadows broke away from the shade of the forest and followed the departing bard.

Traveling east of the Obelisk Hills, Aidan could not shake the unsettling feeling of being watched. Ruby, on the other hand, seemed happy and content as she flew between wildflowers in the grasslands through which they traveled. As the day progressed, a brooding feeling settled into the young bard's mind. Even with the protection of his father's ring, Aidan felt the cursed energy of the ophidian growing inside him again. A nameless fear and sense of melancholy weighed on his heart.

Later that afternoon, Aidan saw strange images out of the corner of his eye. Dark silhouettes seemed to be moving on the periphery of his vision, darting between the shadows of the oak trees that dotted the landscape. Initially, Aidan thought his imagination was getting the best of him, but as the sun dipped low in the sky, and the shadows lengthened, the dark silhouettes circled closer, until he could almost look directly at them.

With growing anxiety, Aidan stopped to drink and consider whether he should summon the aid of the Green Mystics. As he raised the water skin to his lips, he felt a sharp pain in his stomach. Looking down at his belly, Aidan caught a flicker of movement out of the corner of his eye. Spinning around, he was confronted with a disturbing sight. On the ground in front of him, his shadow was being attacked by another shadow. The attacker, thin and wraithlike, had plunged a black dagger into his shadow's gut.

Black ink began to drain from his shadow as the attacking wraith removed the dagger. The cut was bleeding badly, and as the conflict continued, his shadow became paler. Aidan was shocked to find that he felt weak and nauseous from the open wound in his shadow.

Aidan's shadow managed to repel the wraith with a kick to the head. Realizing how badly it was bleeding blackness, it quickly covered the wound with one of its hands, and the ebony blood ceased to flow. His shadow didn't have long to recover before several more wraiths attacked.

The young bard had never been in a fight, so he was surprised to see his shadow fight like a skilled martial artist. It moved like water, dodging blows and counterattacking with deadly precision. It repulsed the wraiths many times with fingertip strikes to the throat and magnificent spinning kicks to the head. Aidan felt aggression and violence rising within him as the wraiths continued their attack.

Aidan unsheathed the Sword of Light and quickly moved to attack the malevolent shadows. Feeling the power of Renshen within him, Aidan sliced through the shadow wraith closest to him. As he did, intense white light shot out from the sword, causing the wraith's form to waver. Then, as if something had snatched it from below, the wraith was sucked into the earth.

Bolstered by the sword's magic, Aidan moved with fluid grace as he fought side by side with his shadow. Between his shadow's whirlwind of spinning kicks, knife-hand strikes, and Aidan's attacks with the sword, they repelled a number of the attackers. But as they did, more wraiths appeared from the lengthening shadow of a nearby oak tree. As the number of wraiths increased, Aidan and his shadow could barely fend them off. In the midst of the melee, a particularly fast wraith penetrated their defenses and slashed Aidan's shadow in the chest. The wound was so severe that his shadow could not fully stop the bleeding.

Intense agitation rose in Aidan. As his shadow continued to bleed, he felt increasingly ungrounded and unable to think clearly. It was as if his soul had become untethered and was in danger of rising out of his body. The number of wraiths continued to grow, and it became clear that he and his shadow would not be able to hold them off much longer. The attackers sensed their advantage and began to assault Aidan's shadow with renewed energy. As the wraiths circled in, Aidan tried to focus his panicked mind, so he could summon one of the Green Mystics.

At that moment, a new shadow entered the fray. Ruby's tiny shadow glowed with intense, pulsing rainbow light. It shot like a rocket into a shadow wraith as it slashed at her with its dark dagger. The wraith's shadow flashed momentarily with rainbow light and then faded to grey, quivering as it was sucked into the earth.

Ruby's rainbow silhouette joined forces with Aidan and ferociously defended his shadow. Rocketing through the air, the tiny warrior pierced one wraith after the next. In rapid succession, the attackers flared with rainbow light, then vanished back into the earth. The wraiths could not defend themselves against Ruby's lightning-quick attacks. Within minutes, the last of the wraiths had returned to the dark soil of Mother Earth.

Ruby had come not a moment too soon, for Aidan's shadow was bleeding badly. A black pool of ink was spreading out at his feet in the lengthening shadows of early evening. Aidan had become more distraught and ungrounded as his shadow faded further, feeling so untethered that his soul was close to leaving his body. Although Aidan knew he needed to tend to his shadow's wounds if he hoped to survive, how could he heal his own shadow?

He calmed his racing mind the best he could and tried to think. Using all of his will and meditation training, he cleared his mind and connected with the subtle knowing of his intuition. A trying minute passed with no response, but then, the warm maternal voice of the Goddess whispered in his mind, "Use the water, Aidan."

The young bard knew immediately what to do. He pulled out the blue crystal amphora Father David had given him from the Garden of the Goddess. Removing the stopper, he knelt and carefully trickled a few drops of the water from the Goddess's spring onto his bleeding shadow. Several tense moments passed before Aidan noticed that a small plant was sprouting from the earth where the drops had fallen. Before his eyes, the plant grew and flowered into a beautiful purple iris. After the plant had come to full flower, the pool of ink began to flow back into his shadow body. Its form darkened as the shadow's life force returned, and Aidan felt himself become rooted to the Earth once again. Clarity returned to his mind, and raw, vital energy flowed up through his feet, filling his body.

Aidan had taken his shadow for granted in the past and never realized how essential it was to his survival. As if in response to his thoughts, the soothing voice of the Goddess came to his ears once again. "Yes, Aidan, the shadow is an essential force in human life. Without your shadow to balance the light, your spirit would have no gravitation to this world you love so dearly. Dark energy is connected with the deep wisdom and power of the Earth itself. Your darkness is a living link with the medicine of the Earth and the natural world. It is a source of primal energy and power, which is crucial for your health and wellbeing.

"The dance between light and shadow creates potent energy and dynamism in this world," the Goddess continued. "Within a human being, neither light nor shadow can exist without the other. Understandably, people are mistrustful of the human shadow's potential to do harm, but fearing and demonizing human negativity only makes it stronger.

"What is needed instead is the courage and honesty to see the negativity within yourself and to surround these wounded parts with love. Nourished with love and acceptance, these demonized aspects of ourselves can feel safe to be vulnerable and begin the process of healing. In this way, the negativity can be transformed back into life energy. This will allow you to reclaim your vital energy in a healthy way and become more whole.

"When people refuse to accept their negativity and are cut off from wounded parts of the soul, wickedness begins to fester like an abscess in the ostracized recesses of the human shadow. Humanity has denied and condemned its shadow for so long that natural darkness has become twisted into profound evil.

"The sinister wraiths that attacked you were manifestations of this type of evil. They were created by Makhol, the demon warlock. He harnesses people's fear and hatred of their dark side to animate their shadows with cruel intent and uses them to do his bidding. By disowning their own shadows, people lose control of them and allow them to be enslaved."

As the Goddess spoke, Aidan remembered the dark emotions that had flooded him during his battle with the shadowy wraiths. He had felt hatred toward the wraiths and hunger for violence. Aidan was concerned about these negative emotions and asked the Goddess how to live with them in a healthy way so they would not become distorted into cruelty and evil.

"The key, my son, is truth and love. Woven together, love and truth are the most potent healing energy in this world. Use the Diamond Mind meditation to look honestly at your hatred and negativity. Accept these feelings completely, but do not feed them. Emotions are like weather systems moving through your being. Watch them with curiosity, as a child would watch wind rustling through the trees. You will find that, like the weather, your emotions will shift and change of their own accord. By observing your feelings with honesty and compassion, you will come to realize that, although emotions are a core part of your experience of living, they do not define what you are. And remember, Aidan, the negativity of your shadow should be an invitation for learning and growth, not fuel for loathing and self-abuse."

Considering his own experience, Aidan felt compassion growing for people whose lives were filled with cruelty and hatred. *For those without love in their lives, how easy it must be to slip into the shadows and curse the cruel world,* he mused sadly. An image of Oscuro came to his mind, and he wondered at the suffering the dark druid must have experienced in his life. *How tortured Oscuro must be to lay a curse on a young bard who has done him no harm,* Aidan thought with a heavy heart.

Aidan thanked the Goddess dearly for her teachings and healing water. She bid him farewell as her presence faded from his mind. A wave of exhaustion overcame Aidan from his ordeal with the wraiths, as he sat down with his back against a nearby oak tree. As the sun began to set, the bard watched dreamily as his long shadow merged with the deepening darkness of nightfall.

That night, Aidan had a dream of Oscuro as a young child. Dressed in the black robes of a druid, the child was playing with worms in the dirt with a delighted smile on his face. Night began to fall, and the young Oscuro became afraid. The black form of Oscuro's shadow rose from the ground and began whipping the boy with a snake until he lay powerless and terrified on the ground.

Then the shadow stepped into the boy's body, and Oscuro was transformed into a demon with a pitchfork in hand, the flames of hell burning behind him. The demon turned to look at Aidan, and he saw his own face staring back at him.

Aidan bolted awake and shuddered at the nightmare. Hoping to shake the residue of the dark dream, he decided to practice the Diamond Mind meditation. Dropping into the meditation, he looked at the feelings of hatred and violence he had felt in his battle with the wraiths. He felt the presence of Akon Aba, Rose, and Renshen come to support him as he worked with his shadow.

Aidan saw clearly how the wraiths threatening his life had fueled his hatred and violence. In that moment, Rose entered his awareness. She stood like a regal queen in her dark-green silk robe and gazed at Aidan with a mother's loving eyes. The large rose blooming from her chest pulsed gently with life.

"As the Goddess said, when you are looking honestly at the shadow sides of your nature, it is important that you do so with love," she said. "Envelope the negative feelings as if they were children in pain. In this way, the shadow can be honored and cared for instead of repressed. When it is repressed, the negativity becomes stronger and eventually erupts into cruelty toward yourself and others."

As Aidan surrounded his anger and hatred of the wraiths with love, his negative feelings began to dissipate. He saw how his anger and hatred had surfaced to protect him and vanquish the wraiths.

Renshen arose in his mind and showed Aidan how his fear and his inexperience in battle had ignited his anger. Then he showed the bard how he could have been fully engaged in the battle without hatred. Aidan saw images of himself fighting the wraiths with fierce aggression, but instead of anger, he felt utterly absorbed in the moment, like an artist involved in their craft. Every move, strike, and defense was an opportunity for mastery and perfection. Aidan was shocked to feel peace in the midst of the battle, as he gave himself fully to the artistry of combat. As the meditation came to a close, Aidan vowed to practice this paradoxical way of being a warrior with peace in his heart if he ever found himself in another battle. Nevertheless, he prayed to avoid any future violence on his journey.

Aidan's heart and spirit felt lighter after his meditation. He thanked the Green Mystics for their support and prepared a quick breakfast, so they could be on their way.

The sun shined brighter that morning without the gloomy presence of the wraiths to dim the light of day. As they continued their journey toward Lochshire, Aidan looked down periodically to check on his shadow. Each time he was relieved to see its healthy black form walking with him instead of battling a dark foe or bleeding profusely. Aidan's parents had always told him that he was born of the light. This new kinship with his shadow made him feel like he was also a child of the night and the mysteries of darkness.

Far to the north in the Sawtooth Hills, Oscuro began his journey to intercept Aidan and prevent him from reaching the Bone King. The dark druid had hovered over his cauldron for two full days to create more ophidian. Although he wanted a great horde, he was only able to spawn a few more of the cursed creatures. Time was running out, and he needed to leave soon to intercept Aidan before he reached Unstan.

Knowing that his sickly horse would never survive the journey to Unstan, Oscuro decided to secure passage with a traveler from Willow's Glen, who was headed out of town. That morning, he went to the village marketplace and began asking merchants if he could travel with them when they departed.

After several unfruitful conversations, Oscuro came upon Raven, the witch, selling her magical wares in the market. Oscuro inquired if she might have space for a passenger when she left town.

"I would love to give you a ride, you handsome devil." Raven winked at him seductively.

Oscuro blushed and stood with his mouth open, unable to speak.

"Don't get too flustered, Oscuro. I'm just having a little fun with you. But yes, you're in luck. My business here is beginning to wane, so I will be leaving Willow's Glen tomorrow for Lochshire. I can take you most of the way to

Unstan. I would be happy for the company on my travels."

The next morning, all had been made ready. Raven had packed her things in the covered horse cart that doubled as her home on wheels. The walls of the purple trailer home were painted with eyes, spirals, six-pointed stars, and other witch-worthy symbols. Raven's little house even had a shingled roof and small wood-burning stove.

Oscuro packed his cauldron, various herbs, magical objects, and all his remaining ingots of haedium steel into the trailer home, then he climbed into the seat next to Raven. He was impressed to see that there were no reins attached to the horses. Raven simply said, "Move out, my friends." The two horses strained for a moment against the load and then started pulling the cart down the main street of Willow's Glen toward the edge of town.

The dark druid was happy to be traveling with Raven. He was more at ease in her company than with most people. Unlike the villagers of Willow's Glen, Raven was not put off by Oscuro's dark demeanor and curmudgeonly ways.

They spent their time on the road talking of divination, magical spells, and herbal medicine. Although he would have been reluctant to admit it, Oscuro actually enjoyed his time with Raven. It was a relief to be in the company of someone who didn't fear him, and it felt good to be out on the open road.

Hours later, as they lumbered through the grasslands on the far side of the Sawtooth Hills, Oscuro mused about the few ophidian that he carried in his knapsack. *This will not do,* he thought. *I will need many more ophidian to insure my victory over the bard and any others foolish enough to stand with him. But I haven't enough haedium steel or time to spend at the cauldron. I must think of some other way to create my serpentine swarm. Perhaps the crisp air and the open road will clear my mind and bring me inspiration.*

SIXTEEN

For two more days, Aidan and Ruby made their way south toward the coast and the town of Lochshire. The rolling hills were covered with tall green grass that rippled and danced in the breeze. Through the leather soles of his well-worn shoes, Aidan relished the feel of the soft earth under his feet. The smell of fresh grass reminded him of the meadows near his home and of lying on his back with Feather watching the billowing clouds floating leisurely across the sky.

On the second day, the land descended toward the coast. Aidan felt fortunate that his journey was allowing him to explore Orkney's countryside and to more fully appreciate his homeland. Bucolic visions of sheep grazing in the rolling hills became more common, and there were occasional houses nestled into the landscape.

Ruby's curiosity was insatiable, and she couldn't resist buzzing into the flocks of sheep to investigate. She startled many sheep by suddenly appearing inches from their faces and chirping excitedly. Later in the afternoon, Ruby rocketed up to a shepherd, who sat daydreaming on a boulder as his sheep grazed nearby. The shepherd cracked a smile at the sight of the curious bird humming happily in front of him. After she sped off, he looked up and caught sight of Aidan. Aidan waved as he approached the man. "Hello, young lad," the shepherd said with a friendly smile. "I am John." He shook Aidan's hand with the strong grip and rough skin of one who works with his hands. John's sun-browned face had a contented smile tinged with curiosity. "What brings you to these parts?"

"I am on my way to Lochshire to meet a friend," Aidan said.

"I see. Well, you still have a full day of walking before you reach Lochshire. My wife, Isabel, and I don't get many visitors. Would you like to join us for dinner? Isabel is making roast mutton, and her cooking is not to be missed. Our home is not far from here. You're welcome to stay with us tonight and continue on your journey in the morning."

"That sounds wonderful," Aidan replied with a smile. "Thank you for your hospitality."

As the late-afternoon sun drenched the rolling hills, they slowly made their way toward a group of oak trees. The shepherd's log cabin was nestled under the trees overlooking the grasslands and the coastline in the distance. Smoke rose lazily from the chimney, and Aidan caught the welcoming scent of roast mutton as they approached the shepherd's home.

After guiding the sheep into a large pen and securing the wooden gate, John led Aidan to the front door of the house. Ruby wanted to stay outdoors, so she buzzed off to explore the area.

Aidan stepped into a small, cozy home filled with the savory aroma of Isabel's cooking. The house was sparsely furnished with rough-hewn oak furniture. A small hearth in the main room glowed with dancing firelight. Mutton roasted on a spit, dripping its savory juices into the flames as it cooked.

"Look who I found, my love," John said cheerily as he walked through the door. "He's been walking all day, and I imagine he could use a

181

home-cooked meal. Isabel, this is Aidan. He's on his way to Lochshire."

Turning around from her work in the kitchen, Isabel wiped her hands on her apron and looked at Aidan with steady, gentle eyes. She reminded Aidan of his mother. Although her skin was much darker than Mary's, her smile was warm and kind like his mother's. Aidan immediately felt at ease in her presence.

"Welcome to our home, Aidan," Isabel said. "I am glad for your company. We don't get many visitors up in these hills. Please, make yourself comfortable. Can I get you a mug of my homemade mead?"

Aidan gratefully accepted the mead and sat down with John on the couch next to the fire. "We have a beehive out back," John said proudly. "And Isabel has become quite skilled at brewing mead."

The mead was crisp, light, and flavored with huckleberries. "It's delicious!" Aidan declared.

John and Isabel were earthy, contented people, and the young bard was grateful for their company. After a delicious meal of roast mutton and potatoes, Aidan brewed them all a pot of rose tea. They passed a cheerful evening playing cards and talking about the life of sheepherders. Aidan was glad to speak of simpler things and avoid the subjects of demon warlocks and dark druids.

"Isabel and I have been living in this home and tending the flock for many years now. We met and fell in love while living in Lochshire. Before long, we both came to feel that something was missing from our lives. Lochshire is bustling with interesting people and things to do, but living there somehow felt empty for us both. So, we bought a flock of sheep from an aging shepherd and moved into this sweet home in the hills.

"Living out here, we found what was missing in the city. Here I feel connected with life in a way I never could in Lochshire. Away from the rushing bustle of the city, I feel my rightful place as part of the natural world. The gentle hills, clouds floating by on the breeze, birds, and animals all bring me into communion with the Way.

"Being aligned with nature and its rhythms makes me feel like I am part of something sublime and mysterious. Too often, the city is distracting and abrasive, but here I can slow down, be awake to the miracles of the natural world, and feel fully alive. Now, when I stay in town too long, the rushing pace of humanity makes me feel like I'm actually being ripped apart from the fabric of the world. I am much happier up here with Isabel, where I feel connected with the great web of life. Here, I feel whole." Isabel smiled knowingly in agreement. Being with the humble shepherds reminded Aidan of the warm feel of his family's home. He yearned to remain with them and live the life of a sheepherder for a time, but such was not his path.

After washing the dishes, Isabel gave him a blanket and pillow, and they wished each other good night. Lying on the couch, Aidan yawned and lazily watched the glowing embers of the fire until sleep overcame him.

After a restful night of sleep, they all shared a breakfast of hot cereal with honey and huckleberries. Aidan thanked them for their hospitality and good company, then stepped out into the crisp morning air. Ruby was soon buzzing around his head, to the amusement of John and Isabel. Aidan waved goodbye and then began walking down the gentle slope, towards Lochshire.

Farther down the rolling hills, they encountered another flock of sheep. The grazing animals were a comforting presence as they made their way along the trail toward the coast.

Around midday, the town of Lochshire appeared below, huddled along the coastline of the North Sea. Lochshire was a port town situated on a finger-shaped bay that protected it from the ravages of the North Sea. The town served as a natural marina for trading ships and the townspeople's fishing boats. The smell of the sea permeated Lochshire's streets.

Aidan and Ruby reached the edge of town while the sun was still high. They made their way through damp, narrow streets lined with grey houses weathered by the salt air. As they approached the center of town, the widening streets began to fill with people. Following the river of townspeople, Aidan and Ruby eventually spilled out into a wide street, where a market was in full swing.

In contrast to the faded grey buildings of Lochshire, the market was an explosion of color. Bright fabrics decorated the merchants' stalls, and textiles and clothing from faraway lands hung from kiosk walls. Aidan gawked in disbelief at the vast array of exotic wares for sale. He had never seen anything like it. Being a lover of vibrant colors, Ruby buzzed excitedly from stall to stall, taking it all in.

The market was filled with a wide range of characters from foreign lands. Merchants from Seville, soldiers and mercenaries, traders from Genoa, fisherman from the north, harlots, thieves, artists, craftsmen, and a host of other rowdy folk wandered the streets. Aidan listened intently to people's conversations as he and Ruby made their way through the market.

"I'll not part with this shawl for such a pittance. This precious silk comes from the far east beyond the land of the Mongols." said a squat, crusty woman haggling with a sharp dressed tailor from France.

Passing them by, Aidan came upon a stall reeking of fish where a ruddy-faced fisherman was showing off his catch to a group of interested customers.

"Ay, the mackerel and haddock fishing was good in the North Sea. Look at these beauties," said the brawny fisherman.

Aidan spent the afternoon exploring the market and chatting with vendors about their wares. He spent a good while at a jeweler's booth, admiring the inspired designs of the treasures on display.

The animated, grey-haired woman at the counter was clearly passionate about her work. Having learned from his father about working with metal and gems, Aidan was soon immersed in a conversation with the jeweler about the details of her craft.

After mentioning that his father made jewelry, Aidan showed her Bran's ring. Looking intently at the ring through her glasses, the woman's eyes opened wide and she said, "Your father is a master of his trade! That is a fine ring, indeed. I would love to meet him some..."

"Excuse me!" barked an overweight, gaudily dressed woman, rudely interrupting their conversation. "You might sell one of your expensive pieces today if you wouldn't mind helping a customer."

The jeweler rolled her eyes at Aidan and then reluctantly turned to help the woman. Deciding to move on, he waved at the proprietor then continued walking through the market.

In the next block, Aidan came upon a blacksmith's stall with swords, knives and horseshoes hanging from the walls. The glow of the forge cast an orange light on two men speaking together next to a large anvil. The proprietor had a concerned look on his chiseled face, so Aidan listened intently as he walked past and heard the blacksmith say, "I've heard tell that Makhol's slave ships are on the move once again. May he stay far away from Orkney's shores."

Aidan cringed when he heard mention of Makhol. A bit shaken by the news, he decided to find some food to settle his nerves. Soon he and Ruby reached a section of the market that opened into a grassy clearing with communal tables surrounded by a number of food vendors. The tables were filled with people talking together and enjoying their meals.

Looking around, Aidan spotted a food stall with a particularly long line and decided it would be a good bet for a tasty meal. The stall was hung with Arabic fabrics and bells that jingled gently in the breeze. The thin, brown-skinned woman at the counter moved with efficiency and precision so the line moved quickly. She had an aquiline nose and a look of noble, exotic beauty.

As Aidan approached the counter the woman smiled at him and asked, "How can I serve you, young man?"

"I would like a plate of the house special," Aidan replied.

Within seconds, a steaming plate of ground lamb and flatbread was handed to him. The aroma of spices from the near east made his mouth water. Among the bustle of conversation and people eating, Aidan found a place to sit at one of the tables.

Digging into his food, Aidan relished the delicious foreign flavors and forgot about everything else until his plate was empty. Looking to his shoulder, he realized that Ruby had disappeared. *How strange having a hummingbird for a friend,* Aidan thought. *One minute she's chirping excitedly in my ear, and the next moment she's gone. Then I blink and she's back on my shoulder.*

By the time he finished his meal, evening was coming, and the merchants were closing down their stalls, so Aidan decided it was time to find the Northwinds tavern.

He approached a stocky butcher, who was wearing a leather vest, and asked the stoic man if he knew of the tavern. The man grunted and pointed a fat finger toward a side street leading away from the market. With the help of a few other townsfolk along the way, Aidan and Ruby eventually found their destination.

Darkness had barely fallen by the time they arrived, yet it appeared that those inside were already deep in the drink, as a loud brawl was going on inside the tavern. The sound of yelling and bodies crashing into tables erupted from the Northwinds open doors. Aidan heard an ale mug explode against the wall, and broken shards rained out into the street. Ruby chirped disapprovingly from Aidan's shoulder and rocketed off to safer airspace.

Aidan was shocked to see a local fisherman walk casually through the tavern's roughhewn open doorway and into the midst of the madness.

This piqued Aidan's curiosity, so he inched toward the tavern's entrance and slipped inside.

The Northwinds was packed with a motley crew of unruly characters. A large brawl was in progress at the center of the room and appeared to be welcome entertainment for the spirited patrons. A group of red-bearded men at the bar cheered the combatants as golden ale dripped from their whiskers. Others couldn't contain themselves and jumped into the melee, armed with swords, mugs, or barstools.

It was then that Aidan saw the lone figure at the center of the belligerent mob. A dozen or so attackers surrounded a single defender. When he got a clear view of the solitary warrior, Aidan was shocked to see it was a brown-skinned woman. Clothed in a black leather vest and dark grey pants, she moved like a cat, with amazing speed and precision. Her sinewy arms brandished two daggers, which she used with frightening skill.

As a burly, red-bearded Scotsman swung at her head with his empty mug of ale, the lithe warrior ducked and plunged her dagger into his foot. The man roared in pain and hobbled back to the bar. Then a dark-skinned trader from Castille lunged at her gut with a capable thrust of his sword. With blinding speed, she darted around the attack and, like a snake, plunged a dagger into his sword hand. The man's sword crashed to the floor as a look of disbelief and pain colored his face. Clearly, the lady was not bent on doing permanent harm to her assailants, even though they seemed intent on her demise.

A huge pirate from the North Sea with long blond hair ran at her with a barstool. He raised the stool into the air and came down with a crushing blow meant for her head. But her head had different plans, and the feline warrior darted backwards as the barstool crashed to the floor at her feet.

Then, to Aidan's astonishment, and the loud applause of the drunken patrons, she ran like lightning up the stool, jumped onto the pirate's shoulder, grabbed his long ponytail, and cut it off. Leaping to the floor behind him, trophy in hand, she slashed the man's pantaloons, causing them to drop to his ankles. The freshly sheared pirate was mortified and turned beet red. He pulled up his pants and slinked off to nurse his pride. The entire tavern erupted into laughter, and the remaining attackers seemed to think better of joining the fight.

The woman smiled, glided to the bar, and wiped the blood off her daggers with a rag. As she approached the bar, Aidan caught sight of her companion waiting patiently for her. In the confusion and activity of the brawl, he hadn't noticed the large grey wolf sitting by the bar until she reached down and scratched the animal affectionately behind the ear.

Apparently, the fight had been a bet of sorts, because many of the patrons dropped coins on the bar in front of her as she laughed with the bartender. The portly, red-faced barkeep obviously knew her and her skills, for he was the only other who had won the wager. After the two swept up their winnings, the barkeep went out back and returned with a rack of lamb on a large platter. The woman took three ribs and put a larger plate on the floor for the wolf.

Aidan approached the bar, giving wide berth to the area where the wolf noisily cracked the bones with relish. Pulling up a stool next to the woman, Aidan ordered an ale for himself as he built up the courage to speak with her. After taking a large swallow of the bitter ale, he turned to the woman.

"That was quite impressive. You are a great warrior, my lady."

"A warrior, yes, but save the lady speak for one more fitting of the description." Her fierce brown eyes looked at him with predatory intensity. "I am Patia Faa, of the Roma people. Ladies tend not to live long in the world of the Roma. My people are known for their sharp blades and razor-edged minds. Beware, for sheep tend to perish in the company of wolves." She fixed Aidan with a knowing' gaze as she stroked the grizzled hair of her lupine companion.

Aidan squirmed in his seat and was beginning to regret he had approached her when she dropped her grim expression and exploded with laughter.

"You should have seen your face!" she howled. "I thought you might wet your pants for a moment there." Calming down a bit, she smiled. "I'm sorry, we Roma are also known to be a bit mischievous at times. Forgive me. What is your name, *fine sir*? You look familiar to me, yet I know not from where."

"I am Aidan, from Willow's Glen," the young bard said, slowly regaining his composure. "I was sent here to find you by a druid you may know."

"Druid you say?" Her eyebrows raised a bit as she fished in her mind for a memory just out of reach.

"Yes, a wise and powerful druid named the Seer. He told me to mention a dream where he came to you."

Patia turned pale and looked as if she had been struck by a blow. "The dream!" she whispered. "How could I forget? Yes, that's where I know you from. And now you stand before me in the flesh. You are the bard I saw in my dream."

Shaken by the unfolding of events, Patia was quiet for a spell while she pensively drank her ale. "When your druid, the Seer, came to me in the dream," she said, "I knew in my heart that my life would never be the same. He spoke to me of many things that night, and his piercing green eyes whispered of much more. The Seer told me of your quest for healing. After his tale was complete, you rose out of a pond in his garden and looked at me with your sky-blue eyes. You smiled at me knowingly but said nothing.

"Then the druid fixed me with his gaze, and I felt that he was looking directly into my soul. He asked if I wanted to understand my destiny. I was afraid, but I said 'yes.' I followed him into his ancient library, and in an empty room, he showed me a large leather-bound tome covered in words that I did not understand. 'This is the Book of Mysteries,' he said. 'Within its pages, the unknown is revealed for those who wish to see.'"

Aidan nodded knowingly, remembering his own encounter with the Scribe and the Book of Mysteries.

"What that book revealed to me has changed me forever," she continued. "I was shown the entire course of human history for the last many thousand years. Most importantly, it illuminated the significance of the times we now live in. We have the opportunity to heal the corruption of our ways and our broken relationship with the Earth. And I was shown the essential role that you will play in this great time of change. Before the book released me, it showed me that you will need protection from the forces of darkness that are rising against you...and that I am meant to be your protector.

"I knew in my bones that what the book had shown me was absolute truth and that I was meant to be your guardian in this life. It is my destiny. Aidan, I offer my sword and my life to your cause, wherever the road may take you."

Aidan felt his chest fill with a warm wave of affection for the courageous warrior. "I gratefully accept your offer of companionship and protection, Patia Faa. I am truly fortunate to have you at my side."

Aidan looked down and saw the wolf's intense blue eyes staring at him. He seemed to have been listening to the conversation and now sat as if waiting for something.

"And, of course, I would be deeply grateful for your support also, noble one," Aidan said.

At that, the large wolf's ears relaxed, and he licked his lips contentedly.

"His name is Byol. We are family, he and I. I found him many years ago being held prisoner by an evil man in Granada. In cruel spectacles of violence, they forced him to fight against bulls and wild dogs. He never lost a fight. From the moment I laid eyes on him, I felt a close kinship with Byol. I was determined to free him from his bondage.

"So, I bet his captor that I could defeat five men of his choice in battle. If I was victorious, he would give the wolf to me. As you can see, I won the bet. I knew Byol would not hurt me and did not fear him when the man released him. I immediately set off for the Sierra Nevada mountains in Andalucía, which I felt would be a good home for a wolf. By the time we reached the mountains, it became clear that our connection was deeper than I thought and he had no intention of leaving my side. He has been my devoted friend and companion ever since."

At that moment, Ruby rocketed into the tavern, landed on Aidan's shoulder, and chirped excitedly in his ear.

"It seems we both keep strange company, young bard!" Patia laughed as Ruby buzzed into the air and hovered within inches of Byol's face. She darted around, examining him from a dozen angles as the wolf's eyes followed her with curiosity. Finally, she landed on his head, ruffled her feathers, and started chattering in his ear. Byol cocked his ear toward her, and a peculiar introduction took place.

"Now that is a sight you don't see every day," Patia said, an amused look on her face.

Over mugs of ale, Patia and Aidan talked well into the night. Patia spoke about growing up as a wandering nomad in a small community of Roma people. She told Aidan stories of the passion and creativity of her people. As a child, she spent many nights outdoors around a campfire listening to songs of love and loss accompanied by the driving, soulful rhythms of flamenco guitar. Her people lived from the heart as if each day was their last on Earth.

Patia's father was a blacksmith who specialized in knives and weaponry. From an early age, Patia showed great aptitude with a blade. Growing up, she had plenty of opportunities to practice her fighting skills. Life was hard for the Roma people. Her family was the target of bigotry wherever they traveled. She honed her abilities as a warrior over the years by defending her friends and family from attacks by those who hated the Roma. She became so proficient with a blade that she was able to make her livelihood by challenging people to fights and waging bets on the outcome. In those matches, Patia rarely parted with her coin.

As the years passed, her reputation spread, and some people began to resent her successes in battle. During her family's travels, she encountered more and more people who were hostile toward her and wished to do her harm. The fact that she was Roma increased their feelings of ill will toward her.

One night, her camp was attacked by a group of people seeking revenge for a powerful merchant Patia had wounded in battle. Her family narrowly escaped with their lives. Patia realized she was a threat to her family's safety and reluctantly decided to leave her community and home in Granada. Soon thereafter, she set off on her own and had been traveling land and sea ever since.

Several mugs of ale later, Aidan told the tale of Oscuro's curse and his journeys since then. Patia listened with rapt attention to his stories about the Alchemist, the Larimar clan, and his many other adventures. Recounting his time at Druid's Keep, he came to the Seer's warning that Makhol, the demon warlock, was bent on his destruction. Upon hearing these words, Patia's smile disappeared, and she looked as if a heavy load had dropped on her shoulders.

"That is foul news, Aidan," Patia said. "I know of no worse enemy on this Earth. I have seen Makhol's raiding ships along the northern Castilian coast. I have seen him take townspeople as slaves...and I have seen what he does to them. I would not wish that fate upon my greatest foe.

"And I'm afraid it gets worse. Two days ago, a fisherman from the north told me that Makhol's raiding ships are on the move toward Orkney. I didn't think much about it at the time. However, now I remember what else the fisherman said: Makhol is hunting for someone in particular: a young bard from northern Orkney. He is offering a large bounty for your capture. We are fortunate that you have not sung a word in Lochshire and that you travel with no musical instrument. Nevertheless, you are in grave danger, Aidan. We must not delay here in Lochshire. Tomorrow morning, we will set out for Unstan. I hope the magic of your plant allies is strong enough, for Makhol will not be easy to defeat."

"I hope so too, Patia...I hope so too," Aidan said with a heavy heart.

SEVENTEEN

Before dawn awakened the morning sky, Aidan and his companions took their leave of Lochshire. Patia insisted they depart before the townspeople awoke, so no one would notice Aidan and his direction of travel. Still groggy from too many mugs of ale, they packed their bags in silence and shuffled out of their room at the Northwinds tavern. As they weaved through Lochshire's narrow streets, Aidan chewed on some of Akon Aba's bitter root to help clear his head.

Taking the west road out of town, they walked under starry skies just beginning to blush with the glow of pre-dawn light. They continued along the empty road for hours until mid-morning, when they came to a wooded area that provided some shelter from watching eyes. Patia had convinced Aidan that they must conceal their movements for the remainder of their journey. She feared not only bounty hunters looking for Aidan but also other servants of Makhol who might be searching for them.

Grateful for the cover of the oak and alder trees, the travelers stopped for breakfast on a cluster of large rocks next to a pleasant babbling brook. As Patia prepared a meal from provisions in her knapsack, Aidan walked down to the stream to wash the hangover and road dust from his body. Finding a spot with some privacy, he stripped off his clothes and waded into the clear, refreshing water.

As he splashed water on his face and body, Aidan felt a growing connection with the stream and slipped into a trance. The flowing water brimmed in his awareness, and he sensed the entire course of the stream as if it were his own body. Feeling the Flow awakening in him, he found that he could see the surrounding landscape miles away downstream.

At that moment, he felt the spirit of the stream rise within him and assure him that the land downstream was safe from danger for the next several miles. Aidan knew this to be true, for he could see every bend in the river until it was reunited with the mighty ocean. Then Aidan sensed Flowing Rainbow Nectar awakening within him to commune with the spirit of the gurgling creek. Water is drawn to water with a powerful magnetism. Flowing Rainbow could not resist bubbling to the surface of Aidan's mind to connect with a fellow member of the water folk.

Their energies intermingled for some time, dancing playfully with each other like flirtatious lovers. Aidan was a bit disoriented from the experience, for having such an encounter occur within one's own skin is a strange thing indeed. During their babbling, wandering conversation, Aidan learned many things about the two streams and the ways of rivers.

The new brook, Shimmering Water Diamond Roots, was expressing a paradox in the nature of rivers. Rivers are beings of strong emotion, and Shimmering Water relished the beauty and mystery of every moment. He loved every cascade, eddy, waterfall, and bend in the river to the core of his being and was enraptured by the perfection of the ever surging now. And yet, woven through his watery adventures was a longing for something more. He sensed the object of his longing pulling him onwards, making him eager to see what was around the next bend in the river. Like all rivers, Shimmering Water longed, above, all to return to the deep mysterious waters of Mother Ocean.

Aidan was surprised to hear the brook express a longing similar to what he had felt his entire life. Although it was not the ocean that called to Aidan, some great mystery that he could never quite put his finger on beckoned his soul. He felt it calling him when he witnessed an especially inspiring sunset or when he pondered the vast, star-filled expanse of the night sky.

The bard was snapped out of his reverie by Patia laughing at him from the shore, "I think you must be plenty clean by now, my fair-skinned friend! You'll miss breakfast if you take much longer. Were you planning on standing there all day with that faraway look in your eyes?"

Aidan looked down at his naked body in embarrassment and turned back to Patia, blushing. That made Patia laugh even harder, and she lost her balance and almost fell into the water. "You are an unlikely hero, *Master Bard,* but you certainly are amusing."

After she walked off, Aidan dried himself and put on his clothes. Walking was an interesting experience with the Flow still strong in him. His body felt like liquid, and he could sense the entire course of Shimmering Water and Flowing Rainbow at the same time. Although he longed to spend more time in communion with his watery friends, he resisted the urge and slowly walked back to join his companions.

Sitting down with his friends, Aidan was grateful for the solid feel of stone beneath him. As

Patia handed out chunks of smoked fish, sharp cheese, and bread, Aidan's mind drifted back to the wandering way of rivers. Having the Flow moving through him was very enjoyable and physically pleasurable; however, it made it difficult to focus at times. He realized Patia was staring at him with mild concern in her eyes.

"You've been acting very unusual since we got here," she said. "Did you eat any strange mushrooms down by the brook?"

Aidan smiled dreamily and then told her the story about Flowing Rainbow Nectar and how the Flow had come to him. After his tale was over, Patia looked at him with curiosity and fascination.

Aidan heard a buzzing over his shoulder and turned to see Ruby hovering within inches of Byol's grizzled head. The wolf was sitting quite still, and Ruby was trying to provoke a reaction from him. She darted in and out and side to side, fearlessly taunting the stoic wolf. In a flash, he snapped at her with his powerful jaws, but she easily dodged his attack. Byol lunged the other way and missed again. The game continued back and forth until Patia and Aidan burst out laughing at how ridiculous it looked. At that point, Ruby landed on the wolf's neck and chirped happily at them. Byol stretched contentedly, lay down, and began eating the smoked fish and bread that Patia had placed in front of him.

"I do believe they like each other," Patia said with an amused look on her face, and I'm not sure Byol is top dog in the relationship."

Ruby let out a series of chirps in response and ruffled her feathers confidently.

Knowing that the path downstream was free of danger, Aidan's companions traveled along the brook's tree-sheltered course for the rest of the afternoon. The day was filled with stories as Patia spoke of her many adventures as a wandering Roma and solitary warrior. The descriptions of her countless battles were the stuff of legend. Aidan was awed by the courage she had shown throughout her difficult life.

Patia also reminisced about her life with the Roma and the rich culture of Granada. She spoke of gatherings of Roma under the full moon, when music and song filled the air and her people danced, as if it were the last night on Earth. Patia told tales of Doña Alma, who danced flamenco with renowned passion and nobility. It was said that Doña Alma danced with such fierce power that the ground shook, and no child or animal could sleep until she returned to her seat. Through her many tales, Aidan realized how much Patia missed her family and the Roma people.

"Perhaps I will return to them after our adventures are over," she said longingly. "It has been far too long since I sat around a Roma fire listening to song and dancing under the moonlight with my people. The Roma have a passion for life that I have never seen rivaled in all my travels. Some part of me has felt empty ever since I left them years ago."

"I too miss my family and my home in Willow's Glen," Aidan said somberly. "Home seems so far away. I will be grateful to walk again in the Whispering Woods and return to the peaceful, simple life of my village."

As Aidan thought longingly of home, he found it hard to imagine that he would actually be healed of his curse and return some day to being a bard in his beloved village. His old life seemed irretrievably lost. Aidan walked in silence for quite a while, musing sadly about the state of his life and wishing he could return to the happier days of his youth.

He was grateful for the company of Flowing Rainbow and Shimmering Water swirling within him as they walked along the brook. Shimmering Water felt Aidan's longing for home, and his watery words rippled up into Aidan's awareness:

> *We rivers say*
> *it is best not to pine for the past.*
> *Remembering the sweetness*
> *of waters left behind*
> *is lovely for a time,*
> *but if our eyes see only what was,*
> *how can we experience*
> *the magic of life's river*
> *unfolding moment by moment,*
> *its beauty vibrant and real?*
> *Allow the stream of time to meet you*
> *in the vital spirit of the now*
> *instead of chasing stale waters*
> *of days gone by as they fade*
> *from the realm of the real.*
> *Embrace each bump, bend, and surge*
> *in the river as if nothing else exists,*
> *and you will live in beauty and bliss*
> *beyond mortal knowing.*
> *The present opens to unimaginable gifts...*

The brook's wisdom percolated into Aidan's being, filling him with appreciation for the mysterious journey of his life. As his spirits rose, a radiant beauty awoke in the forest around him. Everywhere he looked, nature's splendor smiled back at him: the shimmering sunlight on the brook's rippling water, the rustling whispers of a gentle breeze in the leaves overhead, the rich smell of moist soil beneath his feet. Aidan walked along the waterway in awe, reveling in each moment of nature's beauty and perfection.

By day's end, their path took them away from the stream. Before they left, Aidan bent down and pulled some dried rose petals from his pack, spreading them over the water as a gift. After reluctantly saying farewell to Shimmering Water, Aidan climbed the streambed and joined his companions.

Patia was eager to put as much distance as possible between themselves and Lochshire, so they decided to keep walking until nightfall. They walked through the forest until the sun set and twilight descended around them. In the growing darkness, bats began to feed on bugs still careening drunkenly through the air from a long day of sunlight and feasting. Although there were relatively few insects in the forest, the number of bats seemed to increase the farther they traveled.

"Strange," Patia said with a concerned look. "Something doesn't feel right about all these bats." As soon as she uttered those words, figures unfurled from beneath the flying bats like window shades descending to block out the light. The figures had human form and were dressed in black leather armor with thick black capes flapping in the breeze. In the growing darkness, a dozen of them materialized, armed with a variety of weapons.

"Shapeshifters!" Patia shouted, drawing her sword and stepping in front of Aidan to protect him. The shapeshifters attacked with quick, erratic movements. Their swirling capes made it even more difficult to read their attacks. However, Byol's senses were keen, and with teeth bared, he bounded from behind Aidan, leaping onto the nearest attacker and locking onto his arm with fierce lupine jaws.

Right behind him, Patia attacked another with the blinding speed of her lethal blade. The shapeshifter parried her first strike, but the second pierced him in the heart. The creature let out a high-pitched inhuman screech as the life drained from his body. A moment later, the shapeshifter was gone, and impaled on the tip of Patia's sword was the bleeding body of a dead bat. Flinging the bat corpse off her blade, she turned to meet the attack of a half dozen angry shapeshifters surrounding her with weapons raised.

Before she could react, an arrow impaled her chest near her heart. As she staggered back from the impact, another arrow whistled through the air from the canopy above and found its mark in her abdomen. Quick as lightning, Patia threw a dagger into the branches above. Aidan heard a grunt as a shapeshifter with a bow toppled out of the tree and landed dead on the forest floor.

Horrified, Aidan looked back to his injured friend and saw Patia snap off both arrow shafts and raise her sword defiantly to her attackers. Byol raced in with a blood-covered muzzle and stood by her side, growling. Steely anger radiated from the wolf and his Roma companion. Aidan felt his own anger rising as he unsheathed the Sword of Light. "Renshen, be with us!" he shouted before joining his friends in battle.

The next few minutes were a blur of attacks. Patia's sword whistled though the air, while Byol savagely assaulted their attackers. Patia's wounds were bleeding badly, but she continued fighting, as if possessed. As she slashed at one of the shapeshifters, her sword got caught in its cape. The bat assassin spun quickly, trying to wrench the sword out of her hand. Patia used the momentum to throw her own body into the air over the attacker. When she landed, she swung hard and hurled the shapeshifter into a nearby tree trunk.

Aidan felt the power of Renshen surging through him as he attacked the shapeshifters with sword raised. Ruby helped his cause by flying in the face of shapeshifters to distract them. With Renshen's spirit coursing through him, Aidan rapidly struck down three of the attackers. Each flared with blinding white light before transforming into a bat and falling to the ground.

The air was filled with unnerving shrieks as the bat assassins fell before Aidan and his friends. Finally, Patia struck down the last shapeshifter in the midst of its erratic, lethal attack, and a last ear-piercing shriek marked the end of the battle. All that remained of their attackers was a littering of bats across the forest floor.

Looking pale and unsteady, Patia dropped her sword and slumped down with her back against the nearest tree. Concerned, Aidan knelt at her side and offered his water skin. After she had taken a few sips, Aidan reached into his knapsack for the glass amphora of Goddess water, hoping to heal Patia's wounds.

"First we must remove these broken arrow shafts," Patia whispered, her voice weak with exhaustion. Byol seemed to understand perfectly. He reached his head behind her and yanked out the broken arrow with his teeth. She gasped in pain, steadied herself, and then nodded for him to pull out the remaining arrow. After it was done, Aidan poured a few drops of the Goddess water into her wounds. Within seconds, the wounds stopped bleeding and began to close. Patia started to feel better, although she was still pale and weak.

"Tomorrow we will stay put and let you rest. The Goddess water has healed your wounds; however, you have lost a great deal of blood. You will need some time to recover."

Patia was too exhausted to protest. She smiled weakly with an amused look in her eye. "Are all the bards from your village so handy with a blade? And what a blade it is. I have heard tales of magic swords but never seen one in action. Perhaps you missed your calling, young warrior."

Aidan frowned in dismay at the brutality of battle. "I don't think I'm made for the violence of fighting," he muttered.

"You could have fooled me," Patia said softly as she closed her eyes and rested her head on the tree behind her.

Not wanting to ask her to walk any farther that night, Aidan rolled out her bedroll and covered her with a blanket. Patia laid down with a sigh and was asleep within minutes. After scattering an offering of rose petals in gratitude for Renshen's support, Aidan laid down on his bedroll and soon dozed off. Byol faithfully watched over them while they slept.

EIGHTEEN

The next morning, they moved deeper into the forest, where they found a clearing next to a tranquil pond. Patia set up camp near the shore, while Aidan boiled water in his small cookpot to make soup for breakfast. As he cut carrots and potatoes into the pot, Aidan heard a rustling from the forest. He turned to see Byol approaching with a bloody rabbit in his mouth. The wolf stopped in front of him and dropped the rabbit at Aidan's feet.

"Thank you, Byol," Aidan said trying to remain calm with the wolf's bloody jaws so close to his face.

After thanking the rabbit for giving its life so they could live, Aidan skinned the animal and cut the meat into his soup pot. As the soup simmered over the fire, he sprinkled ginseng powder and nettles into it to help build Patia's strength.

After their breakfast of rabbit soup, Aidan and Patia sat against a fallen tree and warmed themselves in the morning sun. Patia was still weak, but the sleep and medicinal soup had brought some life back into her face. Instead of her usual boisterous self, Patia had been quiet and pensive all morning. Looking at her with concern, Aidan asked what was on her mind.

Patia sighed and looked at Aidan with weary eyes. "I think I may be losing my taste for the warrior's life. When I was younger, I reveled in the thrill of battle. I lived to match my skills against those of another and test them in combat. Victory

206

was my greatest joy. But now I begin to feel that, in violence, there is no victory. Even if I am unharmed in battle, what have I gained? To wound or kill another person. The spoils of battle come at a high price. In a way, I envy your path as a bard."

Aidan looked at her with sympathy. "Well, I, for one, am immensely grateful for your skills as a warrior. Without them, I might not survive to our journey's end."

"I suppose saving your skin is a worthy cause," Patia said, a glimmer of jest in her eyes.

Aidan paused for a moment before replying. "May we live to see the day when humanity's darkness can be transformed by love rather than steel. Perhaps when our journey is over, you can retire your sword and begin a new chapter of your life."

"Perhaps," Patia said, her voice trailing off to a whisper.

At that moment, the air in front of them began to glow yellow like a blazing sun. The light then contracted and took the shape of Renshen, Aidan's warrior ally from the plant realm. Through a mane of root-like hair, he looked down on them with fierce, golden eyes.

Patia gasped. She knew a powerful warrior when she saw one and sensed immediately that she could never conquer this one in battle.

"Fear not, Patia," Aidan said. "He is a friend and a revered ally."

Renshen stood before them, radiating the nobility of an ancient king and the strength of a ferocious warrior. With penetrating eyes, like those of a lion, he looked straight at Patia. "The warrior spirit within you is sacred, Patia. It is one of the essential energies feeding the harmony of the Way. There are many ways to embody the warrior without engaging in violence. Unwavering presence, well-honed skills, dedicated training, mental focus, decisive action, courage, devotion to a higher cause…these attributes of the warrior are good medicine for this world. You have trained yourself well, Patia, and cultivated these attributes with dedication.

"The power of the warrior lies not in sword or spear but in heart and spirit. If you were to drop your blade and leave it forever, the warrior within you would not be diminished. There are many worthwhile struggles to engage with in this world. Yet, in most of these conflicts, there can be no true victory through physical aggression and battle.

"As you know, Patia, the time has not yet come for you to drop your sword. You serve a higher purpose in supporting Aidan, so your own needs must wait until the time is right. The most essential element of the warrior's path is devotion to a cause greater than oneself. Without being dedicated to a higher good, one can be a brawler or even a highly skilled fighter but never a true warrior. May you serve your cause with courage and strength, Patia Faa."

Renshen stepped forward and, with the flat of his sword, touched each of her shoulders reverently, as if knighting her. As his sword touched her body, golden light from the blade streamed into Patia, filling her with strength and vitality. When he finished, Patia bowed reverently before the Green Mystic. Renshen bowed in return, then took one step backwards and disappeared in a flash of golden light.

Later that morning, next to the pond, the two companions sat in silence, absorbed in thought. Aidan watched the breeze awaken ripples on the surface of the pond. "When I was a child in Willow's Glen, the villagers used to say that I was like an angel, so loving and filled with light," he said. "I feel sadly disconnected from that light. Oscuro's curse has shown me the darkness living inside me...fear, hopelessness, anger, hatred. I feel sullied by my own shadow. I am certainly no angel."

Patia laughed. "Any angel choosing to live in this world must deal with their shadow like the rest of us. I've heard priests speak of 'original sin,' as if we are fundamentally broken. I don't think this is true. Our world is a place of light and darkness, and the fabric of this reality is woven into us. If God created us, then how can this world and our people not be perfect just as they are?

"Sometimes around the village fire at night, my grandmother would speak of humanity's darkness. She once told me, 'Your shadow follows you wherever you go. It is always with you. Why not learn how it moves so you can dance with your shadow rather than condemn it and make an enemy of yourself?'"

Aidan considered Patia's words, then smiled. "Your grandmother is a wise woman. I wish I could have met her. I will certainly heed her advice.

"I will say that encountering my own shadow has made me more compassionate toward people struggling with their own demons. People who have suffered far more than me in their lives must be haunted by negativity beyond imagining. If I am ever healed of this foul curse, I will write songs to help mend people's relationship with their shadow, so they can love all of what they are."

"*When* you are healed of your curse," Patia said with determination in her eyes. "*When* you are healed."

She paused for a moment and then asked, "What was it like for you to sing for people in your village? I have heard of the bard's ability to channel healing energy through his song. Is this true?"

"It seems so long ago that I sang for my people, almost like another life," Aidan said sorrowfully. "To answer your question, singing is the most perfect thing that I have ever experienced. When I sang, it felt like a river of beauty flowed through me. As if spirit had taken liquid form, and I was a vessel pouring its song into the world. When I sang, my sense of self disappeared, and I became one with the sublime energy of the Way. It was an ecstatic communion with God. I miss it more than you can imagine."

"I look forward to hearing you sing once again after our little site-seeing visit to Unstan," Patia said, slapping him on the back with a playful look in her eyes.

Aidan and his companions spent the day at the pond resting and allowing Patia to regain her strength. Although Patia seemed much more energized after feeling the touch of Renshen's sword, Aidan insisted they go no further that day.

Byol napped in the sun while Ruby hunted small insects flying above the water. After filling her belly, Ruby buzzed up to Byol's ear and chirped loudly to taunt him. The wolf snapped lazily at her with his powerful jaws, then fell back asleep.

While drinking a cup of Akon Aba tea, Aidan wondered if the shapeshifters had been sent by Makhol or Oscuro to attack them. Perhaps he would never know. Thinking about the shapeshifters caused feelings of fiery anger and hatred to flare up within him. Aidan decided the challenging emotions would be a perfect focal point for practicing the Diamond Mind meditation. *What fun!* thought Aidan with amused sarcasm.

Sitting beneath a willow tree, Aidan connected with the anger and hatred inside him. He accepted the feelings completely and bathed them with love, as if they were young children in distress. Although it was humbling to acknowledge such violent emotions, it was also a relief to be fully honest about what he was feeling. After sitting with the anger and hatred for a few minutes, the feelings began to dissolve, and his mind settled into a more peaceful state.

A few minutes later, Akon Aba's spirit appeared in his awareness. The African shaman looked at Aidan, his ancient brown eyes shined with clarity and strength. The Green Mystic's energy was that of a stern, yet loving grandfather.

As Aidan focused on Akon Aba presence, his awareness expanded and the radiant white light of the Diamond Mind filled his consciousness. Sitting in the diamond light was like having his soul bathed in pure spring water.

At the end of his meditation, Aidan found himself drawn to the watery spirit of the pond through his connection with the Flow. The peaceful pond told him its name was Sky Mirror and it was delighted to hear Aidan's stories of his river friends, Flowing Rainbow Nectar and Shimmering Water Diamond Roots.

Aidan found the pond to be much less restless and chatty than the other water spirits he'd met. Sky Mirror was like a river on vacation, content to put its feet up and relax for time. The pond was a calm, meditative soul, happy not to be rushing around all day like rivers do. His greatest joy was to contemplate the vast expanse of the sky above and reflect its azure beauty to the world. Aidan lay on his back in silence on the shore of the pond and joined Sky Mirror in its rapt communion with the heavens. Time dissolved as the bard lost himself in the perfection of the clear blue sky and the leisurely migration of billowing clouds.

By day's end, Patia's condition had improved significantly. More medicinal soup had restored her energy and aided her healing as she rested and slept. The companions decided to spend the night at Sky Mirror pond, then set off first thing in the morning. As they lay down to sleep, a chill breeze arose, sending ripples across Sky Mirror's skin and scattering the light of the moon reflected on its surface.

Off the coast of Orkney in the North Sea, biting winds sent choppy waves rolling through the moonlit water. The waves slapped against the hull of the raiding ship with a drum-like rhythm as it cut through frigid ocean waters. Impelled by a disturbing dream, Makhol, had set sail from his stronghold on Graystone Island with malevolent determination.

Humans typically describe nightmares as dark dreams; however, for Makhol it was the dreams filled with light that haunted him. On the previous full moon, he had dreamt of Aidan. In his dream, Aidan walked through the lands like a radiant sun, bathing the world in his golden light. People laughed and sang as they harvested crops from the fields. Plants, animals, and all life flourished in the light emanating from Aidan's being.

Makhol had awakened from his dream bathed in sweat and seething with anger. Sitting up, he made a silent promise to himself. *I will quell the glowing light of the bard's spirit like a feeble candle flame. My forces will enslave humanity and plunge the world into unending darkness. It is time to prepare my slaves for battle and set sail for Orkney. We will destroy Aidan and all who stand with him!*

Now, weeks later, onboard Makhol's ship, the crew was deathly quiet. There was none of the boisterous talk and laughter one might hear from sailors at sea. The only sounds were wind in the sails, waves striking the ship's hull, and the shuffling feet of the crew. And what a dismal crew it was. Makhol had brought his entire undead army to reap Aidan's demise. The skeletal zombies drearily went about their tasks, longing only for the coming battle.

Makhol's soldiers were the empty shells of what used to be human beings. No one knew exactly what the demon warlock did to the poor souls he captured and enslaved, but the end result was frighteningly clear. His "pets," as he called them, were thin, bony, and hunched over, as if their hearts had withered into nothing and could no longer support them. With grey, opaque eyes, they shuffled about the ship, wearily doing Makhol's bidding. Lifeless as they seemed, the demon warlock had been careful to leave them with the emotions that would suit his dark purposes.

Ruthlessly, Makhol instilled fear in his pets, a paralyzing fear of their master and an even greater fear of living without him. He also cultivated in his slaves hatred and cruelty toward human life. Makhol twisted their minds so completely that his pets believed humanity was responsible for their anguish and suffering. So, they hungered to extinguish the life of the human family they had once called their own.

Makhol's undead army hungered for battle. Their thin, sinewy frames were covered in leather-plated armor, and their dark eyes darted about like cowering dogs. Makhol's zombie pets could smell the anger and hatred swelling within their master as they closed the distance to Orkney. Watching the demon sorcerer as he looked out from the ship's bow, his slaves feared and revered their master's formidable presence and the dark power he emanated.

Even on a sunny day, Makhol was surrounded by an aura of darkness that devoured any light foolish enough to shine near him. Anyone who had the strength of heart (or naive foolishness) to look the demon warlock in the eyes soon realized that Makhol's eyes were completely black, like dark doorways to his origin. Few people remembered the story of Makhol's birth, but if you were to ask the stone people who hold the ancient stories, they might share this tale with you.

Makhol, came to our world in the Age of Iron, drawn by the growing greed and arrogance of humankind. At the time of his arrival, he was but a seed of darkness dropped into the fertile ground of human negativity. This seed had floated for thousands of years through the vast expanse of the Milky Way until its darkness was attracted like a magnet to the shadow growing in the minds of men.

Where did this dark seed come from, you may ask? That is a strange tale indeed. Makhol's mother, if one might call her that, was a gaping black hole at the far reaches of the galaxy. Every few millennia, her pregnant darkness erupted, sending small pieces of herself out into the cosmos like a tree spreading its seed to the wind.

When the seed of Makhol's essence fell to Earth, it was undefined, still a primordial darkness, a part of its mother. Like all black holes, it had a voracious hunger, a dark need to devour light. Humankind's cresting lust for power and domination during the Iron Age was the poison that nourished Makhol's becoming. As his power increased, the seed of his essence grew into the demon warlock, a being formed in the image of humanity's greed, violence, and lust for power. Makhol's mother may have been a black hole, but his father was certainly humankind's negativity.

True to his nature, Makhol sought to devour all light and life on Earth, until there was nothing but darkness in our world. He would not stop until he met his goal and Earth returned to the abyss.

Looking at Makhol's face, you could see his icy hatred for life and feel the destructive magnetism in the black holes of his eyes. But if you looked for too long, you would lose the light of your soul to the abyss and become another of the demon warlock's pets.

The growing light of dawn was powerless to stop the darkness approaching Orkney's shores and Aidan's destiny.

NINETEEN

Aidan and his companions awoke as the pink light of dawn blushed the watery skin of Sky Mirror's face. The air was still, and the pond's surface was like glass, reflecting mountains of clouds painted with the soft colors of pre-dawn light.

Aidan walked to the edge of the pond and began his morning sword practice. As soon as he unsheathed his sword, he felt Renshen's spirit with him. Energized by the power of the Green Mystic warrior, he began to thrust and parry with the Sword of Light. The Flow awakened within him, and Aidan moved like water as he sliced through the air with sweeping arcs and dodged the attacks of his imagined opponent.

Patia watched with curiosity as Aidan surged forward like a rushing river and spiraled to the side to parry with his sword. His magical sword blazed with white light as he continued his fluid dance of attack and defense. Aidan was breathing hard and dripping with sweat by the time his practice came to a close.

"You move well," Patia said as Aidan splashed water on his face at the pond's edge. "Your morning sword training is paying off."

"I have Renshen and this sword to thank for my progress," Aidan replied, still breathing heavily.

"Perhaps Renshen could give me some pointers also," Patia mused.

"I've seen you wield your sword," Aidan said. "You don't seem to need a teacher."

"There is always more to learn, especially from a master teacher like Renshen."

"Fair enough. I will ask him to teach you the next time he comes to me."

After eating a quick breakfast of salted fish and bread from Lochshire, the companions broke camp and set off to continue their journey.

Making their way back through the forest, they returned to the scene of the shapeshifter battle. They walked quickly through the area, not wishing to linger. Soon, the forest opened up into a large grassland. Once out of the trees, they continued west along the edge of the forest. A cold wind blew through the tall grass while dark clouds swept in from the north.

"I hope you like walking in the rain," Patia said. "If not, it looks like you may get ample opportunity to start liking it."

Before long, the mass of dark clouds had overtaken them, and a steady rain began to fall. At first, they tried to stay dry by hugging the tree line, but soon realized there was no avoiding getting soaked. The grey skies and sheeting rain cast a somber pall over the travelers. Byol's fur was dripping wet, and Ruby stood on his back, her shoulders hunched against the downpour. The picture of the somber hummingbird riding a soaking wolf was so unusual that Aidan started to laugh.

Trudging through the mud, Aidan was the only one who seemed to be in high spirits. The sheeting rain awakened the Flow within him, which brought Flowing Rainbow Nectar percolating into his awareness.

Rainy days, not surprisingly, are a time of boisterous celebration for creeks, ponds and other watery folk. While the ocean is mother to all water beings, raindrops are the newborn little ones who grow over time into mighty rivers and majestic mountain lakes. The downpour of tiny liquid tots was a mass birthing for water folk, and Aidan found tears of joy streaming down his cheeks...or were they raindrops? At any rate, the heavy patter of rain was like the music of heaven mixed with the excited whispers of countless liquid fledglings. Aidan danced giddily in the rain, splashing through puddles like a child.

Patia stopped walking and looked at Aidan as if he had lost his mind. Even Ruby and the wolf eyed him warily as they passed him doing a pirouette in an especially large puddle.

"My friends," Patia said, "it appears that, under the pressures of our dangerous quest, our fair bard has gone insane."

Aidan's enraptured communion with the rain lasted through much of the morning. Immersed in the Flow, he realized he was not only family with rivers and lakes but also that the rain connected all water beings with the clouds and sky realm. He felt intimately connected with the Earth as the rain seeped into the dark reaches of the soil beneath his feet. Aidan was overcome with the reality of water's boundless presence and the sublime harmony that exists between all the elements of nature. Never had he experienced the workings of the Way so deeply. It was perfection beyond words.

Just before they stopped for lunch, the Flow finally ebbed from Aidan's body, and he came out of his trance. After a quick lunch under the cover of some trees, they continued their travels through the pouring rain. Feeling somewhat hung-over from the ecstasy of his Flow experience, Aidan soon became weary of the cold rain and the dull grey landscape. Trudging through the mud and sheeting rain, Aidan and Patia talked very little and spent the dreary afternoon in the company of their own somber thoughts.

Occasionally, they caught sight of a sheepherder's home out in the gloomy grey of the grasslands, but they saw neither shepherd nor any other travelers that day. They did see a small flock of sheep at one point, but even they were huddled together under some trees to wait out the rain.

When the darkening skies signaled that the sun was close to setting, the companions looked for a dry place to spend the night. Just before the light failed them, Patia's keen vision spotted a shepherd's hut farther out in the prairie. No candlelight glowed from the windows, and it became clear as they approached that the hut was abandoned. The door hung askew from its hinges, and some of the hut's wooden siding had blown away in the harsh winter winds.

Dilapidated as it was, Aidan and Patia were greatly relieved to be out of the rain for the night. The hut was a single room with a small cot, a table and chair, and a wood-burning stove. They were delighted to find a pile of dry firewood sitting next to the stove. Without delay, Patia began splitting kindling with one of her daggers, and Aidan pulled out his fire kit. Before long, a small fire was burning in the hearth.

After shaking the water out of his fur, Byol lay down in front of the fire and fell asleep. Aidan and Patia stripped off their wet clothes and hung them near the stove to dry. Aidan filled his small pot with water from his water skin and put it on to boil. He shaved slices of ginseng and ginger root into the steaming water. Aidan had enjoyed ginger's spicy, warming nature ever since he discovered the exotic plant in the Seer's garden.

The companions sat quietly in front of the hearth and allowed the fire's warmth to chase the chill from their bodies. Aidan poured them each a steaming cup of tea. The spicy, fragrant aroma lightened their spirits, and the ginseng replenished their energy. The rain's gentle patter had become a pleasant sound now that it fell on the roof of the hut and not on their heads. Ruby had dried off and was preening herself on Aidan's shoulder, chirping in a quiet contented voice.

The orange, flickering light of the flames and the dancing shadows created a homey yet mysterious atmosphere that only a fire can summon. A fire's warm glow has a way of inspiring people to share their stories with each other. Fires are eager to hear the tales of humans and charm them out of us with their hypnotic fingers of flame. Patia soon succumbed to the fire's unspoken invitation.

"Today's rain reminds me of a story my grandmother, Maria, would tell sometimes by the fire. She said the true ancestors of the Roma people were the cloud beings who wander the skies above, following the winds of change. They were wanderers, like our people, free spirits journeying through the heavens as they saw fit. Like the Roma, clouds liked to tell each other stories by the fire, only their fire was the radiant sun that lived in the heavens with them. Clouds can only speak in whispers, and they wanted to share their stories with the people of Earth far below. So, they told stories in pictures by sculpting images in the billowing mists of their bodies. We can still communicate with the cloud spirits in this way and receive teachings from them. All you need is an open mind, like a child, to see their thoughts in the blossoming whiteness.

"Just like the Roma, my grandmother would say, the cloud people were inspired artists. Not only were they accomplished sculptors, they were painters also. To celebrate sunrise and sunset, they would paint the most magnificent skies and cloudscapes with the light of the sun. All the people of Earth gathered at sunset to see what miracles the clouds would paint in the heavens to honor the day's end.

"In those days, the people of the Earth were carefree. Life was peaceful, serene, and filled with joy.

"One night, the moon rose from the horizon, full and luminous in her mysterious beauty. A particularly charming cloud became smitten with the moon and flirted with her as she moved across the sky. He must have courted her well, for the moon fell in love with the handsome billowing cloud. They spent the night traveling the heavens together, painting masterpieces in the cloudscape with liquid moonlight. Painting in the silver light of his beloved moon was a joy greater than the cloud had ever known.

"The night seemed to go on forever. Cloud and moon experienced a love beyond their wildest dreams. As the night came to a close, the contented couple lay down together in the sweet afterglow of their passionate love affair. The moon wished nothing more than to stay with her lover; however, the pull of destiny is strong and her path beyond the horizon called to her. Amid the cloud's desperate protests, the moon said her despairing farewell and disappeared below the horizon. The loss of her lover was so painful that the moon felt she had lost a part of herself. Indeed, in the following nights, the moon became smaller and smaller in her grief, until she was only a slim crescent of her former self.

"The poor cloud was heartbroken. He was so distraught that a consuming darkness overtook him. Anger rose within him, and he sent bolts of lightning and booming thunder upon the earth. His intense longing for the moon was so overwhelming that, for the first time, a cloud wept, and his tears fell to the earth.

"The cloud's lightning bolts of passion caused an entirely new form of life to spring from the Earth. A new people nourished by the bittersweet rains of melancholy and loss was born. They were the Roma.

"To this day, our people still feel the sadness of loss and have intense passion for life, as the cloud did. We are fierce as the stormy lightning and, like the moon's heartbroken lover, we live with a deep sense of longing for something just out of reach. But it is this very longing that inspires us to create music and song and to live every moment to the fullest."

The fire crackled pleasantly as the last words of Patia's story filled Aidan's mind.

"What a lovely tale." Aidan sighed as he gazed at the flickering fire. "Let us raise a cup to your grandmother and the treasure of her words."

Clicking cups with Patia, Aidan looked into her eyes and saw the passion of the Roma people shining like flashes of lightning on a dark night. "You must miss your family, Patia. Will you return to them when our journey is done?"

"Perhaps if I lay down my sword and avoid the public eye, those who have wished me dead will forget about revenge. Maybe then I can return to my family without putting them at risk. It has been far too long since I have been with my people, since I have danced around the fire under the stars and sung the songs of the Roma. Yes, Aidan, I think you are right. After our work is through, I will return to my home."

After speaking these words, a weight lifted from Patia's heart. The burden of her family's absence had become such a part of her that she had forgotten it was there. Patia knew she could no longer live without her family and her people.

Aidan looked down at the ring his father had given him and tenderly touched the heart and vines etched into its surface. He had the sobering thought that he and Patia might never see their families again. The idea of never seeing Mary, Bran, Feather, or the Whispering Woods again was almost too much to bear. Aidan kept his dark thoughts to himself and returned his attention to the cryptic crackling of the flickering flames.

Waves of rain thrummed the roof of the hut late into the night. Although Patia slept soundly, Aidan lay awake with his thoughts and fed logs to the fire when the embers burned low. The comforting warmth of the fire and the steam rising from their clothing soothed Aidan's troubled mind. As morning approached, the rain eased and he finally fell into a restful sleep.

Aidan awoke to a wolf's tongue licking his face and the early morning light filling the hut. The rain had ceased, and Patia was humming contentedly as she sat on one of the weathered chairs toasting bread on the stove for breakfast.

Aidan yawned and looked at Byol's huge head with his light-blue eyes staring down at him.

"Very well, Byol, I'll get up," Aidan said sleepily.

The bard gratefully put on his dry, warm clothes and joined Patia by the fire. "Thankfully, the storm has passed," Patia said. "Traveling in dry clothes will be a welcome change."

As Aidan stretched his stiff muscles by the fire, Renshen's voice came to his mind. "I have come to teach you and Patia. Bring your swords, and meet me outside."

When Aidan told her, Patia smiled like an eager child and snatched up her sword. "Well, what are you waiting for?"

Aidan and Patia stepped outside into the crisp morning air. Scattered white clouds sailed across the blue sky above, and the grasslands sparkled with water droplets in the morning sun. Byol lazily followed them outside and was quickly accosted by Ruby, who was buzzing with energy from her breakfast of flowery nectar.

Aidan spoke the words of Renshen's invocation, and the Green Mystic's imposing form materialized before them.

Renshen looked down at Patia. "I'm glad you wish to learn, Patia. I think you will enjoy today's lesson. Today we will work with your native elemental nature. Every person has an element that is most essential to who they are. Whether it is earth, air, fire or water, one element will dominate. Aidan, as you already know, your native element is water. And yours, Patia, is clearly fire."

A spark of interest kindled in Patia's eyes. As soon as Renshen spoke, she knew his words were true. She had always had a deep connection with fire.

"Channeling your native element," Renshen continued, "empowers the warrior spirit and brings success on the battlefield. It also fuels the expression of your essential nature. But, enough talk. Let us begin."

"First, Patia, close your eyes and connect with the spirit of fire within you. Visualize a fire burning in your belly. Let yourself become entranced by the flames. Connect with the fire's heat, light, and energy. Once you feel a strong connection, let the fire expand to fill your entire body.

"And you, Aidan, do the same thing with water. You are already well versed in how to do this. Simply connect with the Flow, as you have in the past, and you will be channeling water."

After waiting for them to prepare, Renshen said, "Now unsheathe your swords. Staying connected with your native element, I want you to spar with each other. Let the fire or water move you. Release yourself to its energy, but be careful. Channeling the elements can be dangerous. Work with each other, and create harmony between fire and water as you move."

Patia and Aidan faced each other and began to spar with their swords. Patia moved with quick, sharp movements and explosive power, attacking and retreating like fingers of flame. Aidan's movements were more fluid and graceful but his attacks had the strength of a massive, crashing wave.

Brimming with primal power, they both seemed larger than life, like two elemental titans engaged in battle. Fueled by fire and water, they had boundless energy. They attacked and defended with unflagging intensity until Renshen finally called the match to a close.

"That was amazing!" Patia said, fiery passion still burning in her eyes. Breathing hard, Aidan nodded eagerly in agreement. Renshen smiled with satisfaction.

"You both did well. Continue to practice channeling the elements. It will serve you well if you are forced to resort to the sword." The golden aura around Renshen flashed brighter for a moment, and then he was gone.

Sitting out in the morning sun with their backs against the shepherd's hut, Aidan and Patia enjoyed a breakfast of sheep cheese, bread, and dried mutton. After packing their bags and cleaning up, they set off through the raindrop-bejeweled meadow. The fair weather and sparring had energized their spirits, so the travelers walked at a brisk pace through the wet grass.

"By this afternoon, we should arrive at the Ring of Brodgar, a sacred stone circle of the ancient ones," Patia said. "Brodgar is one of the most revered sites in all of Orkney. Thousands of years ago, the people of this land erected the massive stones to track the movement of the sun, moon, and stars. It is said that their understanding of the cosmos was far beyond what astronomers know today.

"The Ring of Brodgar was a pilgrimage site for the followers of the Way who sought to live in harmony with the movements of the cosmos and the cycles of the seasons. They say that the spirits of the ancient ones who created the stone circle will bless those who come to pay homage. Perhaps it will bring us good fortune on the rest of our journey."

By late afternoon, the travelers came within view of Brodgar. The large circle of stones was perched on a rise near a peninsula jutting out into the sea. Like a sovereign crown emerging from the earth, the Ring of Brodgar looked out over the surrounding grasslands toward the distant mountains of Orkney.

As they approached the site, Aidan saw how massive the standing stones were. The monoliths were so masterfully placed that they seemed to have grown out of the land itself. Aidan marveled at the skill and devotion of those who erected them so many years ago. It was a large ring, over three hundred feet across, with an inspiring view of the surrounding countryside. The vaulted roof of the sky seemed much closer than normal, as if one could reach up and touch the passing clouds.

As they crested the hill to the edge of the ring, Aidan felt a sense of absolute peace wash over him. After making an offering of rose petals to the spirits of the sacred site, he entered the circle. Walking slowly around the ring, Aidan felt that the power of the Way was strong at Brodgar. The standing stones were a towering presence, like living beings.

Aidan reached the eastern edge of the circle, which looked out over the remains of a large temple complex. The past was a living presence at Brodgar. Aidan heard it whispering to him. Once he allowed his eyes to relax, visions of the past materialized before him.

Ancient people from the Age of Stone moved about the temple complex. Aidan was struck by their humble nobility. Their every encounter with a plant, stone, or person was filled with appreciation and reverence. They emanated a feeling of natural ease and peace, as if they knew their rightful place of belonging in the world. The people were quick to laughter, and their eyes shined with vitality and joy.

Watching the ancient people go about their lives, Aidan realized their entire reality was aligned with the Way. They lived in communion with nature and knew themselves to be stewards of Earth rather than conquerors of it. These wise beings felt a sense of belonging in the world that most of the people of Aidan's time had forgotten. To see the beauty of the Way so fully expressed in his ancestors brought Aidan to tears.

"May our people live once again according to the Way," Aidan said through his tears, "and heal our separation with the great web of life."

Aidan felt Patia's hand on his back and turned to look into her fiery eyes. "May it be so, my brother."

They lingered at the Ring of Brodgar for a time to connect with the unique energies of the different standing stones. Patia soon found herself drawn to a giant triangular stone that emanated the energy of an ancient warrior. She sat with her back resting on the stone and bathed in its good medicine.

Looking out from the ring, Aidan found himself drawn toward the temple complex. Walking down the hillside, he reached a large patch of angelica, whose white flowers glowed invitingly. Aidan knew the plant wished to commune with him, so he sat down and made an offering of rose petals to the glowing plant. Recalling his teachings from Druid's Keep, he spoke the words of invocation for angelica.

> Keeper of the spirit light
> May your soul burn ever bright

Angels' doorway, realm of love
Gift of grace from heaven above.
Teach us of the ways of peace
Guide us through the long dark night.

No sooner had he spoken these words than a column of white light appeared from the sky above, and a form materialized within it. The spirit of Angelica was a tall, thin, fair-skinned queen dressed in a flowing white gown. Her head was set with a crown of radiant diamonds. In her hand, she held a royal scepter affixed with a small crystal ball.

"Welcome to Brodgar, fair Aidan. I am Angelica, the last of your inner circle of Green Mystic allies. It is good that you have come to this sacred site and received a vision of its past. You must hold this vision of humanity living in harmony with the Way, so your people can reclaim their rightful place as stewards of Mother Earth and all her children. The past is gone, but the power of the Way is everlasting.

"Humanity's true destiny is not to rule Mother Earth but to be her devoted protector. A deep sense of purpose will awaken in your kind when you reclaim your noble role as the loving caregiver for all forms of life. Your people are meant to help weave the sacred fabric of the Way, not tear it asunder."

Aidan nodded knowingly in agreement.

"I wish to share a story with you about my kind," said the Green Mystic. "The Angelica family was planted in the soil of this world by a highly evolved community of celestial beings, who are guardians and protectors of life on Earth. They are light beings of great wisdom and refined energy committed to helping our world grow and thrive. These light beings are like angels overseeing the lives of your people.

"The most essential function of the Angelica family is to bridge the guardians' refined energy into this world and, with our roots, weave it into the living soil of this planet. This angelic energy irrigates our world, nourishing the spirit of the Way.

"Humans were also seeded on this Earth by celestial beings. This is why humanity is so different from the rest of the animal kingdom; you are not entirely of this world. Like the Angelica family, your people are meant to be bridges between the realms of heaven and Earth.

"Your ancestors who built the Ring of Brodgar knew the importance of creating harmony between heaven and Earth. This ring was constructed to track the cycles of the moon, the sun, and the constellations, so the ancients could align their lives with the movement of the heavens. They knew the ideal times to sow seeds, harvest crops, and make plant medicines, and they could sense when specific ceremonies were needed to honor the spirits. Living in concert with the Way and the rhythms of heaven and Earth, your people thrived and lived long, healthy lives.

"These ancient followers of the Way had immense love for life and felt deep kinship with all of Earth's creatures. If they needed trees for building homes or animals for food, they took only what was needed and did so with reverence and gratitude. When your people care as much about the health of the forest and the animals as they do for themselves, you will be well on the way to healing your people's relationship with the web of life on Earth."

Looking into Angelica's eyes, Aidan said, "I look forward to those days returning, wise teacher. Thank you for the role you play in nourishing the health of the Earth."

"It is my purpose and my great joy," Angelica replied. Then her expression became more grave. "I must warn you, Aidan, the road to Unstan becomes more dangerous by the day. Stay here tonight within the Ring of Brodgar, for this place has good medicine for you and your friends that will bring you strength for what is to come. But delay no longer. Continue on your journey soon after dawn.

"Before you leave, please harvest a root of Angelica to add to your herb satchel. We will meet again soon, young bard. Farewell on your journey." With that, the crystal ball on her scepter flashed with blinding white light, and she was gone.

As the sun began to set, Aidan harvested an Angelica root from the hillside. Returning to the Ring of Brodgar, he tied the spicy-smelling root to his knapsack to dry.

Patia was still sitting against the giant, triangular standing stone with her eyes closed. When Aidan approached, she slowly opened her eyes, as if coming out of a trance. Her eyes shined with even more intensity than they normally did. A bewildered smile spread across her face. "This stone has the spirit of a noble warrior," she said. "It has generously shared its wisdom and strength with me.

"Life becomes more interesting and mysterious every day. For most of my life, I learned the ways of the warrior from other people. Then I met Byol, and he taught me even more about fighting and combat. Since I've met you, I now have plants and stones teaching me about the warrior's path. Next thing you know, I'll have snails teaching me sword fighting techniques."

Aidan laughed and sat down beside her. He pulled some bread and cheese out of his knapsack, and they ate while Aidan told Patia of his experience with Angelica. Byol soon materialized out of the surrounding bushes, with Ruby buzzing around his head. Byol lay down at Patia's feet and lazily closed his eyes. He had clearly been successful in finding prey for dinner. His belly was swollen and his muzzle stained with blood. Ruby flew off to fill herself with nectar before the darkness of night fully descended.

Soon after nightfall, they moved into the center of the ring and pulled out their bedrolls. Patia quickly fell asleep, but Aidan lay awake for a long while looking up at the vast starscape. The night sky was clear and crisp, and the stars shined brilliantly in the heavens above.

Marveling at the Milky Way's celestial river of light and darkness, Aidan saw beams of light connecting the different constellations and lines of energy from the stars descending into the Ring of Brodgar. He felt totally connected with the movements of the constellations and sensed what an intimate relationship his ancestors must have had with the dance of the cosmos. Remembering his earlier visions of the ancient inhabitants of Brodgar, he felt how their lives moved in perfect harmony with the mysterious workings of the universe.

Lying on his back in a state of awe, Aidan heard words pouring into his mind from the starlit muse of the Milky Way.

Entranced my eyes behold wonder
Elegant workings, graceful movements
Beauty's brush paints the night sky
Inspired strokes, perfect lines
Creation's canvas of flawless design
Celestial mobile of luminous souls
Starlight rays weave harmony's tapestry
Life's unfolding, mysterious majesty

Stars dancing dervishes
Whirling us home
Musical rapture, melodic ecstasy
Earthen stones dance my bones
Face to the sky, soul dances destiny

Far above, the ancient craftsman
Sits back from his workbench
Laughing, delighted

The celestial mechanism's
Inconceivable intricacy
Timeless golden gears
Music of the spheres
Life forever more
The dream that never ends...

A shooting star shot across the night sky. Aidan gasped like a child as he marveled at the beauty and mystery of the cosmos. Before long, his eyes grew heavy, and he drifted off to sleep under the vast canopy of stars.

TWENTY

Oscuro had made good time traveling across Orkney with Raven in her horse-drawn carriage. Knowing Aidan's destination, he made straight for Unstan rather than following the bard's trail. A fortnight before summer solstice, they arrived at Unstan, and Oscuro parted ways with Raven. Delighted that Aidan had not yet arrived, he made camp under cover of an ancient oak forest that bordered the stone cairn of Unstan.

"Here we will wait for that troublesome bard," Oscuro said to a red-eyed metal ophidian serpent coiled on his shoulder. The ophidian hissed malevolently in reply.

"Yes, we must prepare a worthy welcome for the great bard. I need to create many more ophidian for his welcoming party. But how can I create a swarm of shadow serpents in such short time?"

Looking around at the canopy of oaks surrounding him, a clever spark kindled in the dark druid's eyes. "Hmm, perhaps..." he whispered.

Miles from Oscuro's scheming, Aidan and Patia awoke more deeply rested than they had felt in a long time. The energy of Brodgar had blessed their dreams and renewed their spirits. They spent the morning walking at a brisk pace, and by midday, they had reached the edge of an oak forest. Grateful for the cover of the trees, they entered the forest and decided to stop for lunch at a rock-strewn area near the foot of a hill. While eating cured fish and bread from Lochshire, Aidan told Patia of the vision of the ancient ones he had received at the Ring of Brodgar.

After listening to Aidan's story, Patia realized their water skins were nearly empty and decided to look for a stream where she could refill them. Connecting with the Flow, Aidan opened his senses to the water spirits and pointed into the forest. "Two hundred feet in that direction, you will find a stream."

Raising her eyebrow, Patia hesitated and then turned and walked off in the direction Aidan had pointed.

Aidan placed the fire sprite on top of his knapsack to soak in the sun while he ate. As the bard sat chewing a piece of dried mutton, he caught a movement out of the corner of his eye. He turned his head just in time to see a small, brown-skinned gnome with clever eyes and a pointed nose snatch the lapis box containing the fire sprite and run off into the forest.

"Stop, thief!" Aidan yelled as he took off running after the gnome.

Terrified of the fire elemental falling into the wrong hands, Aidan ran like the wind after the thief. With branches and bramble scratching his face and arms, he just managed to keep the fleeing gnome in sight. Then, as they approached a rocky hillside, the gnome disappeared into a cave entrance hidden by bushes.

Breathing hard, Aidan sprinted after the gnome into the cave, which opened into a network of torch-lit tunnels. As they raced through the underground passageways, they descended deeper and deeper into the earth. Although Aidan sprinted as fast as he could, the gnome was always just out of reach. Just as his pace was beginning to slow from exhaustion, Aidan burst into a vast stone chamber. He gasped in shock at what he saw within.

At the far end of the cave sat a dragon. The massive creature was illuminated by red light emanating from a deep fissure in the stone. Steam billowed forth from the magma-filled rift and swirled around the dragon's serpentine body. Its red and orange scales shined like metal in the misty light of its lair. The dragon sat perched upon a large mound of gold coins and treasure.

Aidan was shocked by the sheer size of the creature. Its long, massive head was the size of a small house. With its ferocious jaws, it could have eaten a cow in a single bite. Aidan's stomach dropped as the dragon's undulating body and powerful legs snaked with frightening speed toward where he and the gnome were standing.

"What treasure have you brought me today, faithful servant?" the dragon rumbled as he coiled his head to peer at the short, wiry gnome. Still puffing from exertion, the gnome relaxed noticeably with his master there to protect him. The dragon tilted his head toward Aidan with a bone-chilling smile.

"I recommend you not try to escape, unless you want Pip here to have roasted Scotsman for dinner. So, Pip, what do we have here? What a beautiful lapis box." The dragon practically purred with satisfaction over his newfound treasure.

Smiling wide with a giant mouthful of sword-like teeth, the dragon lowered his head to get a closer look at the lapis box sitting in the gnome's hand. When he realized what was inside, he recoiled, and his eyes widened in shock. "You fool!" he bellowed at the gnome. "You've stolen a fire sprite. What kind of dimwit are you?"

Pip cringed in fear at his master's anger and unsuccessfully tried to withdraw into his own skin, like a turtle retreating into its shell.

The dragon swiveled its head to within feet of Aidan's face. His menacing, yellow eyes pierced Aidan's soul. "And why have you brought a fire sprite into my territory?" he asked, cold malice dripping from his voice. "Did you hope to destroy me and steal my treasure?"

Aidan stood terrified, engulfed in the steaming stench of the dragon's coal-furnace breath. Paralyzed with fear, he closed his eyes and helplessly awaited his fate.

"Hmm..." the dragon said, narrowing his eyes. "That's an exquisite ring you have. I recognize the workmanship. The craftsman is a true master. I have several amulets in my horde from the same maker."

Aidan slowly opened his eyes. "It was made by Bran, my father."

"Interesting..." the dragon purred. Lowering his head to Aidan's face, the dragon studied the bard. Aidan resisted the urge to flee as the creature's golden, penetrating eyes fixed on him. Then recognition dawned on the dragon's face.

"Aidan of the Golden Light," the dragon whispered. "The Bard has walked into my lair. What good fortune. Pip, you have been wise in your foolishness to lead this one here."

Pip smiled weakly in response.

"You are the Bard, are you not?" the dragon asked.

The Flow rose in Aidan as Flowing Rainbow assured him that the dragon was not a servant of Makhol. "Yes, noble dragon, I am Aidan the bard, but the golden light you speak of has faded. I am cursed by black magic."

"I am Belloc, the Stormbringer," the dragon rumbled. "You need not fear me, for I serve only Creator. For the time being, you and I serve the same cause. As for the light of your spirit, it is like moonlight during an eclipse...temporarily hidden in shadow. When the shadow recedes, the light will be born anew. But tell me, bard, how does one who channels the Flow come to travel with a fire sprite?"

Impressed by the dragon's ability to sense the Flow, Aidan told Belloc of his time with the Alchemist. When his story was finished, the dragon smiled. "Of course, Cambius is part of this. Earth is poised for an immense transformation, and nothing interests the Alchemist more than times of profound change. The era of the Great Shift is upon us."

"Belloc, I'm afraid I don't understand. How is it that you and I are aligned with the same cause?"

Belloc smiled enigmatically as a shimmer of electric light rippled through his body. He fixed his penetrating gaze on Aidan. "We are both here to help give birth to a new world. Your work is to support the healing of your people's hearts and minds through music and song. The healing of humanity is essential if your people are to survive the Great Shift. My role is a bit different...and difficult to explain."

After a long pause, Belloc slowly began to speak, "Deep within the womb of existence lives a primordial rainbow serpent. Spiraling endlessly beyond time and space, this Cosmic Serpent is the primal energy from which all life springs. It is the source of all change within the cosmos.

"We dragons are servants of the Cosmic Serpent, bringers of change and magic. When life falls out of balance, as it has in the human realm, this connection with the Cosmic Serpent becomes weak. Without a clear, strong connection to this primal energy, your world has become sick and distorted. It is the Cosmic Serpent that feeds the roots of the Way and supports the health and vitality of all life.

"We are approaching a time when Earth will be born anew. Its connection with the Cosmic Serpent must be renewed. Soon, the dragons will awaken from their long period of dormancy and take flight. Then we will breathe the transformative power of the Cosmic Serpent into your world. This blazing light of creation will cleanse and renew life on Earth."

Aidan's mind was filled with questions for the dragon, but Belloc continued before he could put words to them. "I can tell you no more at this time. Your fate awaits you, and I must rest and prepare for when my own destiny calls." Belloc's steely gaze left no doubt that their conversation was over.

Aidan nodded slowly. "I am honored to have met you, Belloc the Stormbringer, and am grateful to know that we serve the same cause."

"Be well, young bard," the dragon said. "And please...take the fire sprite with you," he added with a razor-toothed smile.

With his thin, brown, trembling hands, Pip returned the lapis box to Aidan. Before Aidan left the chamber, he looked back and saw Belloc once again illuminated in the glowing red light of the Earth's magma, shrouded in steaming mist.

When Aidan emerged from the forest, Patia was clearly relieved, and Ruby buzzed excitedly around his head. "Where did you wander off to?" Patia asked.

"You can't imagine," Aidan replied. "I'll tell you as we walk."

They spent the rest of the afternoon climbing through the forested hills beyond Belloc's lair. After hearing Aidan's story of the dragon, Patia was speechless for a time.

"Belloc called himself the Stormbringer, did he? I fear any storm that a dragon might bring. If he is going to help give birth to a new world, as you say, it doesn't sound like it will be an easy birth."

"I have seen women give birth," Aidan replied. "It can be painful. Besides, storms bring renewal and new growth to the land. Howling winds blow down dead tree branches, and rain nourishes the soil."

"And lightning burns down entire forests," Patia said with a smirk.

"Yes, but then life rises again from the ashes, and a new forest is born," Aidan replied.

As evening approached, they reached a ridge that looked down into a wide valley carved into the surrounding hill country. Aidan looked at his map and then turned to Patia. "We follow this valley to Unstan. Let's make camp soon before night falls. We can enter the valley in the morning."

TWENTY-ONE

Aidan awoke before dawn and practiced the Diamond Mind meditation until sunrise. Rising from his meditation with stiff legs, he found Patia awake and eager to practice channeling the elements as Renshen had taught them. After warming up, Aidan opened up to the Flow, and Patia connected with her native element of fire. Aidan moved like water, attacking with fluid grace. His movements were relaxed yet relentless, like a raging river.

Patia moved with the quick, sharp, explosive energy of fire. She attacked with lightning speed, then retreated like flame in the blink of an eye. Channeling fire, Patia was truly frightening to behold. If Aidan hadn't been bolstered by the power of water and the Sword of Light, he would have surely turned and run in the face of Patia's blazing attack.

As they sparred, Patia slapped Aidan in the back or belly with the flat of her sword whenever he left himself open to an attack. Although Aidan did not once get inside Patia's defenses, he was a worthy opponent nonetheless and kept Patia on her toes.

Breathing hard, they finally took a break from sparring. Patia smiled. "I like this elemental practice. It has renewed my love for the way of the sword. Channeling fire is an ecstatic experience. And your water sparring was amazing. You did not let me rest for a moment, oh great river warrior."

With sweat dripping from his brow, Aidan smiled as he sheathed his sword. "Come, let us have some breakfast and break camp."

After eating, Aidan pulled a length of thin rope out of his knapsack and started to weave together a small net satchel.

"What is that for?" Patia asked.

"I'm going to put the fire sprite's box in it and attach it to my belt. After the gnome stole the box, I realized I wasn't being careful enough. I won't let the fire sprite out of my sight again. He can soak up the sun while tied to my waist."

After he finished making the net satchel and tying the lapis box to his belt, Aidan and his companions packed their bags and made their way through the hills and into the valley below. Ruby buzzed about, sampling the local wildflowers, and Byol stopped regularly to sniff the trail of animals that had passed by earlier that morning.

Later that afternoon, when the sun was at its height, the travelers came to a bend in the serpentine valley. Byol growled, and Aidan saw something unlike anything he had ever seen. Farther down the valley, perched on a cluster of rocks was something akin to a black sun. Instead of emitting light, an ominous darkness radiated from its center. The darkness surged into an even deeper shade of black, then ebbed to reveal a massive being looking at Aidan with a cruel smile.

Makhol, the demon warlock, stood over ten feet tall with a broad muscular torso and legs as stout as tree trunks. He wore leather armor studded with small spikes of haedium steel. His dark grey face was broad and thick boned. Curved teeth like the tusks of a boar sprouted from his sneering mouth. A large haedium ring pierced the septum of his squat wide nose, while other smaller rings adorned his pointed ears. Emerging from the sides of his head were two horns, like a bull. His eyes were orbs of the deepest darkness, beckoning like gravity from the edge of a sheer cliff.

"Makhol!" Patia exclaimed.

Aidan felt his stomach drop in fear as Makhol's ebony eyes bored into him. Surrounded by his band of restless undead soldiers, the demon warlock approached to within earshot of the travelers.

"At last we meet, young bard," Makhol said, his voice steeped in icy malice. "How appropriate that the forces of light have such a cowardly weakling representing their cause. And look at your pathetic band of companions. I should have left my pets at home and simply destroyed you all myself. Hmm...perhaps I will let the wolf live. He could be a useful servant."

Growling, Byol bared his teeth, and the spirit of the wild blazed in his eyes. The wolf clearly intended to fight to the death before submitting to Makhol as his master.

"As you wish, young pup," Makhol said. "My pets will be happy to dine on dog flesh tonight. And what about the rest of you? I am not unreasonable. If you surrender now, I promise to let you live and offer you my protection,"

"So you can steal our souls from our bodies like the rest of your zombie pets?" Patia said, her voice full of disgust.

Makhol smiled wickedly. "For such as yourselves, I can offer a different fate. You are clearly a formidable warrior of the Roma people. I will make you a general in my army and bestow upon you power beyond anything you have ever known. And you, Aidan, will become my trusted advisor and help to shape the writing of history. The battle for supremacy of the world has begun. Only a fool would align himself with those who are destined for defeat. You must know that darkness will be victorious. Darkness has been on the rise for generations. Its power will continue to grow and dominate. I offer you a place at my side in this new world. Choose wisely, my friends. If you refuse, I will not be forgiving, and you will know unimaginable suffering before you die."

As Makhol spoke, his dark sorcery penetrated Aidan's mind. He began to doubt the power of the light and its ability to prevail over the evils of the world. Fear rose within him as Aidan thought of what Makhol might do to his friends if they were captured alive. Sharp pain seared through Aidan's heart as the ophidian fed on Makhol's dark magic.

Knowing he needed help, Aidan whispered the invocations for his Green Mystic allies. To his right, a glowing yellow orb appeared and materialized into the tall, imposing form of Renshen. His sword blazed with golden light as he stood rooted like an immovable tree at Aidan's side.

In a flash of diamond-white light, Akon Aba appeared on Aidan's left. The ancient African shaman stood dressed in a saffron robe with a gnarled wooden staff at his side. Turning to look at Aidan, the piercing light of the Diamond Mind shined brilliantly from Akon Aba's eyes. In another moment, Rose, in her deep-green silk robe, and Angelica, in her long white robe, had materialized by his side.

His confidence bolstered by the Green Mystics, Aidan said, "Indeed, you are right, Makhol, these are pivotal times in the history of our people, and darkness certainly has its place in this world. But you do not. You will never sit on the throne of this world. We already have our queen, our dear Mother Earth. The long, dark night of humanity's cruelty and ignorance is coming to a close. You are no longer welcome here. The sun rises on a new dawn for our beautiful planet. The radiant light of love and truth will chase your shadow from our world."

Seething with anger, Makhol's dark aura swelled and dimmed the light of the sun around him. "You are an idealistic fool!" he spat in disgust. "Your plant allies can do nothing to stop the ocean of darkness that I will unleash on this world."

Makhol raised his hand, and black magic exploded from his palm like a torrent of tar and smoke. Images of skulls and scenes of horrific violence proliferated in the smoky darkness of his raging plume of sorcery. Before Aidan could react, Angelica stepped in front of him protectively. Her luminous aura of light pulsed outwards like a brilliant sun, surrounding Aidan and his friends. Angelica raised her scepter, and a beam of blinding white light filled with diamonds shot out from the crystal ball at its tip. The white light cleaved Makhol's magic like a blade and deflected the attack away from Aidan's companions.

Makhol paused for a moment, then erupted with cruel laughter. "Very well, defenders of the Way. Prolong your demise, if you wish, but know that I will cut you down like weeds nevertheless."

He looked out at his army of zombies. "My pets, it is time to feed. Kill them all!"

With sadistic hunger in their eyes, Makhol's undead soldiers surged forward to attack.

Scurrying forward like rabid vermin, the hunched forms of Makhol's zombies raised their dull gray swords for battle.

Aidan's band leapt into action. Akon Aba and Rose spread out to each side to prevent Makhol's forces from surrounding them. Renshen and Angelica remained with Aidan to meet the main thrust of Makhol's attack.

As the undead army surged toward them, Patia drew her two short swords and courageously faced her attackers. Channeling fire, she attacked Makhol's soldiers with frightening intensity. With a sword in each hand, her attacks were quick and sharp. A spinning whirlwind of steel, Patia plowed into the undead soldiers, leaving corpses in her wake. Byol fought ferociously at her side, leaping at the undead attackers. His powerful jaws tore into their flesh and snapped the bones of sword-wielding arms.

Makhol's army was over two hundred strong. The undead attacked with fury, knowing they vastly outnumbered Aidan's forces. Their cruel eyes shined with the fire of hatred as they scurried around the field of battle like rats hungry for a meal. Makhol's forces were unrelenting in their attack. As soon as one fell to Patia's sword or Byol's crushing jaws, more rushed in.

With the Flow coursing through him, Aidan attacked with the fury of a raging river and sidestepped zombie sword thrusts with liquid grace. Ruby aided his cause by flying into the face of his attackers and distracting them.

At Aidan's side, Renshen fought like a noble warrior king. His sword blazed like the sun as he cut sweeping arcs into each wave of attackers. When his Sword of Light sliced through one of the undead, it severed the root of Makhol's spell, and a shadowy wraith fled from the soldier's body. The soldier did not die but rather, Renshen's Sword of Light reignited the pure soul essence within them.

Aidan's sword had the same effect on his attackers. After sidestepping a zombie sword thrust, Aidan plunged his Sword of Light into the heart of a snarling attacker. He watched as the soldier transformed in front of him. A spark of realization dawned in the man's eyes, and his back straightened as Aidan saw the man's human nobility return to him. A moment later, the man picked up his fallen sword and exclaimed, "I am with you, brother! My name is Robert. May my sword defend your cause." With that, Robert jumped to Aidan's side and raised his sword against the surging undead horde.

Every slice and thrust of Aidan and Renshen's swords that found their mark expelled the evil from one of Makhol's soldiers. As they reclaimed their power and clarity of mind, more soldiers raised their weapons in Aidan's defense.

Despite their aid, the numbers of the undead were too great. Patia and Aidan were pushed back under the relentless advance of Makhol's forces.

While defending herself against multiple attackers, Patia failed to see an undead soldier slip behind her with his sword raised. Sensing the attack, Patia spun out of the way; however, the sword still sliced through her leather armor, cutting into the flesh of her back.

Cold fear seeped into Patia's bones. She rarely felt fear in battle and was confused as to why the feeling had arisen so powerfully. What she didn't know was that Makhol's soldiers wielded tainted swords. He had coated their swords with the same poison he used to break people's souls and transform them into zombie slaves. The poison led to a growing feeling of inescapable terror. Patia had spent her life facing fear, so she fought on valiantly in the face of her rising terror. Sensing her weakness, Byol redoubled the fury of his attacks.

As the first of the undead reached Akon Aba, he wielded his staff like a club. When he struck the first soldier's head, bolts of white lightning discharged from his staff into the zombie's grimacing face. The soldier's body twitched convulsively, then he collapsed to the ground. Like a bolt of illumination, Akon Aba's magic shattered the curse that Makhol had laid upon him. The Diamond Mind flooded the soldier's awareness as he was forced to see the truth of what Makhol had done to him and what he had become. Overwhelmed with this horrific revelation, the soldier leapt to his feet in a panic, dropped his sword, and fled the battlefield. With every blow from Akon Aba's staff, the power of truth awakened another undead soldier from the delusion of Makhol's dark spell. In the face of this painful reality, they ran for the hills in horror.

On the other side of the battlefield, Rose faced the relentless assault of Makhol's forces. Standing weaponless in her dark-green cape, she was far from defenseless. As the undead soldiers raised their swords to attack, she looked down upon them with love and compassion in her eyes. From the rose blossoming from her chest, the rich red light of love radiated out towards her attackers. As the red light touched their eyes, the soldiers stopped dead in their tracks, confused, as if having awoken from a horrible dream. Makhol's dark spell relied on fear for its power, and fear cannot exist in the presence of pure love. Rose's love broke Makhol's spell in every undead soldier that she bathed in her light.

When the soldiers' hearts reawakened, vitality returned to their eyes, as realization of their plight dawned in them. With Makhol's curse broken, they were flooded with traumatic memories from their years of enslavement. One by one, they fell to their knees and wept at Rose's feet. Bathed in the glow of her radiant love, their hearts began to heal on the bloodied soil of the battlefield.

As the battle raged, Makhol stood perched on a giant boulder behind his undead army, bellowing commands and threats to motivate his soldiers. Seeing the growing mass of weeping soldiers surrounding Rose, he commanded his pets to cut their fallen comrades with their tainted swords. Cut with the poisoned blades, their fear returned, and, once again, they fell under Makhol's evil spell. Faces twisted with hatred, they seized their swords and rose to their feet. Makhol commanded them to avoid Rose and directed them toward Aidan and the main thrust of the battle.

Seeing her healing work undone, Rose called out to Renshen in her mind. *Great warrior, bring your Sword of Light to my aid! Restore the courage to the pained hearts of these dear soldiers. Empower them with your sword, so they may rise from their mourning and join us in battle against Makhol!*

Asking Angelica to protect Aidan, Renshen marched toward Rose. His mane of root-like hair blew in the wind, and his eyes shined with golden light. Reaching Rose and the mass of weeping, awakened soldiers, he touched each one with his enchanted blade. Courage and strength returned to each one he touched, and, one by one, they reclaimed their swords and joined Aidan's forces. They formed a line of defense around their mourning comrades, protecting them from the undead attackers' poisoned blades, while Renshen continued to empower them with his sword.

With Renshen preoccupied, Makhol unleashed the full force of his evil sorcery on Aidan. Torrents of black magic erupted from his hands. Angelica responded with a blinding beam of white light to repel his attack. For several moments, the streams of light and dark magic collided and wrestled for dominance. Beads of sweat formed on Makhol's leathery face from the strain of such intense magic. Realizing he could not destroy Angelica so easily, he stopped his attack. Weary from her clash with Makhol's magic, she was grateful for the reprieve.

Searching for a more cunning means of attack, Makhol sensed Aidan's weakness and decided to exploit it. Using his mind, he fed the strength of the ophidian in Aidan's heart with his dark energy.

Aidan staggered on the battlefield, grabbing his chest as searing pain tore into his heart, and fear flooded his mind. Steeling his resolve, Aidan refused to let his fears control him. Using the Diamond Mind, he focused his awareness on what he needed to do. He brought his left hand with his father's magic ring to his heart and felt the pain in his chest diminish slightly. With one hand over his heart and the other wielding his sword, Aidan launched himself back into the battle.

Patia, Aidan, and Byol had struck down many of the undead, and a growing number of Makhol's soldiers had fled after encountering Akon Aba's staff. Many others had turned against Makhol and fought with Aidan after being healed by the Green

Mystics. However, Aidan's forces were still painfully outnumbered and were beginning to tire in the face of the undead army's relentless attack.

Makhol's soldiers managed to flank and surround the Green Mystics. Rose and Akon Aba were corralled toward Aidan and Patia. Patia continued to resist the fear poison from her sword wound, but the effort had cost her dearly, and she looked weary as she fought on. Aidan was also suffering as Makhol continued to feed the cursed ophidian in his heart. Despite their efforts, the battle was turning against them.

Sensing victory, Makhol brought the full fury of his sorcery upon the defenders of the Way. Aidan's forces were hammered with the seething darkness of the demon warlock's magic. It took all the Green Mystics combined power to repulse the relentless barrage of Makhol's dark sorcery. The ground shook as each blast of magic detonated against the Green Mystics' energetic shield. Makhol's hunger to destroy Aidan fed his power, and his dark aura flared outwards like a ravenous black hole. He harnessed his growing power into a massive orb of darkness, which he shot at the Green Mystics' shield. The dark magic exploded against their shield like a bomb. Aidan's plant allies staggered back from the force of the impact, and the energetic shield flickered and then disappeared.

Although Makhol had broken their defenses, he had weakened himself through the effort and could no longer muster the energy to attack. The explosion of magic had stunned his undead army, so, for the moment, they were not attacking Aidan's forces. Akon Aba saw their opportunity.

"This is our chance!" he whispered to the other Green Mystics. "We must use the combined power of all our magic and attack Makhol while he is still weak."

Angelica, Rose, Renshen, and Akon Aba clasped hands and stood in a line facing the demon warlock. As their hearts and minds became one, they knew what they had to do. Their collective power grew until it became a cyclone of pulsing rainbow light swirling around them. With each passing moment, the rainbow cyclone grew larger and began to coil out like a giant serpent toward Makhol.

"Fight, you fools! Fight!" Makhol roared at his stunned undead soldiers.

A moment later, the rainbow cyclone reached its full power, spinning like a ferocious tempest. With her crystal scepter raised, Angelica's commanding voice rose powerfully into the air. "Makhol, your reign of evil in our world is over. I summon the spirit of the Green Mystics and the power of the Way to our cause. You are banished from this world. May you return to your origins in the far reaches of the cosmos!"

With her words, the rainbow cyclone surged forward, surrounding Makhol. Its tail shot out far behind him, and its magic pierced the fabric of space. A wormhole opened behind him into the massive black hole of Makhol's birth. Within the rainbow wormhole, the immense pull of the black hole was impossible to resist.

"No!" Makhol howled, a look of rage and disbelief on his face. "It can't be!"

Then, in the blink of an eye, Makhol vanished into the depths of the wormhole and returned to the mighty black hole of his origins. The trailing rainbow cyclone followed him into the far reaches of the cosmos and then, with a rush of wind, the wormhole slammed shut.

Silence hung thick in the air over the battlefield. Makhol's departure broke the poisonous spell of his undead soldiers' enslavement. They looked around in a daze, unsure what had just happened. Aidan breathed a sigh of relief as the ophidian loosened its grip on his pounding heart. Slowly, a smile broke on Patia's face, and she raised her swords in the air, shouting,. "We have defeated Makhol!"

A cheer erupted from Makhol's soldiers as they realized they were no longer slaves of the evil demon warlock. The Green Mystics looked at each other and smiled with relief. Aidan embraced Patia and looked into her eyes. "Thank God, you're alive!"

"Quite alive, my friend. Only a couple of minor scrapes."

Aidan's hands were covered in blood from the wound on Patia's back. Looking closely, he realized Patia was bleeding from several battle wounds. He frowned. "Minor scrapes indeed."

"Worry not, Aidan. I have received worse and lived. You seem relatively unscathed, young warrior. You fought well for a bard from Willow's Glen."

"I would not have fared so well without the Green Mystics at my side," Aidan said, looking gratefully at the group of noble plant spirits next to him.

Angelica surveyed the battlefield. "We are victorious in battle, yet our work here is not done. Many have sustained injuries...in body and soul. We must tend to the wounded."

Aidan gathered yarrow to treat people's wounds, while the Green Mystics tended the injured with their healing powers. Rose turned to a group of Makhol's soldiers, whose souls had already been healed by her and Renshen. "Go find your comrades who have fled from the battle. The truth of their enslavement with Makhol was too much for them to bear. Bring them to me, and I will heal their broken hearts."

They spent the rest of the day tending the injured. Aidan cleaned people's wounds and applied yarrow poultices to stop bleeding. Angelica worked at his side, her peaceful presence allowing the men to rest and heal. Rose, Renshen, and Akon Aba worked together to heal the hearts and souls of Makhol's soldiers. Together, they held the three great medicines of love, power, and truth. For each of Makhol's former slaves, Akon Aba laid his hand on the soldier's head, while Rose worked on his heart and Renshen on the power center in his belly. Their powerful magic flowed into each soldier, bringing healing to his heart and mind and restoring his inner power and human dignity.

With immense relief and tears of joy in their eyes, the soldiers thanked the Green Mystics for their potent medicine. One by one, they realized not only that they had been healed from the poison of Makhol's enslavement, but they felt more vital and whole than ever in their lives.

The sun was setting by the time all the soldiers had been tended to and the dead had been buried. People gathered wood, and groups of soldiers lit several campfires in the valley. Many of the soldiers spoke excitedly of returning home to their families and communities.

Later in the night, a group of men came to the fire, where Aidan and Patia sat with the Green Mystics. A stout, dark-haired, bearded man stepped forward. "Noble plant spirits, I am Paul. We can never thank you enough for healing us of Makhol's curse. If it is not too bold, we have a final favor to ask of you. Several of my brothers here have no families to return to. We have decided to establish a village here in this valley. Our village will be called Freedom to honor our liberation on this blessed day.

"Your love and generosity has inspired us to establish our village as a stronghold of the Way. We wish to live in harmony with nature and the plant world and to build our village in a way that honors the spirits of this land. We humbly ask that you teach us the timeless wisdom of the Way, so we may be stewards of this land and help all life to thrive here."

Bathing him in her radiant light, Angelica smiled. "Your words are sweet nectar to our ears. Yes, we will help you to establish your village in harmony with this land and all its creatures. You are humble and wise, my son. I have no doubt that Freedom will become a beloved sanctuary for the spirit of the Way.

"Before we depart, we will leave you with the seeds of our kind to plant in this land. If you tend these seeds well and help them grow, the Green Mystics will have a home here, and we will share our knowledge with the villagers."

"My deepest gratitude to you all," Paul said, tears welling in his eyes. "You have bestowed a profound blessing on us all."

The fires burned late into the night as the men spoke excitedly of their plans for the future. Aidan and Patia were exhausted yet content as they sat next to the fire. They spoke little as they watched the dancing flames.

Aidan's relief at Makhol's defeat was short-lived, however. Angelica reminded Aidan that solstice was only two days away. Soon, Aidan's mind turned to the next leg of their journey. They were only a half-day's travel from Unstan, yet Aidan dared not delay their departure. He resolved to leave as early as possible the next day. Exhausted and battle weary, Aidan lay down and watched the hypnotic dance of the fire until he fell fast asleep.

TWENTY-TWO

When Aidan and Patia awoke early in the morning, he brewed a strong pot of ginseng and nettle tea to renew their energy. After eating a quick breakfast, they packed their bags and approached Paul and the Green Mystics, who were farther down the valley discussing plans for building their new village.

"I wish we could remain longer, but Patia and I need to move on," Aidan said.

"Yes, Angelica told me of your need to make haste," Paul replied. "I wish you well on your journey. I can't thank you enough for helping to liberate us from Makhol's bondage."

"You're welcome, Paul. I wish you well in building your new village and creating a home for yourselves in this valley. I'm glad the Green Mystics are staying here to help you begin the process. Hopefully, I can return one day to pay you a visit."

"You will always have a home here in Freedom," Paul replied with warm smile. "Safe travels, Aidan Bourne."

Aidan turned and looked at the circle of Green Mystics. "My profound gratitude to you all for helping us defeat Makhol. We would have been doomed without your support. I look forward to the next time our paths cross."

Aidan's beloved family of Green Mystics looked at him with their wise, caring eyes. "Farewell on the rest of your journey," Rose said with her gentle, maternal voice. "May you find the healing you seek."

Aidan and Patia shouldered their bags and, with Ruby flying ahead and Byol at their side, made their way down the valley. They were sore from the battle, but walking did them good. Patia's wounds were healing well after being tended by Rose's hands.

Aidan looked at Patia walking next to him and noticed she had a huge smile on her face. "What are you so happy about?" he asked.

"We're both still alive!" she replied. "Isn't that wonderful?"

Aidan laughed. "Yes, it is wonderful. Thank the Way, we are both alive."

The morning sun warmed their skin as they wound through the valley. Aidan felt excited and a bit nervous, knowing they were close to Unstan and their journey's end.

Around midday, they came out of the valley and caught their first glimpse of the stone cairn of Unstan perched on the next rise. Aidan looked at the ancient stone building in disbelief. "I can't believe we're actually here," he said. For a moment, he dared to hope he might actually rid himself of Oscuro's cursed ophidian and be able to sing as a bard once again.

The cairn was a wide, low building made of stone and dotted with multi-colored lichens. Like many of the structures built by the ancient followers of the Way, Unstan was a harmonious part of the landscape and seemed to emerge from the ground itself.

Aidan's ancestors had built Unstan as a sacred site to guide souls in and out of this world. Unstan's inner chambers were a liminal space of peace and harmony, which eased people's passage through the process of dying. Pregnant women would also spend time in the cairn to help facilitate the birth process and support a newborn's transition into the physical world. Birth and death midwives were highly respected in the Age of Stone. Their work was considered essential for tending the health and wellbeing of souls as they arrived and departed from Earth. The followers of the Way knew the manner in which people came in and out of this world impacted whether or not their souls would flourish in this life or the next.

Aidan felt the peaceful, nurturing presence of Unstan as they approached the structure. Drawn to enter the cairn and steep in its energy, Aidan approached the doorway. Suddenly, a searing pain cut into his heart, and he dropped to his knees.

Patia rushed to his side. "What's wrong?"

"The ophidian," Aidan gasped. "Its power surged as I stepped toward the cairn." A foreboding feeling took hold of Aidan's mind. With Bran's ring over his heart, the pain subsided a bit, and he could stand once more. Looking down the grassy hill toward the surrounding forest, Aidan saw something inexplicable. Although there were no clouds in the blue sky above, a large shadow had emerged from the forest and was advancing across the meadow.

"I've got a bad feeling about this," Aidan said, holding his chest.

Patia frowned in confusion. "What is that?"

Aidan did not reply, for he was already bowed in prayer, whispering the invocations to call forth the Green Mystics. As his plant allies materialized around him, he looked up again, recoiling at what he saw. At the trailing edge of the approaching shadow, like a shepherd of darkness, stood the black-robed form of Oscuro.

"We meet again, golden boy!" Oscuro shouted from across the meadow. "I thought you and your friends could use some company. Perhaps you are familiar with my companions?"

As the darkness approached up the grassy slope of the hill, Aidan saw it was indeed no shadow. The dark mass resolved itself into a swarm of slithering snakes with bright red eyes.

"Ophidian!" Aidan exclaimed. "And so many of them."

The ophidian were much larger than the tiny one in Aidan's heart. Some were up to six feet long, and their metallic bodies moved with frightening speed. The nearest snakes opened their mouths to reveal fangs, sharp as knives. Aidan's heart sank as he gazed in horror at the slithering swarm of serpents.

Angelica looked at the approaching ophidian with apprehension. As the haedium snakes approached, she summoned a protective shield of magic around Aidan and his friends. When the ophidian reached the energetic shield, they stopped and hesitated around its perimeter. Then, one by one, they wriggled onto the dome of Angelica's magic, looking for weak spots in the field.

Oscuro approached Aidan's group, pouting sarcastically. "What poor manners! I had hoped you would welcome my friends with tea and biscuits. It appears you may have offended them."

Oscuro stood in the midst of the writhing snakes and examined Aidan's companions with a curious eye. In his hand was a sorcerer's staff that looked like a tree branch made of haedium steel. "So, these are the fabled Green Mystics.

How quaint. You should have remained in hiding. Your time on the stage of history is long gone. Humanity has moved on. We have no more use for your childish teachings about the Way. We have taken hold of our own destiny. No longer are we slaves to the whims of nature. With the power of Black Metal, our kind can forge our own destinies, as we see fit, and bend the natural world to our purposes. We are the rightful rulers of this world."

With unwavering clarity in his brown eyes, Akon Aba looked at Oscuro. "You are an arrogant child, Oscuro. Listen to yourself...'rulers of the world'. Mother Earth rules herself. Your people are her children, like all life in this world. The Black Metal tradition is based on the delusion that humanity is separate from nature. This lie is a foul poison of the mind. With your weapons of Black Metal, you would kill your own brothers and sisters in our dear family on this planet."

"You are not my family!" Oscuro said. "Soon enough, you will understand the true power of Black Metal. No tree or pesky weed can withstand its cutting blade."

Oscuro's haedium staff pulsed with shimmering, black energy. In response, a group of ophidian slithered onto Angelica's protective dome of white magic. Using the power of Black Metal, they attacked the energy field with their sharp fangs. Sparks flew as they tried to pierce the shield's protective energy.

"The power of Black Magic is strong in Oscuro's forces," Renshen said to Aidan and his companions. "These ophidian are made of haedium steel. There are too many of them. Angelica's magic will not be able to hold them off for long. We need to disperse the ophidian and go on the offensive before they drain all our energy."

261

Angelica looked to her friends. "Prepare yourselves!"

The defenders of the Way raised their weapons and readied themselves for battle. With a surge of blinding white light, Angelica's protective shield erupted with magic. The force of it hurled the ophidian snakes into the air in all directions. An instant later, she lowered her shield, and Aidan's companions stepped out to meet the ophidian swarm.

Wielding their swords, Aidan, Renshen, and Patia fought side by side. Crawling quickly through the grass, the red-eyed ophidian serpents attacked their legs with razor-sharp fangs. Aidan and Renshen's Swords of Light sliced through the serpents like lightning, raising a spray of sparks amidst the sound of ripping metal. With his blazing golden sword, Renshen made large sweeping slices into the serpent swarm, destroying several ophidian with each attack.

To her dismay, Patia soon realized that her swords could not harm the ophidian's haedium steel bodies, so she adopted a new game plan. With a short sword in each hand, she flung ophidian into the air in front of Aidan and Renshen, where they could easily destroy them. Channeling fire, she moved with speed and precision. It was a bizarre scene, with metallic snakes flying through the air and being cleaved in two amidst a spray of sparks.

The haedium serpents were especially drawn to Aidan and the ophidian parasite living in his body. Patia positioned herself to intercept the surge of ophidian scurrying through the grass toward Aidan. Thankfully, the magic of Bran's ring had diminished the pain in Aidan's chest.

The ring weakened the ophidian's power enough that Aidan could fight with all of his strength.

The ophidian fought together as an organized unit. As Aidan attacked one, another slid in under his defenses. The snake coiled its metallic grey body to strike. With its mouth open and fangs bared, the ophidian shot toward Aidan's ankle. At that moment, Byol appeared, snatched the ophidian with his teeth, and tossed it into the air. Before it touched the ground, Renshen cleaved the serpent in two with his sword.

Byol continued to snatch each ophidian that made it through their defenses, tossing it into the air, where Renshen or Aidan could destroy it. Ruby played her part by distracting the ophidian. She taunted several of them at once by flying into their faces and darting away when they attacked. This distracted the serpents until Aidan or Renshen could dispatch them. They worked well as a team, and a growing mound of ophidian carcasses rose around them.

Thirty feet away, Angelica battled another group of ophidian. Angelica's staff shot beams of white light at the attacking serpents. Each ophidian touched by the beams blazed white and then fell dead to the earth.

Seeing that Aidan was distracted with fighting the ophidian, Oscuro smiled maliciously, raised his haedium staff, and pointed it at the bard. A pulsing orb of dark magic swelled at the tip of his staff and erupted into a black beam of energy filled with haedium daggers.

In a flash, Rose and Akon Aba materialized out of the air between Oscuro and Aidan. Akon Aba raised his own wooden staff to meet the incoming attack of black magic. Blinding diamond light flared from the staff, striking Oscuro's foul magic with a sound like two colossal swords clashing. Oscuro's magic sprayed to the sides as it dispersed into the air.

Oscuro was furious. Before he could attack again, Rose sent a beam of red light out from the blossoming flower in her chest. As it surrounded Oscuro, his look of fury changed to terror. Nothing is more threatening to one who uses Black Metal than the energy of love. Black magic is rooted in fear. Love dissolves fear and erodes the foundation of Black Metal's power. For the followers of the Way, there is no power greater than love.

"Why have you closed off your heart, dear man?" Rose asked Oscuro in her warm, soothing voice. "You have cut yourself off from humankind and imprisoned your soul in a black metal cage. What heartbreak led you to choose this lonely path?"

"Shut up, you crazy witch! You know nothing about me!" Oscuro spat with venomous hatred. "Your words are poison!" With that, his anger flared, and black magic surged from his staff, forming into slithering tendrils of darkness that ate away at Rose's blanket of magic.

Again, Oscuro's staff shot Black Metal at them, like a cannon. Akon Aba's staff surged with light, and his magic clashed with Oscuro's attack, repelling it once again. Rooted in the Diamond Mind and the pristine power of truth, Akon Aba's magic was a potent defense against the dark druid's attacks.

Patia and Aidan were both bleeding from multiple snakebites inflicted by ophidian serpents that had breached their defenses. With razor-sharp fangs, the ophidian had bitten viciously at their legs or climbed higher to attack their arms and torsos. With the foul magic of their haedium fangs, the wounds were already beginning to look infected. Even so, Aidan and Patia fought with ferocity and speed, causing the number of ophidian serpents to dwindle.

Angelica had also destroyed most of the ophidian attacking her. Feeling that the tide was turning in their favor, Aidan risked a quick look at Oscuro. The dark druid was defending himself against a beam of Rose's magic. Then a movement at the edge of the forest behind Oscuro caught Aidan's eye. As he squinted to focus on what it was, his heart sank. Moving out into the meadow was another swarm of ophidian nearly the same size as the one they had just fought.

"Where are they all coming from?" he asked in disbelief. He ran to Akon Aba's side. "Something is very wrong. Another swarm of ophidian serpents just emerged from the forest. We need to know how many more lie in wait."

"I will go see what there is to see," the African shaman replied as he vanished in a flash of light.

"Prepare yourself!" Aidan yelled to his friends. "More ophidian are coming!"

Hearing Aidan's anxious words, Oscuro laughed cruelly. "Did you think you would defeat my forces so easily, foolish bard?"

Having destroyed the ophidian attacking her, Angelica stood at Patia's side, helping to dispatch the last of Oscuro's serpents. As Aidan approached them, he realized something strange. The mounds of destroyed haedium snakes had disappeared. Before he could think about it further, Akon Aba reappeared.

"Bad news from the forest," he said. "Oscuro has poisoned the trees with his foul magic. A group of oaks has been twisted into servants of

265

Black Metal. Instead of growing acorns, they grow ophidian from their branches. The latest crop just dropped from the trees and is almost upon us."

With his cunning, twisted mind, Oscuro had devised a way to create an endless source of ophidian. He put a potent spell on the trees, using the power of Black Metal. The huge oaks were forced to dig deep with their roots in search of deposits of haedium steel. When they found a vein of the metal, Oscuro had them pull it into their roots and weave it into the fabric of their wood. The oaks took on the dull black color of haedium steel, and their trunks were almost indestructible. Oscuro had turned them into slaves of Black Metal. Instead of life-giving acorns, death-dealing ophidian fell from their branches. After an ophidian was destroyed on the battlefield, its haedium body slowly dissolved into the air, and the Black Metal particles were drawn like a magnet back to the trees. Then the trees reused the haedium to create another crop of ophidian.

"We must destroy the trees," Aidan declared. "We need to get to the forest now, before the next swarm picks us apart." Another swarm of slithering ophidian serpents was already approaching from up the hill, effectively blocking their path to the forest.

"Gather close together," Angelica said. "The other Green Mystics and I will use our combined magic to repulse the swarm while we make our way to the forest."

The Green Mystics raised a protective shield of their combined energy as they ran toward the forest. When they passed Rose, she fell in next to them.

Seeing them run toward the forest, Oscuro's rage erupted, and he sent a massive beam of black magic at Aidan and his friends, which detonated against their protective shield with so much force that the ground shook, and Aidan was almost thrown off his feet. Shaken, they continued onward.

Moments later, the ophidian swarm reached them and wriggled onto the dome of protective energy. Sparks flew as the ophidian serpents began piercing the energetic defenses.

"Come, we must hurry!" Angelica said. "We can't hold them off for long."

Running at full speed, they plunged into the swarm as the ophidian flowed around and over the dome of magic like a river around a boulder. Reaching the edge of the forest, Akon Aba led them to the grove of haedium trees.

The oaks were massive, their bark the dull black color of haedium steel. In the past, the grove had been a peaceful place infused with the calming presence of the guardian oaks. However, now a sinister presence filled the area, and Aidan's skin crawled as they entered the forest.

"I don't like the feel of this at all," Patia said with a troubled frown.

The ophidian swarm gained strength as they entered the grove and attacked the Green Mystics' protective shield with savage determination. Fed by the energy of the haedium trees, the ophidian in Aidan's chest unleashed an unbearable pain upon him. Gasping, he fell to his knees clutching his chest. The Green Mystics knew they had to act quickly.

"We must destroy the trees with our combined magic!" Renshen said, his golden sword raised.

With one mind, the Green Mystics looked at each other, gathering their energy. The protective shield pulsed with light, sending the ophidian flying into the air away from them. With the shield down, they raised staff and sword, unleashing their full power into the nearest tree. Nothing happened.

"It can't be," Aidan said, his hopes plummeting.

Oscuro appeared from behind the oak tree, a look of grim satisfaction on his face. "Now you see the true power of Black Metal. Not even the Green Mystics can destroy my creations. The power of the Way has faded. So begins the dominion of Black Metal!"

A hideous torrent of blackness teeming with daggers exploded from Oscuro's haedium staff. The Green Mystics raised their energetic shield just in time to deflect the attack. The concentration of haedium in the oak grove had strengthened Oscuro's power immensely. As the blast of dark magic collided with the shield, its energy flickered and dimmed. Sensing their advantage, the ophidian swarm attacked the dome with renewed vigor.

"We can't hold them off for long!" Angelica said, her voice strained.

Aidan knew they could not survive another battle with the ophidian swarm. As he stood there frozen, time stopped, and Aidan suddenly flashed back to a memory from his childhood. He was back in Willow's Glen helping his father in the foundry. Bran was teaching him about the power of the elements.

"Each element has its strength and its weakness," his father said. He pointed at the molten metal glowing in the forge. "You see, although metal is an incredibly strong element, fire melts metal."

In that instant, Aidan knew what he must do. Returning to the present, he pulled the fire sprite's box out of the net satchel tied to his waist. He looked through the rune box's tiny window.

"Great fire sprite, we are in dire need of your magic. Please, help us defeat Oscuro's forces of Black Metal!"

The wild red-haired sprite cracked a wide smile and rubbed his hands together in anticipation. Swallowing nervously, Aidan turned to his friends. "When I say 'now,' drop the protective shield, and sprint for the meadow."

Looking down, Patia saw the fire sprite's rune box in Aidan's hand. "There must be some other way."

"It is our only choice," Aidan insisted. Then he whispered the words releasing the rune box's spell of containment. As he placed it on the ground, the sides of the box opened.

"Now!" Aidan yelled.

In a flurry of motion, the protective shield pulsed once again, sending ophidian serpents flying in all directions, and then vanished. Aidan and his friends sprinted toward the entry of the grove. Seconds later, a blinding flash of light flared behind them, and Aidan was thrown to his knees by an explosion from the grove.

Disoriented, Aidan turned back toward the forest and gasped in horror. A massive wave of fire hurtled out from the tiny fire sprite's raised palms. Like a scene from Armageddon, the monstrous tsunami of flame sped across the grove. The ophidian swarm, haedium trees, and Oscuro were engulfed in a raging wall of fire. The last thing Aidan saw before he turned to flee from the unbearable heat was the wave of fire crashing through the forest like a furious dragon incinerating everything in its path. It showed no signs of slowing down.

Hair singed and clothes smoking, Aidan staggered out into the meadow, gasping for air. Patia was inspecting Byol's scorched fur, making sure that nothing was still burning. Ruby came to rest on Aidan's shoulder as he approached Patia and the Green Mystics. When he reached them, they all turned toward the forest. Aidan felt utterly sickened by what he saw.

"Please, no!" he exclaimed in dismay. The sprite's wave of fire had destroyed hundreds of acres of the oak forest in a matter of minutes, and it would have destroyed much more, but the inferno stopped when it reached the coast. A massive plume of steam rose from the Loch of Stenness, where the fire had boiled off the last of its fury. Between Aidan and the coast was nothing but flames.

Aidan and his friends watched helplessly as the inferno raged through the forest. Mountains of thick grey smoke rose from the fires, obscuring the sun and casting a reddish light over everything. Sitting next to Patia, his head in his hands, Aidan was miserable. Being a lover of trees, he felt that he had committed an act of mass murder. To make matters worse, he felt the spirit of a river out in the burning wasteland, mourning the loss of its beloved trees.

"I can't believe I burned down the entire forest," Aidan cried, sobbing. "How could I have been so stupid?"

Patia put her hand on his shoulder and looked at him with compassion. "If you had not summoned the fire sprite, we would have all been killed. You did the right thing."

Aidan looked up at the raging forest fire in despair. "I'm not so sure I agree with you."

Angelica kneeled next to Aidan. "That forest was doomed," she said. "The poison of Black Metal that Oscuro awakened would have spread through the rest of the trees. Over time, this forest would have become a foul, evil place."

Aidan sighed. Her words soothed his sadness somewhat. "I just wish it didn't have to happen this way. I feel like an agent of death."

"Sometimes there is no good choice to make...only the best choice," Angelica replied.

By evening, the intensity of the blaze had subsided. The smoke was not so thick, and instead of one giant sea of flame, the forest had become a charred black wasteland dotted with tangled masses of burning trees.

"I need to find the fire sprite," Aidan said, his voice full of concern. "I've got to return him to his containment before he burns the whole world down. Ruby, can you help me search for him?"

The tiny hummingbird chirped affirmatively into Aidan's ear from her perch on his shoulder. Then she shot off toward the destroyed grove in search of the fire sprite.

Picking his way through the ash and embers, Aidan reached what used to be the grove of haedium trees. The trees had been melted, so nothing remained but puddles of dull black steel. Smaller puddles of hardened haedium were scattered everywhere from the remains of the ophidian swarm.

Looking up, Aidan saw Ruby flying about excitedly. She was buzzing around one of the large fires still burning in the area. Aidan made his way toward her and, at the edge of the fire, spotted the fire sprite. The elemental spirit was sleeping on his back next to the fire with a contented smile on his face. His head rested on a red-hot ember, and he seemed to be warming his feet by the fire. As Aidan watched, the fire sprite's muscles twitched excitedly, undoubtedly from some flame-laden dream.

Seeing his chance, Aidan looked around for the rune box and found it lying not far away. The box was impervious to fire and wasn't even singed. Feeling no heat radiating from the box, Aidan picked it up and found that it was cool to the touch.

As quietly and carefully as possible, Aidan set the rune box down next to the sleeping fire sprite. Under his breath, Aidan whispered the words to activate the containment spell. The top of the box opened, and a vortex of blue-and-purple light coiled out. The fire sprite opened his eyes sleepily, but before he could react, the light vortex sucked him back into the box, and the top locked shut. Aidan breathed a sigh of relief.

Looking through the small window, Aidan was surprised to find that the fire sprite did not look angry at all. He smiled a jolly, red-cheeked grin, winked, and blew Aidan a kiss. Obviously, the raging forest fire had put the fire sprite in good spirits. A bit shaken, Aidan smiled back at it weakly. After collecting himself, he looked the fire sprite in the eyes. "I will never be able thank you enough for saving all of our lives," he said.

The fire sprite waved his hand, as if it were nothing, sat down in his stone recliner, kicked up his legs, and fell fast asleep.

Dusk was approaching by the time Aidan returned to the others. Patia sat around a campfire talking with the Green Mystics. Renshen was talking with her about the path of the warrior. Patia nodded as Aidan approached. "Have some rabbit," she said. "We found it pre-roasted at the edge of the forest."

Aidan prayed that the rabbit had died quickly in the inferno and then gratefully helped himself to the roasted meat. Looking pensively into the fire as he ate, he reflected on all that had happened in the previous days. It dawned on him that the following day was summer solstice and his appointment with the Bone King.

With food in his belly, Aidan's exhaustion caught up with him. He turned to the Green Mystics. "Good night to you all. I can never thank you enough for all you have done for me. Thank you for protecting me and teaching me about the Way. You are family to me."

Rose looked at him lovingly. "You are welcome, dear Aidan."

Gazing around at the circle of noble, wise Green Mystics, Aidan felt like the luckiest man alive.

He rolled out his blanket next to the fire and lay on his back, looking up at the stars. The skies were clear, thanks to a breeze blowing the remaining smoke out to sea. Aidan's mind spun with excitement and anticipation about his meeting with the Bone King. But soon, exhaustion took over, and he was swallowed by the rising tide of sleep.

TWENTY-THREE

In a dream, Aidan found himself outside the castle of Robert the Bruce, King of Scotland. The king sat on horseback in chainmail armor with a broadsword at his waist. Surrounded by an army of mounted soldiers, Robert was preparing to lead an attack on a rival king's castle to the north. The air was charged with his men's anticipation of battle.

A shadow swept across the courtyard, where Robert and his warriors were gathered. Aidan looked up to the terrifying sight of a dragon diving from the sky toward the men. Its red-and-orange scales shined like polished metal in the morning sun. It was Belloc, the Stormbringer.

Belloc opened his massive wings and hovered above the terrified soldiers. His wings stirred up a powerful gust of wind and dust, temporarily blinding Robert's forces. With a bone-chilling smile, the dragon's ferocious predatory eyes surveyed Robert the Bruce and his warriors.

At a command from the king, a barrage of arrows shot into the air toward Belloc. The dragon's armored scales deflected the arrows as if they were flimsy twigs.

Belloc roared with laughter, then his eyes narrowed in anger. Inhaling a huge breath into his belly, the dragon opened his mouth wide. With dark storm clouds growing behind him, Belloc breathed a jagged bolt of lightning at Robert the Bruce. Striking the king in the chest, the lightning shot out from his body, sending bolts of electricity into every one of his soldiers. The air crackled with electricity as Robert and his men convulsed on the ground from the lightning coursing through their bodies.

A moment later, the lightning ceased, and Robert the Bruce and his men were suddenly on their feet again. Looking at each other in bewilderment, they realized they were no longer dressed for battle. Their armor, swords, spears, and other battle gear were gone. They now wore the humble homespun clothing of peasant farmers. Instead of swords and spears, their hands held plows, hoes, pickaxes, and other farming tools. With contented smiles on their faces, they walked toward the fields to tend their crops.

As a gentle rain began to fall, Belloc turned from the castle, soared up into the stormy sky, and disappeared into a dark grey cloud.

Aidan awoke with a start. A crescent moon shined overhead, dimly illuminating the meadow. Looking up the hill, he could faintly see the cairn of Unstan waiting for him and the coming dawn. Sitting up, Aidan realized he was not the only one awake. The Green Mystics had departed, but Patia was sitting on a rock looking at him, so Aidan walked over and sat down beside her.

"Couldn't sleep either?" he asked.

"No. Too much on my mind."

Bathed in the dim light of the moon, Aidan and Patia spoke of their battle with Oscuro and the ophidian swarm. Wispy plumes of smoke still rose from the smoldering remains of the forest. Watching the tendrils of smoke being blown out to sea, Aidan caught a movement out of the corner of his eye. Looking up at the clouds bathed in moonlight, he gasped at what he saw.

Following Aidan's gaze, Patia saw a dragon emerging from a cloud. Wings extended, the dragon circled above them. Aidan and Patia sat transfixed, unable to move. They could feel the dragon watching them with its keen eyes. It was Belloc, the Stormbringer. With a powerful flap of its wings, the dragon altered course and sped off to the east.

"Was that..."

"Yes," Aidan replied pensively. "Belloc."

"I'm glad he has no quarrel with us. I wonder what has awakened him from hibernation."

"If Belloc has taken flight, Earth will never be the same," Aidan said. "Who knows what he has in mind? But one thing is clear. The time has clearly ripened for the rebirth of our world. Belloc's purpose is to initiate change and support the dawning of a new age on Earth. If dragons and the Green Mystics are awakening, what other magical beings will appear to aid this era of transformation? Thank God these powerful beings are our allies and servants of the Way."

"Indeed," Patia replied. "I would not want to be at the receiving end of Belloc's storm."

After the shock of seeing Belloc wore off, Aidan's thoughts drifted to his meeting with the Bone King. "It's hard to believe we're actually here. I had my doubts that we would live to see Unstan. I hope it wasn't a wasted effort. What if the Bone King doesn't come? I started this journey based on a dream. What if it was only a dream and nothing more?"

"As you remember," Patia replied, "I joined you on this crazy adventure because of a dream. In my heart, I knew that my dream of the Seer was more real than this rock I'm sitting on. Some dreams are so powerful, they can alter your destiny. What does your heart say about your dream of the Bone King?"

Aidan instantly felt the answer. "My heart says the Bone King is as real as you or me and that he will come."

"Good. Be at peace, my friend. We will see what dawn brings."

Aidan looked at the mysterious cairn of Unstan perched on the hill, marveling at the wisdom and skill of his ancestors, who built doorways between worlds. Patia too was looking at the cairn with curiosity. Looking at her face illuminated in the moonlight, Aidan felt a wave of gratitude wash over him.

"Patia, dear friend, I can never thank you enough for joining me on this journey. Without your protection and companionship, I couldn't have survived."

Patia looked at him and smiled. "Only a fool resists destiny. Mine was clearly to walk this road with you." She laughed. "We'll certainly have some good stories to tell by the fire when we return to our families!"

"Indeed, we will," Aidan said, laughing.

The two companions spoke of their many adventures until the pre-dawn light began to blush the night sky. They sat on the boundary between two worlds. To the south, smoke still rose from the charred remains of the forest. The morning breeze blew the wispy plumes out over the Loch of Stenness, away from Unstan. To the east, the gentle light of the coming day was filled with the promise of new beginnings. Aidan's excitement brought back images of the Bone King from his dream encounters with the ancient being.

As dawn approached, Ruby still slept nestled in the fur of Byol's neck while the wolf's legs twitched from a dream. Leaving their animal companions to slumber, Aidan and Patia slowly made their way up the hill to the ancient cairn of Unstan..

As they approached the cairn, reality took on a surreal quality and the air wavered and became more fluid. They entered the cairn as the first rays of dawn illuminated the inner chamber. Stone benches lined the sides of the room. At the far end of the chamber, an archway twice the height of a man was built into a solid wall of rock. Aidan wondered if this was the doorway to the Bone King's realm.

Aidan and Patia sat to the side on a stone bench and waited for dawn's light to fill the chamber. Golden rays of sunlight touched the stone archway, as nervous anticipation fluttered in Aidan's stomach.

The sound of a footstep off to the right broke Aidan's concentration, and a sharp pain gripped his heart. He whipped his head around to a horrifying sight. Oscuro stood in the doorway to the chamber with his haedium staff raised. A look of cruel malice twisted the dark druid's quivering lips.

Black magic exploded from Oscuro's staff and hurtled toward Aidan. Time slowed. Aidan had no time to react, watching helplessly as the beam of dark magic crossed the room toward him. From the corner of his vision, he saw Patia leap in front of him to intercept the attack. Oscuro's black magic struck Patia full in the chest, and its shadowy tendrils engulfed her body like a predator swallowing its prey. Her body froze in mid-air directly in front of Aidan, then crumpled to the stone floor.

"No!" Aidan screamed, dropping to her side in anguish.

Oscuro pointed his staff at Aidan with a twisted smile. "Your story ends here, boy."

At that moment, a blinding gold light blazed from behind Aidan. Whipping his head around, Aidan saw that the arched doorway in the chamber wall was glowing like the sun. From the doorway, a bolt of lightning erupted and shot over his head. Crackling with electricity, it struck Oscuro and slammed him into the stone wall, pinning him a foot above the ground.

Aidan watched in awe as a hand emerged from the blazing doorway. The lightning erupted from the pointing finger of a giant fleshless hand, whose skeletal fingers were adorned with rings set with diamonds and rubies. The Bone King stepped through the doorway and into the cairn. Over ten feet tall, his crowned head nearly touched the ceiling. His regal robe was woven with countless gems that shined brilliantly with rainbow light. The chamber shimmered with light, as if the air was filled with gemstone dust.

The Bone King's fleshless face looked down upon Oscuro with fierce unwavering presence. Where eyes would have been were deep pools of darkness, like portals into the bottomless depths of the vast cosmos. Still pinned to the stone wall by the electrical bolt of magic, Oscuro looked back in wide-eyed terror at the ferocious majesty of the Bone King.

"You have used your evil power for the last time, dark druid," the ancient monarch said in his commanding voice. "In your ignorance, you have behaved like a cruel, selfish child. Your arrogance and hatred have convinced you that you are justified in harming others. You can hide behind the walls of blind delusion no longer. May the balm of truth exorcise the evil from your soul. I release you from the curse of Black Metal!"

The lightning surged in intensity from the Bone King's finger. Oscuro's face paled in horror, and he struggled in vain to release himself from the Bone King's power. "Please, no!"

Oscuro's eyes opened wide in fear, as if in a waking dream. Images flooded his mind of all of the cruel actions he had taken against others. Even worse, he saw the long-term effects his actions would have on his victims. Oscuro saw with perfect clarity how his lust for power and domination had turned him into a monster.

The Bone King's magic reawakened feelings he had long hidden under the armor of Black Metal. Oscuro felt the crushing sadness of his childhood and the loneliness of living in isolation with his father. He saw how his father's family line had become poisoned with fear and the twisted energy of Black Metal. Shame blossomed in Oscuro's heart as he was forced to face the sickening truth of his ancestry. A soul-wrenching scream erupted from Oscuro as this realization shined its uncompromising light within him.

Aidan saw a giant shadowy wraith rise out of Oscuro's body. It looked around frantically for a moment and then dissolved into the radiant light of the Bone King's magic. Oscuro's body went limp, and he began sobbing like a child. The Bone King dropped his arm, and the lightning ceased as Oscuro crumpled to the chamber's stone floor.

"Please, don't kill me," Oscuro whimpered.

"Death will find you another day, Oscuro," the Bone King replied. "Today, you have been given a priceless opportunity. The cruelty you have wrought upon others cannot be undone; however, you can find redemption, if you so choose."

As if awakening from a nightmare, Oscuro looked in horror at Patia's body lying on the stone floor. "Surely you can heal her, great one!" Oscuro said, desperation growing in his voice.

"Patia is gone from this world. Neither I, nor any other being, has the power to bring her back now."

Oscuro was crushed with the reality of what he had done. He looked as if he wanted to die. The Bone King tilted his fleshless head to the side as if thinking and, a moment later, Rose walked into the chamber.

"Go with Rose, Oscuro, and begin the healing of your heart," said the Bone King. Be grateful that you have seen the truth of your life while you still have time to change your ways. Many people remain in denial about their lives until the moment of death, when clarity dawns. No one leaves this life without facing the reality of their actions and how they have affected everyone they have touched. You have been given a second chance, Oscuro. I hope you use it. I leave him in your care, Rose."

Rose took Oscuro's limp childlike form into her arms. She looked down at him lovingly and then looked into Aidan's eyes with compassion and concern. "I am so sorry for your loss, Aidan," Rose said before she walked out of the cairn with Oscuro's sobbing form in her arms.

Aidan sat next to Patia's body in a state of shock. After she fell from Oscuro's attack, Aidan had held out hope that the Bone King could heal her. Hearing that he could do nothing to help her was more than Aidan could bear. Anger rose in him, and he turned to the Bone King in disbelief. "How could you let Oscuro live after killing Patia? He spent his entire life spreading cruelty and evil, and now he has killed my friend. He deserves to be punished!"

Surrounded with rainbow gemstone light, the Bone King looked down at Aidan and spoke with unwavering clarity. "Now you see the roots of evil, my son. In your anguish over the loss of your friend, you wish for revenge. When actions are rooted in anger and hatred, the shadow gains dominion over your life. The human shadow is an integral part of each person; however, it is meant to follow, not to lead. Oscuro is an example of what happens when the shadow rules someone's life. By killing Oscuro, we would only feed the hatred of the world and empower the spirit of Black Metal. This is a crucial time for you to guide and care for your shadow as you heal from your grief."

Still seething with anger, Aidan tried to remain open to the Bone King's words.

"If you truly wish to live from the heart, you must eventually forgive Oscuro. This is where life becomes painfully real. From this place of torment over Patia's death, you must ask yourself, 'Am I truly devoted to love?' The answer to this question can then guide your path forward.

"You see Aidan, this Earth is, above all, a training ground for cultivating devotion. Your devotion to what you hold most dear is strengthened through life's many hardships and obstacles. Each devotional path reveals different lessons and truths about life. No path is superior to any other.

Whether you are devoted to the mind, the heart, money and power, music and art, love or fear...all paths are sacred. Above all, choose a path that is aligned with your authentic nature, for life is fleeting and precious. This is the crossroads at which you now stand. What path will you choose for your life?"

Aidan lowered his head, realizing his desire to punish Oscuro was the same poison of violence that fed the wicked ways of Black Metal. His anger wrestled with his commitment to walk the path of love. The turmoil and confusion in his heart was unbearable.

The Bone King recognized Aidan's anguished state. "Do not force yourself into forgiving Oscuro before you are ready. Be honest about your feelings, and surround them with love. Be gentle with your anger. Little by little, seek to put yourself in Oscuro's shoes, and imagine how tortured his soul must have been to commit such horrific acts. Over time, you will grieve the loss of your friend, and when the time is right, you will come to a place of forgiveness."

Internalizing the truth of the Bone King's words, Aidan took a deep breath, and the fire of his anger became less oppressive. With a sigh, he asked, "But what if Oscuro returns to the ways of Black Metal? Can't you at least use your power to ensure he can never return to a life of evil?"

"It would go against my nature to do so," the Bone King replied. "I and all the beings of my world are committed to freedom. I would never take away an individual's freedom to choose his or her path in life. Your world is a place of learning, where people are free to make choices and discover their consequences. Freedom is essential for the flowering of a human soul.

"What I have done is accelerate Oscuro's learning. I have rid him of the poison of Black Metal. He now sees the horrific acts he committed while blinded by arrogance and lust for power. His heart has opened, and his vision is clear. From this place, it is unlikely that he will return to the path of hatred and cruelty. With Rose guiding him, he has an opportunity to transform his life."

Aidan sat for a moment and considered what the Bone King had said. He looked at the ancient teacher standing before him like a mountain. His skull glowed with pale white light but his eyes were pools of darkness. Aidan felt himself being drawn like a magnet into their bottomless depths. With some effort he returned his focus to their conversation and said, "Please tell me, without your power to aid us, how are we to rid our world of the poison of Black Metal?"

"As you saw with the sprite, the fire element has the power to transform Black Metal. However, its influence need not be destructive, as it was with the inferno you witnessed. The fire element in its refined state is the essence of love. Love is the medicine that is needed to heal the world of Black Metal and restore your people's connection with the Way.

"It is essential to understand that a battle against the forces of Black Metal could never be victorious. Attacking with swords and anger, people would poison their own hearts and strengthen the energy of Black Metal. Only love can heal this soul sickness."

Aidan sat on the floor with Patia's head in his lap, stroking her hair. His anger had subsided, and he only felt the crushing loss of his dear friend. Tears streamed down his cheeks as the immensity of Patia's sacrifice sank in. "Thank you for protecting me, Patia. If only I could have done the same for you. I will miss you, dear friend."

"I know this is a painful time for you Aidan," the Bone King said, "but know that for Patia, this is simply the end of one journey and the beginning of the next. She is fortunate to have died here in Unstan, while I am present, for this cairn was used by your ancestors to ease the passage of souls in and out of this world. The energy in this chamber will support Patia as she leaves the physical world and enters the realm of spirit. You can help me midwife her soul through the portal of death, if you choose to do so."

"I would love to help her however I can," Aidan replied.

"Very well. But first we must deal with your curse."

With Patia's death, Aidan had forgotten his purpose for coming to Unstan. The ophidian parasite in Aidan's heart had grown quiet since the Black Metal poison was exorcised from Oscuro, but as the Bone King spoke of his curse, Aidan felt a wave of pain in his heart. Hope sprouted in Aidan's mind. Could the Bone King rid him of Oscuro's evil curse? Would he actually be able to sing again?

"Tell me what I must do," he said.

"Just relax, and see your heart healthy and strong," the Bone King replied. With that, he held out his skeletal palm toward Aidan's chest. Radiant gemstones swirled from within the rainbow light, emerging from his palm. As the Bone King's energy entered Aidan's body, he was flooded with all the dark emotions he had felt during his journey to Unstan. He relived the fear, doubt, despair, anger, and his challenging encounters with his own shadow. The negativity surged through his heart and mind like a cresting wave, growing in intensity. The painful emotions continued to build until he could bear it no longer, and then they suddenly disappeared.

Aidan opened his eyes to see the ophidian serpent suspended in mid-air in front of his chest. With its glowing red eyes and fangs bared, the small metallic serpent looked at Aidan and hissed menacingly. The Bone King's gemstone magic began to swirl around the shadow serpent. As the energy spun faster and faster, the ophidian dissolved one particle at a time, until it vaporized into the swirling vortex of rainbow light. A moment later, the rainbow light withdrew back into the Bone King's palm and disappeared.

Aidan sighed. He felt as if a huge weight had been removed from his heart. Tears flooded his eyes as conflicting feelings of gratitude for his healing and grief for Patia overcame him. "Great one, how can I ever thank you for helping me?"

"Help me to midwife Patia's soul into the Beyond," the Bone King replied without hesitation. "Death is an immense opportunity for healing and growth, which continues after the physical body dies. We can bring significant benefit to Patia's soul by supporting her passage through the dying process."

He pointed to a doorway in the stone wall. "This door leads to a chamber that the ancient ones called the Womb of Peace. It is the ideal waystation between this world and the next. Come, let us move her body."

As they carried Patia toward the doorway, Ruby flew into the cairn and landed on Aidan's shoulder. Concerned, he asked her about Byol's whereabouts. Ruby chirped back that he was still asleep while she hovered anxiously near Patia's face.

Aidan and the Bone King gently laid Patia's body on a stone bench in the center of the chamber. A profound stillness permeated the space. Although small, the chamber felt vast, as if it extended into the far reaches of the cosmos.

"As we work together, connect with your love for Patia and hold the intention of supporting the highest good of her soul," the Bone King said, his deep, ancient voice filling the chamber. "Feel your communion with the healing energy of the Way, and from this place let yourself sing once again. Let us begin."

Aidan felt a moment of uncertainty about whether he would really be able to sing, but he laid his doubt aside, closed his eyes, connected with his heart, and opened himself to the life-giving energy of the Way. When he opened his eyes, the chamber was filled with the Bone King's radiant, gemstone magic. Its rainbow light surrounded Patia's body like a cocoon. From Aidan's shoulder, a beam of golden light appeared from Ruby's tiny body. Its light merged with the Bone King's energy and rippled above Patia's body.

Aidan brought an image of Patia's smiling face into his mind. Her dark-brown eyes sparkled with mischief and the fiery passion of her soul. He felt Patia's spirit clearly in the room.

Aidan inhaled deeply...and began to sing. Tentative and faint at first, his voice slowly grew in volume and strength until it filled the chamber. He sang a song of peace and love, which was dearly loved by the villagers in Willow's Glen, yet Aidan's voice had changed since he last sang in his village. His voice was richer and more complex than it had been in the past, expressing the bittersweet reality of human existence.

The healing energy of the Way filled Aidan's body, and tears of joy streamed down his face. It was ecstasy to sing again and feel the divine move through him! He was flooded with gratitude for Patia, Ruby, and the Bone King for helping to free him from the curse of the ophidian. Once again, Aidan could serve his purpose in the world. He had never felt more alive.

Blue and green light flowed out of the bard, a river of healing energy that wrapped Patia's body in its embrace. As his energy merged with that of Ruby and the Bone King, Patia's soul appeared in the space above her body. Looking down at the lifeless body beneath her, her face displayed the shock of acknowledging her own death.

Patia looked disoriented and distraught as she came to terms with her death. However, surrounded by such potent, healing energy, it wasn't long before her face softened, and she relaxed into a more peaceful state. Patia closed her eyes, and for several minutes, she seemed to be resting deeply. When she opened her eyes, they shined once again with the playful spark that Aidan knew so well. Looking at her while he sang, Aidan noticed that the light of her spirit contained patches of darkness.

The healing light swirled into a dark area in her chest as Patia's face contracted in fear. Slowly, the darkness began to unwind, as if a knot were being loosened. It became larger and more diffused and then dissolved completely. As it did, a glowing light filled her chest, and Patia's entire energy body became more radiant. After the healing was complete, her face was infused with nobility and strength.

The process repeated itself in different areas of darkness within her energy body. Each time her spirit shined brighter after the process ended. Aidan had the distinct feeling that he was watching Patia's soul flower through this healing. She seemed more whole, more complete, more fully herself. Without thinking, Aidan let his song come to a close.

Patia looked down at Aidan with love in her eyes. "It is such a gift to finally hear you sing. Thank you, Aidan, for helping my soul to heal. " A playful sparkle danced across her eyes. "What a wonderful adventure we have had together in this life! Thank you for the gift of your friendship."

"I am so grateful to have known you," Aidan replied, barely able to speak. "I love you, dear friend. Farewell in your travels, wherever they may lead."

With that, she winked at Aidan and gave him one last smile. Then, with a child's curiosity and excitement in her eyes, Patia Faa's soul flew through the roof of the cairn and passed from this world.

From outside the cairn, the plaintive howl of a wolf rose into the sky. Ruby shot out of the chamber to comfort Byol. As Aidan stepped toward the door to lend his support to the wolf, the Bone King's voice stopped him. "There is nothing you can do for the wolf. He is already gone. Byol will run many miles, fueled by his grief. Ruby will catch up with him and offer what support she can. You and I have more to discuss before I return to my realm.

"We must speak of the healing of your people and the Earth. As the Seer told you during your time at Druid's Keep, you live in a pivotal moment in human history. Immense potential exists for the flowering of human consciousness. If this growth in awareness is to occur, it will sprout directly from the hearts of your people. This is because love unifies all things, and the greatest obstacle to humanity's growth is the delusion of separateness.

"For generations, your people have sought to distance themselves from the natural world and claim ownership of the Earth. Of course, removing yourselves from the interwoven fabric of the Way and the web of life is impossible. This vain effort has twisted the human mind and withered the hearts of your people. Humanity can no more live outside of nature than one's feet can walk severed from the rest of the body.

"These times are auspicious for the healing of humanity's relationship with Mother Earth and the family of all sentient life. Along with your cry for healing, it is these winds of change that have drawn me to your world. My people are guardians and protectors of life on Earth. With conditions so ripe for change among your people, we are called to support the flowering of human potential.

"You, Aidan, and the other followers of the Way are part of a rising tide of change that swells in the souls of your people. With caring hearts and open minds, you can heal humanity's rift with the natural world and restore your kind's love for all life on Earth. People can remember the fundamental truth that All is One. Living in accord with this truth is the key to awakening humanity's full potential. For how can consciousness truly evolve when it clings to the lie of separation?"

Aidan marveled at the connections he had made with the spirits of nature during his journey: the Green Mystics, the Larimar clan, and the river spirits. Communion with these beings had opened his eyes to a reality he could have never imagined. The wisdom of the Way infused all their teachings and stories. Aidan saw how reconnecting with these non-human spirits was essential for the healing of humanity and restoring harmony on Earth.

The Bone King moved slightly, creating a ripple in the fabric of his shimmering black robe. The movement sent a cascade of tiny filaments of light between the gemstones woven into the fabric. It was as if the Bone King's robe was alive, a sentient network of gemstone energy woven into cloth. Aidan watched, transfixed, for a moment before returning his attention to the Bone King's words.

"Your tragic encounter with Oscuro," the Bone King continued, "sheds light on another essential element of humanity's liberation; healing humanity's relationship with its shadow. Oscuro shows us clearly the horrors of not tending to one's shadow. If one's darkness and negativity are not looked at honestly and guided as a parent teaches a child, the seeds of evil will begin to grow. This unwillingness to take responsibility for healing the shadow has led many of your people to become like selfish children ruled by greed and violence. You have seen how easy it is to fall into righteous anger when you lose someone dear to you.

"Part of healing your people's sense of isolation lies in healing your relationship with your own shadow. As much as you seek to deny the dark sides of your nature, the shadow is essential for your existence. Creating a healthy relationship with these dark forces is a fundamental aspect of the human journey.

"The wisdom of the Way teaches that darkness and shadow are integral to life in your world. There is primal power and depth in the realm of the shadow. Even the colossal darkness of Makhol contributes to the harmony of the Way when it takes its rightful place in the fabric of creation. In the human realm, Makhol created evil and poisoned your people's hearts. However, when he returned home to the immense black hole of his birth, he became a harmonizing force, balancing the brilliant light of the stars in the vast tapestry of the cosmos. It is the same dynamic harmony between light and darkness that creates the rich beauty of life on Earth.

"For humanity to become whole, you must embrace the shadow, surround it with love, and seek to understand it without judgment. Dancing with the shadow brings vitality, creativity, and mystery to life. However, putting the shadow at the helm of the ship will eventually shatter your life on the craggy shores of self-destruction."

Aidan reflected on the Bog of Despair. His shadow had created an internal hell of self-judgment and abuse that had nearly led to his death. He shuddered at the disturbing memory.

"You have already learned a great deal about dancing with your shadow," the Bone King continued. "This dance will certainly bring depth and vital energy to your work as a bard. Continue to love and guide your shadow, and the power of the Way will open itself to you like an ever-blossoming flower. If all your people take responsibility for parenting their own shadow in this way, the human heart will finally know the healing it longs for. Your people must have compassion and understanding for each other as they move through this period of healing.

"As your brothers and sisters wholeheartedly engage this process of healing themselves and their relationship with Mother Earth, the door will open to a future beyond your wildest dreams, and humanity will feel a profound sense of wholeness and belonging on Earth. Fear will dissolve, and life in your world will be bathed in the beauty of love. Living once again according to the Way, your people will recover the inner peace and freedom that is their birthright.

"As the new world dawns, your people will find what they have sought for many, many lifetimes. Complete liberation of the heart and mind is within reach during this time of transformation.

"This all may seem like a fantasy, too good to be true, but it is not. Countless beings in your world and many other worlds have already attained the treasures of which I speak. The ingredients are simple: honesty, humility, dedication, and love for all beings. May humanity leave its selfish adolescence behind and finally claim the noble maturity of the human soul. May your world join the family of liberated beings blazing trails of consciousness in this vast cosmos. Life's greatest adventure awaits you."

"I hear the wisdom of your words, Bone King," Aidan said. "But this goal seems so far from reach. How can we bring this flowering of our people into reality?"

"One person at a time, Aidan. Your brothers and sisters must support each other to heal the frightened, wounded children within. Also, you must reclaim the initiation rituals that guide each person through life's seasons of childhood, adulthood, and eventually into the priceless role of elder. Many of humanity's problems result from the stunted growth of your people. Too many of your kind live like selfish adolescents ruled by fear, greed, and self-deception.

"Your people must reclaim the noble medicine of true maturity and their essential role as caregivers for all life on Earth. When your brothers and sisters' actions arise from a place of wisdom and love for all life, your people will be well on their way to the full flowering of human potential. The truth that All is One is not an abstract philosophy of the mind. It is a prayer that must be lived and made real through every word and action. This is how to honor what is most sacred in life and heal humanity's connection with the Way.

"Yes, Aidan, each person must play his or her own humble part in this flowering of humanity, just as you must play yours. In seeing this journey through to its end, you have shown great devotion to your path as a bard. Do your part. Share your songs and your stories with your people. May your music encourage others to give their gifts to the world.

"One by one, may your brothers and sisters stand up, claim the wholeness of their beings, and open their hearts to each other. These ripples will become a giant wave of transformation, giving birth to a beautiful new world on this Earth."

The Bone King paused for a moment in thought. "Before I return to my realm, I have a task for you. The fire sprite's inferno has cleansed the forest of the foul poison of Black Metal. Now what is needed is the healing regenerative energy of water. A river runs through the burned remains of the forest. Its waters irrigate and nourish these lands. Pour the rest of the Goddess water you received from Father David into the river. This will begin the process of healing the forest."

Aidan's eyes shined with excitement. "I gratefully accept your request."

"Excellent," said the Bone King. "I will wait here for your return."

Reaching into his knapsack, Aidan pulled out the blue crystal amphora with the remaining Goddess water. Leaving the stone chamber, he took a deep breath of the fresh air blowing in from the east and began walking toward a line of hills at the edge of the burn zone. Scattered smoke from the scorched and blackened forest still blew out over the Loch of Stenness on the morning breeze.

Aidan's emotions ebbed and flowed with the changeable weather of his heart. Tears filled his eyes from the sadness of losing Patia and the sheer overwhelming nature of all he had been through on his journey. Yet, the next minute, his heart warmed with the joy of knowing he had been able to support the healing of Patia's soul as she passed from this world.

Aidan also felt immensely relieved to be free of the ophidian. Being healed of the curse had lifted an oppressive weight from his heart. The fear and doubt that had plagued him throughout his journey was gone. An expansive feeling of peace suffused him even in the midst of his grief for Patia. He felt boundless gratitude for all those who had helped him on his quest for healing.

As he climbed the blackened hills, he saw where the river flowed out into the charred forest from a valley farther ahead. Dropping into the valley, he spotted the river. Aidan felt the Flow awaken within him and sensed the river's excitement as it became aware of why Aidan had come. Approaching the river's edge, Aidan placed an offering of rose petals into the ash-muddied water.

"Sweet river spirit, I am Aidan. I come to you today with hope in my heart, for we have been given the opportunity to bring healing to this land."

The watery words of the river's spirit gurgled into Aidan's mind. *I know who you are, Hearth of the Rainbow Light. You are part of the water tribe, and the story of your adventures has traveled through cloud and rain to all the rivers in this land. The Flow moves within you. You are family with all of my kind.*

"Thank you for welcoming me, brother river. Please, tell me why do you call me Hearth of the Rainbow Light? Flowing Rainbow Nectar used to call me Hearth of the Golden Light."

It seems you have not looked at your reflection lately, the river replied. *Here, look into the water along my banks.*

Aidan looked into the water and gasped in surprise at what he saw. Freed of the ophidian's curse, the radiant light of spirit surrounded his body once more. However, his aura was no longer golden, as it had been when he was a boy. His reflection was surrounded with brilliant white light, shimmering with all of the colors of the rainbow.

"Hmm...I see," Aidan said in wonder. "And what is your name, fair river?"

"Thanks to you, I too will receive a new name today. You may call me Life Giver. And now, sweet brother, let us see if I can live up to my new name."

With that, Aidan opened the amphora and trickled the remaining Goddess water into the river. A shimmer of green light rippled across the water's surface and continued downstream into the land that had been scorched by fire. Looking down the hill, Aidan saw the river returning to its crystalline purity as it snaked through the forest's charred, smoking remains. Downstream, green healing light from the Goddess water rippled into the blackened landscape from the banks of the river.

As the Goddess energy continued to spread out from the river on its path to the sea, something awakened in the earth. In the area closest to the hills where Aidan stood, he saw new plant growth sprout from the land. Captivated by the scene, Aidan watched as trees and bushes grew at an incredibly accelerated rate. Before his eyes, the entire forest became carpeted with green. Oak, ash, willow, and alder trees matured to full size in the forest below. Fed by the healing energy of the Goddess, years of growth happened in the span of minutes. Aidan stood in awe of the miracle taking place in front of him. In no time, the forest had grown to full maturity, as if the trees had been there for decades. Joy and relief flooded Aidan's heart as he witnessed the healing of the forest.

"Thank you, Life Giver," Aidan said. "Thank you for helping to heal this blessed forest."

"Thank you, water bearer. You have bestowed upon my waters the blessing of the Goddess. Life will thrive in these lands for many years to come."

Remembering the Bone King, Aidan said goodbye to the river and then began the walk back to Unstan.

When he entered the cairn, he found the Bone King sitting in meditation next to a human skeleton lying on a stone bench against the wall. Remembering that there were no bones in the cairn earlier, he realized it must be Patia's skeleton. Looking confused, Aidan sat across from the Bone King.

"I have allowed Patia's flesh to return to the Earth," the Bone King said. "Now her bones can remain here and bask in the good energy of this cairn for years to come. This will provide continued benefit to Patia's soul as she moves toward her next life.

"My time here has now come to a close. But before I return to my realm, I have a gift for you."

The Bone King stood and walked across the chamber. Towering over Aidan, he reached down with a long skeletal arm and placed his bony hand on Aidan's head. Rainbow gemstone colors flooded Aidan's vision as the Bone King's blessing filled him with a river of light. After a few minutes, the Bone King removed his hand from Aidan's head. "Know that I will always be with you, Aidan Bourne, whether or not we meet again in the flesh.

"I wish you many blessings as you walk your path in this world. May you and your people flower into your immense potential during this time of transformation and remember your noble destiny as followers of the Way and caregivers for life on Earth. May your people's actions be guided by love, humility, and wisdom. And remember that you are never alone. I and the other Guardians of Earth will always watch over your world and return in times of need."

For a timeless moment, the bard and the Bone King stood facing each other in silence, beings from vastly different dimensions united by their devotion to the path of the heart.

"Farewell, Aidan Bourne. Farewell."

Light blazed in the far end of the chamber from the doorway to the Bone King's dimension. Old as time itself, the Bone King walked slowly through the doorway of light and returned once again to his gemstone realm. With a flash of light, the doorway closed, and the cairn returned once again to darkness.

Aidan sat on a stone bench in the dimly lit chamber to let the events of the day sink in. As the peaceful energy of Unstan settled his racing mind, he realized how exhausted he was. Lying down on the stone bench, he closed his eyes. "Maybe I'll rest for a bit," he murmured.

Within moments, Aidan was fast asleep.

TWENTY-FOUR

It was pitch black in the cairn when Aidan awoke. After saying his final farewells to Patia, he felt his way along the rough stone walls and slowly returned to the chamber's entrance. As he stepped out into the crisp air, the eastern skies were painted in the soft colors of pre-dawn light.

"That was quite a nap," Aidan said rubbing his eyes.

He found himself touching the rune stone around his neck nostalgically. As he stroked the smooth, glassy stone, an idea came to him. "Perhaps I will pay Daphne a visit before I return to Willow's Glen. A few days at the Pools of Peace would serve me well. I could use some time to replenish my energy before the long journey home."

At that moment, Ruby rocketed in from behind and perched on Aidan's shoulder. Chirping in his ear, she told him that Byol would not return. In his grief over Patia's death, the wolf no longer wanted human company, so he had returned to the forest to search for a new family among wolves.

Aidan's heart went out to the wolf, and he wished him well in his new life. "And what about you, Ruby? Will you join me on my journey back to Willow's Glen?"

Ruby chirped excitedly, and Aidan was delighted to hear that the hummingbird wanted to continue their travels together.

As the first rays of dawn illuminated the eastern horizon, Aidan took a deep breath of the crisp morning air and drank in the golden light of the sun. The fiery beauty of the rising sun filled him with the feeling that anything was possible.

Looking at Ruby he asked, "Where will destiny take us from here, my friend? What world will we create with our brothers and sisters? What stories will we write in the pages of history for the generations to come? The future is wide open before us."

With Ruby perched on his shoulder, Aidan walked forth into the dawn of a new day.

Made in the USA
Las Vegas, NV
19 February 2022

44242821R00178